Tied Up,
Tied Down

Praise for Lorelei James's *Tied Up, Tied Down*

Rating: 5 Hearts "From the tempting cover to the final page, Tied Up, Tied Down is one terrific read. ...This story touches all your emotions and lightly deals with issues real people face every day. Just as Skylar is Tied Up, Tied Down physically in this story, they are both Tied Up, Tied Down emotionally and that's what makes it an excellent read for everybody."

~ *Lisa Freeman, The Romance Studio*

Rating: 4.5 Nymphs "Tied Up, Tied Down is Ms. James' newest release in her ongoing *Rough Rider* series, and it's just as fast paced, sexy and fun as its predecessors. ... This well-written western romance pulls at the heart-strings, but ultimately it offers hope for the future, making it an excellent read for anyone."

~ *Mystical Nymph, Literary Nymph Reviews*

Blue Ribbon Rating: 4.5 "...The story is a perfect blend of endearing romance with super hot love scenes that leave the reader cheering for a happily ever after between Skyler and Kade. I love the characters in the Rough Rider series and look forward to future works from Ms. Lorelei James. TIED UP, TIED DOWN is not to be missed."

~ *Lacey, Romance Junkies*

Rating: 4 Cups "Cowboys! Cowboys and more Hot and sexy Cowboys! ...Stubborn men and even more stubborn women make this a story that will have you laughing, crying, swooning and panting all at once, taking you on an exciting traipse thru cowboy country, one you will not want to miss."

~ *Matilda, Coffee Time Romance*

Rating: Grade A "...And I enjoy Ms. James' writing. She catches the "cowboy" attitude and way of talking perfectly. She's made me yen for my local rodeo again, but I have to wait until next April. I'm in the mood for some Levi-wearin', buck-broncin', grinnin' cowboys after reading this latest Rough Rider installment!"

~ *Sandy M., The Good, The Bad, The Unread*

Rating: 4 Angels "...I loved this book. ...I found *Tied Up, Tied Down* to be exceptionally well written. The flames between Skylar and Kade leapt off each page. I could feel a connection with them and their emotions. I will definitely be looking to more books by Mrs. James. I would recommend this book to every reader who loves strong, sexy cowboys!"

~ *Kim N., Fallen Angel Reviews*

Rating: 4 ½ Hearts "...Lorelei James is the complete package. Characters, plot, emotion, heat—even laughter—it's all there. One question I might have is that how can one family be so front-end loaded with hot, charming cowboys? Answer: Who cares? Count me in as a member of the James Gang!"

~ *Seanachie, Erotic Romance Writers*

Look for these titles by
Lorelei James

Now Available:
Rough Riders Series
Cowgirl Up and Ride
Rode Hard, Put Up Wet
Long Hard Ride
Tied Up, Tied Down
Rough, Raw and Ready
Branded As Trouble

Running With the Devil
Dirty Deeds
Beginnings Anthology: Babe in the Woods
Wicked Garden
Mistress Christmas
Strong, Silent Type

Coming Soon:
Rough Riders Series
Should Have Been a Cowboy

Wild West Boys
Miss Firecracker

Tied Up,
Tied Down

Lorelei James

A Samhain Publishing, Ltd. publication.

Samhain Publishing, Ltd.
577 Mulberry Street, Suite 1520
Macon, GA 31201
www.samhainpublishing.com

Tied Up, Tied Down
Print ISBN: 978-1-60504-294-7
Digital ISBN: 1-60504-064-9

Editing by Angela James
Cover by Scott Carpenter

First Samhain Publishing, Ltd. electronic publication: July 2008
First Samhain Publishing, Ltd. print publication: June 2009

Dedication

To those of us who've realized a surprise pregnancy isn't the end of the world...but can be the start of something magical.

Prologue

Skylar Ellison hated being naked in public.

Not that she was positioned on a bridge waving her hoo-hoos and va-jay-jay at passersby, but damn, wearing just her birthday suit made her oh-so conscious of the flaws in that aging suit. The paper covering the patient's exam table crinkled beneath her sweaty thighs. A cold breeze from the air duct wafted across her bare butt exactly where the itsy bitsy cloth gown gapped.

That wasn't as bad as having her lower half completely exposed, her knees spread wide, her feet in metal stirrups as she stared at the "Hang In There, Baby" poster plastered to the ceiling.

Skylar dreaded pelvic exams, pap smears, shots, and teeth cleanings—anything resembling a medical procedure. So far she'd been poked, prodded and they'd taken a sample of damn near every bodily fluid imaginable: blood, urine, saliva, a throat culture, earwax, toe-jam—not so much the last two, but it'd sure seemed like it.

She'd been cooling her heels in this sterile room for thirty minutes. Which gave her plenty of time to wonder: What the hell was wrong with her?

For the last month she'd experienced constant nausea. Not enough to make her barf, but wooziness, usually worse at night. She didn't feel like eating, yet, according to the doctor's scale, she'd managed to pack on five pounds since the last time she'd weighed herself at home.

She could attribute her physical changes to stress. Owning her own business was nerve racking, even when her all-natural, made-in-Wyoming beauty products contained aromatherapy properties. Construction delays caused her extra anxiety, but she'd finally opened the retail store of Sky Blue in Sundance. The manufacturing plant outside of Moorcroft was in full swing filling holiday orders.

Still, stress wouldn't make her skin hurt to the touch. Tension might push her to the edge of exhaustion, causing her to sleep for twelve hours straight. She'd missed two or three periods—who kept track? She'd always been irregular. But that didn't explain the weird vaginal discharge. Plus, she was moody. She couldn't regulate her body temp; she was either too hot or too cold. It was all so eerily familiar. She recognized the signs, though never on herself.

Cancer.

Skylar closed her eyes. Please. Not cancer. She couldn't have cancer. The universe couldn't be that damn cruel. Eight years ago her mother had been diagnosed with uterine cancer. Her mom believed she'd hit menopause. She'd exhibited all the signs—signs Skylar recognized because she'd been experiencing them herself recently.

A cancer diagnosis would decimate her sister, India. Ironically enough, their father had been a victim of prostate cancer eleven years ago. Sky's thoughts flashed to the rounds of chemo and radiation. The endless trips to the hospital. If anything would send India back to the shady world of booze, drugs and random sexual encounters, it'd be dealing with another cancer-stricken family member.

The door made a metallic *snick* and Skylar's stomach lurched. She peeled her eyes open to look at the doctor, a striking petite redhead.

"The tests are back," Doctor Monroe said.

"And? Do I have cancer?"

Doctor Monroe frowned and studied the pages inside the file folder. "Why on earth would you think...oh, I see. A family history of cancer. Huh. A *lot* of cancer. But no. It's not cancer."

Skylar stifled the urge to weep with relief. "Then what on earth is wrong with me? Is it a bug or something I picked up someplace? Is it contagious?" For some reason the impulsive event from a few months back clicked front and center in her mind.

Contagious.

Kade McKay. That rat bastard. He'd given her the clap.

"I have to say, Skylar, I'm not particularly surprised."

Skylar's mouth dropped open. "Not surprised that I have an STD? I have unprotected sex *one time*, one freakin' time in all the years I've been sexually active and you're not surprised that the jerk I slept with gave me crotch crud?"

Doctor Monroe smiled—grinned actually. "Oh, he didn't give you an STD. He gave you a baby."

"WHAT?" Skylar shrieked. "I'm...I'm... Omigod. I'm *pregnant?*"

"Three months, does that sound right?"

Skylar nodded dumbly. Numbly.

Pregnant. Good God. She hadn't seen Kade since that blow up at Ziggy's three and a half months ago. The night they'd done the deed in his pickup in the parking lot of a honky-tonk. Immediately after that romp she'd found out he'd tricked her. She'd cut him out of her life, dodged his phone calls and eventually he'd stopped calling.

Yet, recently she'd found herself thinking of patient, sexy-as-sin Kade McKay at the oddest times, wondering if she hadn't gone off half-cocked. Although he'd never corrected her assumption he was pretending to be his identical twin brother, the time they'd spent together never seemed like a trick or a joke, or forced but something promising. Something real.

Right. It didn't get any more real than a baby.

A baby. Jesus.

"Any excessive drinking or other substances I should be worried about that might've affected this pregnancy?"

"No. My sister is a recovering alcoholic and she's been living with me, so I haven't had a drop of alcohol for months."

"Good." Doctor Monroe scooted forward and clasped Skylar's hands in her own. "A surprise pregnancy isn't always a pleasant surprise. You understand as your physician there is no judgment on my part on the decision you make. You're a healthy thirty-four-year-old woman. Pregnancy and childbirth isn't a risk to you healthwise.

"That said, if this pregnancy isn't something you want, you'll need to schedule an appointment with the clinic in Billings or one in Denver within the next week to terminate it. After that, you're starting the second trimester and the health risks to you double."

"So I'm a third of the way through?"

Dr. Monroe nodded.

A baby. Growing inside her. How weird. How...cool.

And suddenly Sky wanted this baby fiercely. "Well, Doc, I'm looking at this as a good surprise."

"I thought you might say that."

"Why?"

"Because we're the same age and if I had the same surprise, I'd be over the moon."

Sky definitely felt as if she'd been launched into another galaxy, spawning a new life form inside her. "Guess I'd better bone up on Mr. Spock's pregnancy and childbirth books."

"*Doctor* Spock, the baby expert. Not the Vulcan Star Trek character," Doc Monroe said dryly. She reached into a cabinet, pulling out a big white plastic bottle. "Prenatal vitamins. I'll write you a prescription, but this should get you through until I see you next month."

Then she rattled off a spiel about unnatural bleeding, swollen tissues, tingling in arms and legs, when to come in— Sky heard it all, but through a fog of disbelief.

The word *pregnant* kept repeating in her mind.

In a daze, she wandered to her car, keeping her coat wrapped tightly against the cold November wind.

Kade had a right to know about this baby. She'd have to steel herself against his reaction—most likely not positive. They'd had sex one time. One. Freakin'. Time. What were the odds she'd end up pregnant? Would he even believe her that the kid was his?

Only one way to find out. She fished her BlackBerry from her purse and scrolled down the contact list.

Dammit. In a fit of anger she'd erased his cell number. Last she knew he'd temporarily moved in with his parents. Even if that was no longer the case, they'd know how to get in touch with him.

Skylar punched up the local phone directory, narrowing it to Sundance before she attempted the surrounding Wyoming counties. McKay. A shitload of them were listed:

McKay, Bennett

McKay, Calvin and Kimi

McKay, Carson and Carolyn

McKay, Carter and Macie

McKay, Casper and Joan

McKay, Charles and Violet

McKay, Chase

McKay, Colby and Channing

McKay, Colt

McKay, Cord and AJ

McKay, Quinn and Libby

No Kade. No Kane. *Think, Sky.* What were his parents' names? No clue. What was up with all the "C" names anyway? That was confusing as hell. She scrolled and started with the couple at the top of the list. Calvin and Kimi.

She dialed. Her heart jumped into her throat, nearly choking her when the phone was answered on the second ring. "McKays."

"Hello. I'm looking for Kade McKay."

Deep male laughter. "Look elsewhere."

"Excuse me?"

"My brother is gone."

The man speaking had to be Kane, Kade's twin. "Gone? What do you mean gone?" Then Sky remembered Kade's cousin had died in a tragic ranch accident and the blood drained from her face. "Is he...dead?"

A snort. "No, he's gone, as in, he moved."

"When?"

"Three months ago."

Damn. Wasn't that a coincidence? Was that irony laughing in the background or just the rude man on the phone?

"Before you ask where he's gone, he might as well be livin'

15

in Timbuktu because there's no way to get a hold of him. Try back late next summer." And he hung up.

Skylar stared at her cell phone in astonishment. How had she ever mixed up Kane and Kade McKay? They were different as night and day.

Which mattered not a single whit.

Call back next summer.

Right. Looked like she was on her own. Again.

Skylar patted her stomach. "Just you and me, kiddo."

After five minutes of aimless staring at the gray nothingness outside her window, she laughed until tears poured down her face.

"A case of mistaken identity with identical twins, unprotected sex in a pickup truck, and now, a secret baby. Heck, with your cowboy daddy MIA, if I moved into a trailer and bought a shotgun we'd be living the redneck anthem."

The fluttery sensation in her stomach solidified as the baby moved.

Chapter One

Nine months later...

The door slammed hard enough to shake the whole house.

"Kade West McKay. I want to talk to you right now."

Kade sighed. He wondered what he'd done to invoke his mother's wrath this time. Left the toilet seat up? Parked in her spot? Forgot to wipe his boots? Did she know how mortifying it was to be treated like a naughty eleven-year-old boy, rather than a thirty-two-year-old man responsible for running a ranch the size of Rhode Island?

A thirty-two-year-old man who was living at his folks' house. Again. *Temporarily*, he silently amended. He'd been back from the yearlong grazing experiment for just two days, and it felt as if he'd gone back in time twenty years.

All five-feet-one inches of Kimi McKay barreled around the corner into the living room. Whenever she got her mad on, he and his brother Kane snickered and called her the blonde tornado—behind her back, of course.

Nothing about the mean glint in her eye invoked his secret chuckle today. Something serious had put the starch in her spine. Out of reflex, he sat up straighter. Rather than risk saying the wrong thing, Kade said nothing.

She bent close to him, her face a mask of fury. "I don't know what the hell is wrong with you. I raised you better than that."

"Better than what?"

"Don't you get smart with me."

Count to ten. "I'm not."

"Don't you lie to me, neither."

"Ma. Calm down. Lie about what? What's wrong?"

"What's *wrong*? Your behavior is what's wrong."

"What are you talkin' about?"

"I'm talking about you being such a..." She tossed up her arms. "A McKay!"

"Huh?"

"I never pegged you as the love 'em and leave 'em type, Kade. I'd hoped you were different."

"Ma—"

"Why is it so damn hard if you can't keep your damn pants zipped to remember to wear a damn condom?"

Baffled, he just stared at her as she ranted and swore a blue streak.

"So you were caught up in the moment of passion, I understand that. But I expected you'd do the right thing, Kade, not walk away. Or run away as the case may be."

"Have you lost your mind? What in the *hell* are you babblin' about?"

"You—" she drilled his chest hard with her index finger, "—neglecting to tell me you'd knocked up a woman and then flitted off to the north forty of the McKay ranch, leaving her to deal with the pregnancy and the baby all alone."

"What woman? What baby?"

Kimi McKay snapped upright. Her pale blue eyes searched his. A mixture of surprise and resignation replaced the anger on her face. "Oh, good Lord. You really don't know, do you, son?"

"Know what?"

"Know that you're a father."

"What? Run that by me again."

"You heard me right. You're a father."

Kade remained calm in light of his mother's delusions. "Remember where I've been the last twelve months. I've barely seen a woman in that long, let alone touched one."

Why don't you just brag about your lack of a sex life to your mother of all people?

18

"Which fits, because that baby is over three months old."

Kade's heart damn near stopped. His mouth dried up like a summer stock dam as he did the math in his head. Last time he'd had sex was last year with Skylar. In their single, spontaneous, passionate bout of lovemaking, they'd forgotten to use a condom.

Not that they'd talked about the "oops" incident afterward. She'd been livid when she learned of his duplicity; he'd resigned himself to losing her for good after she wouldn't return his phone calls. He'd left town within two weeks. Kade realized—for the first time—it was entirely possible that he might've gotten her pregnant.

Oh yeah? If that's true, then why didn't she contact me after I sent her that letter?

Whoa. Talk about acting like a surly eleven-year-old.

"Kade?"

"You saw Skylar?"

"Aha!" She shook her finger in his face. "You aren't denying it?"

"No, but you'd better start at the beginnin' and tell me exactly how *you* came across this information."

"Fine. I popped into Sky Blue in Sundance for a bottle of hand cream. India always helps me. So imagine my surprise when I see the owner working the cash register. Imagine an even bigger surprise when I see a sweet baby nestled in her arms. And that baby sports a shock of black hair and looks at me with blue eyes, *McKay* blue eyes. I've seen my share of McKay babies in the last thirty-six years and there wasn't any doubt I was lookin' at one.

"When Skylar saw the name on my check, she stammered and couldn't get rid of me fast enough. I knew that baby had to be yours. Or Kane's." A pause. "But Skylar is too classy and ambitious to be Kane's type. Then something triggered my memory. Kane mentioning after Dag died you'd suffered a bad break-up with a woman. Is she the reason you were so eager to disappear last year and take a job in the boondocks that no one else wanted?"

"Partially, but I sure didn't know she was pregnant because I never woulda left. Never. You know that, Ma." This was so unbelievable he was having a devil of a time focusing. "Did you ask her if...?"

"Of course I didn't ask her." She leaned forward again. "Do you know how hard that was? To see that darlin' little girl baby, all pretty in pink ribbons and bows, smilin' and cooin' at me, knowin' she was my granddaughter?"

"Skylar had a *girl?*"

"Yep. Only the second McKay girl born in a hundred and twenty-three years. And she's yours."

His. He had a baby daughter. "Holy shit." If Kade hadn't been sitting down, he'd've been falling down. He repeated inanely, "A baby? Skylar had a baby? I'm a father?"

"It appears so."

"What's her name?"

"Eliza."

Eliza. Pretty. His head spun. "Why didn't she tell me?"

"I don't know, son, but I suspect you'd better find out."

Kade heaved himself out of the chair. "Damn straight." He snagged his hat off the coat rack and stormed out to his truck.

Chapter Two

On the drive into town, Kade replayed his first meeting with Skylar Ellison. He'd thought of her and his dumb mistake in the endless days he'd lived alone up on the most remote part of the McKay ranch. He'd obsessed about her to the extent he'd memorized every damn word of every encounter. Every kiss, every touch.

That afternoon from last summer floated into his mind in perfect detail.

As Kade had stood on the sidewalk debating on whether to eat lunch before heading home, *click click* had sounded and he'd turned to see a woman in heels hustling down the sidewalk.

Mercy. She was all curves: hips, ass, thighs, and breasts. He loved women who looked like women and not a skeleton with skin. Her straight brown hair had a hint of red in the bright sunlight. Kade tipped his hat to her and stepped out of her way, figuring she'd pass right on by.

But Miss Sexy Curves bumped her pointy-toed purple shoes against his shit-covered boots and glared. "You were a total jerk to me the other night, Kane McKay. I don't appreciate you ditching me at the restaurant. What kind of shithead—"

"Whoa. Wait a second. I'm not—"

"—the least bit sorry, yeah, I can tell. Why are you here? Trolling for a new woman who'll give you a piece of ass on the first date since I wouldn't?"

That fucker Kane was such an asshole. At times like this it plain sucked they were identical twins and few people could tell them apart. This woman must have been Kane's date from the other night.

His brother was an idiot too. He'd just up and walked away from such a smoking-hot firecracker?

"Got nothing to say, McKay?"

A really good idea occurred to him on how to make this right.

No. It was a bad idea. A terrible idea, his conscience warned.

The devil on his shoulder screamed, *Do it. You and Kane used to switch places all the time. You're not misleading her; you're protecting the McKay name from another round of nasty gossip.*

Big surprise the pitchfork side won the battle.

"Actually, I do have somethin' to say to you." What the hell was her name again? Something hippyishly weird. Aha. "*Skylar.*"

"I'm listening."

"I'm sorry. I lost your number or I woulda called to apologize for bein' a first class jerk. But I'd...ah...taken some allergy medicine and did it do a number on me. Normally I don't act like that. Not that I remember a whole helluva lot besides goin' home and crashin'."

Skylar stared at him skeptically.

Crap. She wasn't buying it. "Can I make it up to you? Buy you lunch? I swear I won't run out again."

"When?"

"How about now?"

"Sure. You don't mind vegetarian?"

Fuck. Kade slapped on a fake smile. "Not at all."

She laughed; it made him think of bells. "You are such a liar. Your family raises cattle. You probably shoot vegetarians."

"Only if they're part of PETA protestin' inhuman treatment of our stock. That pisses us off."

"I can imagine."

"Besides, I eat salad. Not crazy about tofu. Or beans ground up and passed off as burgers. A burger is supposed to be meat. Beans are only good in tacos and chili." Kade looked up. Damn. He'd been babbling.

Her lips curled in a cat-like smile. "Too bad you weren't this honest the other night. I know just the place. Let's go."

Ten minutes later, Kade lowered the menu. "I hate to break it to you, Skylar, but this ain't a vegetarian restaurant."

"I know. It's the most expensive restaurant in town. And since you said any place, I figured you owed me the very best."

"Bit of a hard ass, ain't ya?"

She shrugged. "What're you having?"

"Eggplant parmesan."

"Really?"

"Yeah. Why?"

"I figured you'd order the porterhouse."

"I don't eat beef twenty-four/seven. I eat lots of other things." He'd sure like to nibble on her. Scrape his teeth down to the base of her neck where her throat curved into her shoulder. Flick his tongue across the pulse point beating beneath her jaw. Sniff back up to see if she dabbed perfume behind her sweet little ears or if it was just the natural scent of her skin that smelled so heavenly.

"You're gawking at me, McKay."

Kade glanced up at her eyes. "Sorry."

Skylar folded her menu. "We aren't going to do this again, are we? Sexual innuendos and you ogling my boobs?"

"I wasn't oglin' your boobs. I was oglin' your neck."

She blinked.

"What I meant to say, is you have a sexy—I mean, a nice neck, Skylar. Wasn't my intention to make you uncomfortable."

After the waitress took their order, Kade fiddled with his silverware, wondering how many more times he'd stick his boot in his mouth over the course of the meal.

"So they let you off the ranch today?"

He frowned. "Whaddya mean?"

"The other night, you made it sound like you never get to town, you're always stuck out in the middle of nowhere by yourself."

Kane would play the I'm-such-a-lonely-cowboy-on-the-range angle, figuring she'd be inclined to take a tumble with him if she thought he wasn't a horndog whooping it up all the time—which is exactly what Kane was.

"There's enough guys workin' I can take off now and again."

"It's a family operation, right?"

"Sort of. There are four separate spreads. Ours, my Uncle Carson's, my Uncle Casper's and my Uncle Charlie's. My cousins help my uncles, they've all bought land of their own, but we do ranch together. So the original homestead is twenty-five times the size it was when my great-great-grandfather settled in Wyoming territory and it's spread out in three counties."

"So, did you always want to ranch? Or was it another one of those family legacies where you didn't have a choice?"

How did he explain to someone who didn't possess the same mindset that there was no choice? And it didn't bother him most days his path in life had been set the day he was born? "It's what I've always wanted to do. The only thing, actually."

"How many acres do you guys have?"

Kade shifted and reached for his water glass.

"Did I say something wrong?"

When he didn't elaborate, she angled across the table. "I'm new here, remember? Cut me some slack if I've broken a code of the West or something."

"Truth is, you don't ask a rancher the size of his spread. Or how many head of cattle he runs. Kinda like askin' someone how much money they make."

"In other words, crass."

"Yep."

"Sorry. Tell me more about your family."

Did she suspect he wasn't Kane? "Why?"

"Big families fascinate me, since mine is so small."

"What I've told you don't even take into account my ma's side. The Wests have been ranchin' in Wyoming almost as long as the McKays. Sort of a Hatfield and McCoy rivalry goin' on there. But there's just me and my brother in our immediate family."

Skylar stirred sugar substitute in her iced tea. "Older or younger brother?"

"Younger." By about four minutes. "What about you?" After he asked, he kicked himself. She'd probably told Kane. And wow, hadn't he been babbling like a spring creek? Did she really care about every damn member of his family and their sordid history? His cheeks grew hot.

"I have one younger sister. India. She defines rebellious since she works in a tattoo parlor." Skylar grinned. "She's awesome. Now that I'm settled and out of LA, she's relocating here from Denver."

"Not a lot of tattoo artists round these parts."

"Hopefully that means her business will thrive. My mother grew up here and moved to the coast. Grandma died two years ago and left the small acreage to me and my sister."

"She didn't leave the homeplace to your mother?"

Skylar shook her head. "Mom died seven years ago. Dad four years before that."

"I'm sorry."

"Thanks. After Gran passed on I needed a change from the rat race. The state of Wyoming offered me a financial incentive to expand my hobby into a business, so I did. It's taken over a year to get it up and running."

Kade picked at his salad. "Will you think I'm a total jerk if I tell you I don't remember what business you're in?"

"That's because you didn't ask me."

His head shot up. "That makes me even more of a prick."

That sweet, bellish laughter sounded again. "I'd lay off the pharmaceuticals in the future before a date."

"Deal. What is it that you do?"

"I created a line of all-natural beauty products made right here on my grandma's place."

"Sky Blue?"

Her mouth dropped open. "You've *heard* of it?"

"Sort of. That's why I'm in Moorcroft. My ma sent me to DeWitt's to pick up a bottle of lotion. They don't carry it in

Sundance."

Skylar's mossy green eyes lit up. Kade found himself staring at her again, absolutely taken by her earthy beauty.

"I'm trying to rectify that by opening a store in Sundance. So, which lotion?"

"Ah. Smells kinda like lemony dirt."

She shuddered. "Spoken by a man who probably washes with Lava soap."

"Don't knock Lava, darlin'. It gets the dirt off. And I'm plenty dirty at the end of the workday."

The food arrived. Instead of blathering on, Kade let the silence linger until they finished eating. Then the flirty waitress swung by with a tray of decadent desserts. "The chocolate cake looks good." He prompted, "Skylar?"

"None for me, thanks."

Kade frowned. He'd swear she'd been eyeballing that same piece of cake. "You don't like sweets?"

"I love sweets. I'm trying to watch what I eat so I don't have more of a weight problem."

Being polite flew right out the window. "What weight problem? You're perfect, all curvy and sexy and feminine like a woman oughta be. You're gorgeous and if I wasn't tryin' so damn hard to be a gentleman I'd..." *Nice going, now she'll really think you're reverting to Kane-like behavior.* Kade sighed. "Never mind."

Skylar angled closer, her eyes burned with interest. "No. Tell me, gentleman McKay. What would you do?"

"I'd feed you the cake just to see your lips wrap around the fork. Then I'd watch your beautiful throat muscles work as you swallowed the sticky sweetness, fantasizin' about smearin' chocolate frosting down your neck so I could lick it off. Slowly. And when I finished feedin' you, I'd press my mouth to yours for a thorough taste of you and the cake."

She didn't draw back or recoil.

"Shocked, darlin'?"

"I'm more than a little turned on, if you want to know the real truth."

"Lucky for you I'm willin' to share." He enjoyed the first few bites, then shoved the plate in the middle of the table. "I wanna see you eat up."

"Is that an order?" Skylar dug the tines of the fork into the mound of vanilla ice cream. "If I don't eat a bite will you force feed me?"

"Do you want me to force feed you?"

"What if I said yes?"

"I'd be on your side of the table faster than you could blink."

Skylar said, "Yes," loud and clear.

Kade zoomed around and stretched his left arm along the back of her side of the booth, pressing his thigh to hers.

"You weren't kidding."

"Nope. I never turn down the opportunity to share a taste of the sweet stuff in life." He swirled the fork through the thick chocolate frosting and held it to her mouth. "Open for me."

Her full lips parted slightly.

He slipped the fork inside. "Suck the sweetness off the tip. Just like that. Then I wanna see that pretty throat movin' as you swallow every bit of sticky goodness."

Kade broke eye contact only to watch her swallow. He groaned. "Again. Don't know why I'm torturin' myself, but I can't help it. Lord, you have the sexiest neck I've ever seen."

"First time a date has waxed poetic about the area above my nipples," she said huskily.

"Sweetheart, you've been datin' the wrong man." She didn't know how true that was.

"I get that now."

Kade scooped on another forkful and teased it across the seam of her mouth. "Lick it a little."

Her tongue darted out.

"You want the whole thing, not just a dainty taste."

"It's too big."

"You can take it. Open wide. You know you want to take it all."

Those luscious red lips divided and her moist chocolate-scented breath drifted out.

He set the fork on her tongue. "Suck it off. Oh yeah, just like that." His gaze zoomed to her throat. "I wanna sink my teeth into that hot spot where I see your pulse poundin'. I wanna lick it from bottom to top."

"Stop."

"What?" He dragged his eyes back to hers.

"I think the crotch on my nylons melted you've gotten me so hot. And suddenly I could care less about cake."

Kade swept his thumb across the pouty swell of her bottom lip. He showed her the dab of chocolate he swiped before he brought it to his mouth and sucked it away. "Mmm."

"You are the devil."

"Devil's food, baby, the best kind." Kade allowed a smirk. "That mean I've redeemed myself?"

"Uh." She cleared her throat. "Yeah."

"Will you go out with me again, Skylar? For coffee. To a movie." He smiled slyly. "Or just for dessert? Whatever you want."

She appeared to consider him carefully. "How about if you meet me out front of the feed store at seven the night after next?"

"I'd like to pick you up at your place if it's a date."

"Not a good idea."

Damn. Kade thought he'd been making progress with her. "Don't you trust me?"

Skylar nudged him so he scooted out of the booth and she stood next to him. "After the way your sweet-talkin' activated more than my sweet tooth? I don't trust myself." She swept her fingers over the brim of his hat. "Stay out of the drugstore aisle, McKay, and don't be late." A swish of her hips and she was gone.

Kade shook the memory away. He parked and studied the revitalized Sandstone Building. On the far end was Dewey's Delish Dish, a family restaurant his cousin Carter's wife Macie managed. On the other end was Healing Touch Massage, owned by AJ McKay, his cousin Cord's wife.

Smack dab in the middle was Sky Blue and India's Ink.

And inside that space was his child.

Sweet Jesus. He'd never been so damn nervous in his life. He climbed out of his truck and sauntered up the wooden plank stairs. At the ornate metal door, he took a second to breathe, realizing the woozy sensation was from lack of oxygen to his addled brain.

A set of chimes tinkled when he entered the store.

Scents bombarded him. Not heavy and cloying like expensive perfume, but simple and sweet. Natural. Reminiscent of the wildflowers on the wide-open Wyoming prairie. Reminiscent of Skylar.

Speak of the devil... Right then Skylar came around the corner and froze.

They stared at each other in complete shocked silence.

Lord, she was easy on the eyes. An earth goddess in a floaty turquoise dress, which exposed her swan-like neck to perfection. A scarlet sash tied around her waist brought his attention to the sexy curve of her hips. Be-ringed bare toes peeped out from beneath the jagged skirt hem. Her auburn hair was longer, curling near the bottom of her full breasts, but it suited her gypsy image.

Kade cleared his throat and met her wary gaze head-on. "Is it true, Skylar? Do we have a baby?"

Her response was a long time coming. Finally, she nodded.

"Why didn't you tell me?"

"I tried to, Kade. I called your parents' house. You weren't there. I was told you'd moved. I didn't know where. I didn't know if you'd care."

Rather than snap *bullshit* at her, he expelled a frustrated sigh. "That means you didn't get my letter?"

Her green eyes narrowed suspiciously. "What letter?"

Shit. "I sent you a letter about a month ago. Tellin' you I was comin' back. Askin' if we could let bygones be bygones and start over."

"Start over as in... Start dating?"

"Uh. Yeah."

"I didn't receive any such letter." She squeezed her eyes shut for a second. "What else did it say?"

Her expression clearly said she thought he was lying. He had sent the damn thing. It'd taken him nearly a week to pen a few lousy paragraphs. "We can talk about all that later. Right now, I'd like to see my daughter."

"She's sleeping."

"I don't care. Wake her up."

Skylar's mouth opened. Then closed. "I'll be right back."

That had to be the longest, most excruciating minute of Kade's life. His whole body shook. He even had to lock his damn knees to keep them from quaking like a newborn colt's. Sweat dripped down his spine and soaked the waistband of his jeans. He clenched his teeth and his fists.

Just when he thought he couldn't stand the wait another second, Skylar appeared.

She approached him cautiously, holding a bundle wrapped in a fluffy yellow blanket, nestled against her lush breasts.

Kade couldn't breathe. He couldn't think. He couldn't take his eyes off that tiny bundle. Lord. It was so damn small. How could there be a living, breathing human baby in there?

When Skylar sidled up next to him and peeled back the blanket, revealing a sweet, perfect, beautifully pink face, Kade had a moment of utter pride and joy before his vision dimmed.

He swayed and everything went black.

Chapter Three

Terrific. One glimpse of his fifteen-pound baby daughter and the big, tough cowboy had passed out cold. Skylar rocked Eliza side to side, waiting for Kade to come around on his own. She was half afraid to rouse him because he might come up swinging, as the McKays were rumored to do when backed into a corner.

Finally, he groaned. "What happened?"

"You fainted."

Kade pushed to his knees. "Can you blame me? Ain't every day a man learns he's a daddy."

Huh. No macho posturing. No excuses for his swooning behavior. That surprised her. "You okay?"

"I guess. Good thing I gotta hard head." He rolled to his feet and snagged his hat. "What's her name?"

"Eliza."

"Eliza what?"

"Eliza Belle."

"No. What's her last name?"

"Ellison."

"Like hell. That's the first thing that's gonna change."

"Kade—"

"Give me a second to think."

The more Kade paced and muttered to himself, the more nervous Skylar became.

Suddenly he stopped and was right in her face. "Fine. We have a baby. You can change her name the same time you change yours. We'll get married."

"What!"

"Married. As in you and me are gettin' hitched as soon as possible." He looked down into Eliza's face and the hard line of his mouth softened. "She needs a mother and a father and luckily she's got both."

"That doesn't mean we're getting married, McKay."

"Why not?" Kade lifted those blue eyes, eyes identical to their daughter's. His dark gaze seemed to pierce a hole in her resolve.

"Because you cannot barge in here and make demands. It may work riding roughshod over cattle and horses but it won't fly with me. We don't even know each other."

"The hell we don't."

"Think about it. We had what? A dozen dates? We haven't seen each other in a year? We are basically strangers."

"Strangers? We created a child together. That makes us one helluva lot more than strangers."

"I disagree."

"I don't give a rat's behind whether you agree or not. This little gal," he pointed a thick finger at Eliza's dark head, "ain't gonna be a stranger to *me* any longer." That fiery blue gaze snagged hers again. "Maybe you're right. You don't know me. So let me tell you something. I ain't walkin' away from her. Ever. I take care of what's mine. Period."

"What is that supposed to mean?"

"You don't wanna get married? Fine. We'll get to know each other better first, since that's what's got you all fired up, thinkin' that we're strangers." He paused. "In fact, that'll work out better anyway."

"What will?"

"I'll just move in with you. We'll see how that goes first."

Warning bells clanged in her head. "Oh no. Absolutely not."

Silence.

Kade sighed. "Look. Be reasonable. This ain't about you and me, what we were, or weren't, or what we will be in the future. This is about her. I know it ain't easy bein' a single parent. I watched my cousin Cord struggle with it. You've been doin' all this pregnancy and baby stuff on your own and for that I'm truly sorry, Sky. I can't change the past. But I *am* here now. I will be a hands-on father, not to help you out, but because I wanna be in my daughter's life all the time, not just as a weekend daddy.

"So, for now, it'd be best if we didn't pass her back and forth between us, until I get to know Eliza where you and she are both comfortable. And that is in your house, under your watchful eye so I don't do something stupid or wrong." He smiled shyly. "To be real honest? I don't know nothin' about girls. Especially baby girls."

When Kade looked at her like that, she remembered how she'd ended up pregnant in the first place. The man oozed an earnest sexuality that still packed a wallop. Evidently time away from his intense eyes and devilish grin hadn't made her immune to his considerable charms because she found herself agreeing. "Okay."

Eliza squirmed and emitted a disgruntled cry.

Rather than retreat from her squawking, Kade tenderly touched Eliza's plump cheek. "Hey there, beautiful girl. What's got you fussin'? You hungry?"

Skylar melted a tiny bit at his immediate acceptance and interest in his daughter. "She's always hungry when she wakes up."

"I imagine." He kept stroking Eliza's face, staring at her with an expression resembling awe.

"You wanna hold her?"

"Like you wouldn't believe."

"You have held a baby before, right?"

"Not for a long time. And never mine."

Sky shifted sideways and gently placed Eliza in his arms.

Kade stiffened.

"Relax."

"Am I doin' this right?" His panicked gaze sought hers. "Or am I squeezin' her too tight?"

"You're doing fine, Daddy. Just make sure you support her head." Sky fussed with Eliza's blanket and murmured, "She likes to be snuggled close to your body."

"Like this?"

"Uh-huh." She studied his rapt face, bowled over by the raw emotion he didn't bother to hide. "Be warned. She is squirmy."

"She don't weigh much, does she?"

"You won't be saying that when you've been walking the floor with her all night because she won't stop crying. Those fifteen pounds feel like a hundred."

He smiled and brushed his thumb across Eliza's plump cheek. "I can't wait. I can't wait to do it all. Good Lord, she's so beautiful."

Not the response Skylar expected and it brought a lump to her throat. "I'll warm up a bottle."

That terrified look returned. "You're leavin' me alone with her?"

"I'll be in the back if you need anything."

After grabbing a bottle from the mini-fridge, Skylar heated a pan of water on the hot plate. She considered Kade's suggestion of moving in with them. Much as she'd been inclined to argue, it made sense. Not only could she use his help, she'd never intended to deny Kade contact with Eliza. She'd been too startled by his mother's unexpected appearance in the store this morning to ask Kimi McKay her oldest son's whereabouts. But she'd been thinking about it ever since. Wondering how she'd react when she saw him again.

Skylar remembered every little detail of the last time she'd seen him on that sultry evening last summer, sadness from a family tragedy had been weighing on him. They'd been on their way to dinner and the heavy silence in his truck had gotten too much for her to bear. She'd said, "Will you think I'm pandering if I say I'm worried about you?"

"No. It'd be nice to have someone worry about me for a change." He'd shot Skylar a sheepish look. "Sorry. Just feelin' low. Never thought I'd be thirty-one, single, and livin' back at home, wonderin' if my future is as bleak as it looks right now."

He seemed embarrassed by that admission as he parked at the far edge of the lot at the restaurant. "Hang tight. I'll come around and help you out. The damn interior light is broken. It's awful dark out here for you to be stumblin' around in them ankle breakin' shoes."

He opened the door. Skylar swung her legs to the running board, but didn't hop right out.

"What?" His hands tightened on her waist.

"You look like you could use a hug." She wreathed her arms around his neck. Scooting forward, she trapped his hips with her knees, which brought them pelvis-to-pelvis, chest-to-chest and almost mouth-to-mouth.

"Skylar—"

"Ssh. It's okay." She kissed him, wanting to chase away his melancholy. He relaxed into her like she'd given him exactly what he'd needed.

He was so sweet. So big and solid and sturdy. Such a contradiction with his hungry kisses and tentative touches. And he smelled like a million bucks. If she could bottle that elusive manly scent, she'd be filthy rich. He tasted of tobacco and toothpaste and Sky decided she could stay right there pressed against his firm body, secure in his strong arms, all night.

The kiss intensified. His rough palms slid up her thighs. She didn't bat away his roving hands. Neither did she protest when he cupped her breasts and stroked his thumbs across her hard nipples.

He kept touching her. Kissing her. God. She was dying for him to put his mouth to good use everywhere on her body. His lips tracked moist kisses down the sensitive line of her throat.

The stretchy material of her top gave way when he tugged. Her breasts popped free with one flick to the front clasp of her bra. Her bared skin was putty in his oh-so-capable hands. He sucked her nipples, one after the other until she couldn't think beyond the next thorough curl of his tongue around the puckered tips.

Amidst teasing bites to her mouth and throat, he rubbed his face over her neck and breasts, marking her with his suckling kisses and scratchy beard.

Reluctantly, he retreated to brush his lips across her hair. "Sorry for maulin' you. But you are so damn sexy you make me lose my ever lovin' mind. Give me a sec to clear it and we'll go in, okay?"

"I don't want to go in."

His head snapped up. "Then what do you want?"

"You. I want you. Right now. Like this." She whispered, "Please. Touch me. Don't stop this time."

He kissed her hard, as he eased her flat on the bench seat and slid her silky skirt up to the curve of her hips. He reached between her thighs and found her soaking wet, practically growling his pleasure. "I want my mouth on you."

"Next time."

"No. Now. Right now."

Never had a man been so forceful, so demanding of her submission. Never had she dreamed she'd...love giving in.

He twisted her panties in his fingers and yanked aside the flimsy cotton. No easing her into the intimate kiss. His wet tongue lapped her slit from top to bottom. Swirling. Tickling. Tasting. He tongued her relentlessly, jamming deep in her pussy, returning to flicker the very tip across her clit until her whole body shook. When he finally sucked that bit of protruding flesh, she came in a throbbing rush against his mouth.

As she attempted to regain her sanity, he feathered unbearably gentle kisses across the tops of her trembling thighs. He breathed heavily and muttered against her slick flesh.

Skylar lifted up on her elbows and looked down at his dark head nuzzling her.

His hot gaze met hers across the clothes bunched around her middle. "If I don't get inside you I'll go crazy."

"Then you'd better hurry up, huh?"

In record time he'd stepped up on the running board, unbuckled, unzipped, shoved his Wranglers to the tops of his boots and levered himself over her.

Skylar circled her legs around his waist and canted her pelvis for easier and faster entry, mindful of not nicking him with the razor-thin heels of her red stilettos. Her fingers dug into his tight, muscular ass.

Witnessing the ecstasy on his face as he slowly sank inside her to the root was one of the sexiest things she'd ever seen.

He pressed his forehead to hers. "Do you know how perfect you feel? Tight. All creamy wet, soft and hot for me? Do you know how long I've been achin' to be with you like this?"

"Oh, so *now* you wanna talk, McKay? When we're naked?"

He laughed, if a bit shakily.

"Talk later. Sex me up first. Kiss me. God, your kisses undo me."

He kissed her with the same vigor as he made love to her. The heat in the truck expanded, making for a sticky, hot and intense coupling, yet, retaining the balance of comfort they both needed.

His thrusts became more frantic. Deeper. Faster. He pulled away from her mouth to whisper, "Skylar. Take me with you this time." Lifting her hips higher, he slammed home three more times.

When she came in a series of juicy ripples, he buried his face in her neck, repeating her name, and followed her over the edge.

She frowned. Now that she thought about it, she hadn't said *his* name. She'd taken to calling him McKay on their previous dates. About an hour after that fateful incident, she'd learned the truth about who he really was.

Wrong. His name may've been different, but the man was the same.

Eliza cried, jarring Skylar back to the present.

Kade entered the small backroom. "Is that bottle ready yet?"

Damn. She'd been so lost in the vivid memory of him, of them, of heat and sex and need and lust, she'd forgotten all about the bottle. She popped it in the pan. "Just about ready."

He took one look at her flushed cheeks and bright eyes and somehow knew she'd been reliving their brief—but glorious—naked past.

Defiant, she raised her chin a notch. "What?"

Kade's look held more steam than the pan of boiling water. "I think about it all the time too. Some days that's all I can think of."

"Do you want to feed her?"

"Later. I'd best get back to my folks' place and pack up my stuff. What time will you get home?"

"Around five-thirty."

"I'll be there earlier than that."

"Wait. You'll need a key." She removed the front door key from the massive key ring and set it on the counter. Skylar watched as Kade kissed Eliza's wrinkled forehead and murmured, "Later, sweet baby," before he awkwardly snuggled her back in Skylar's arms.

Then he did the strangest thing: he kissed Skylar's forehead and whispered, "Later, sweet baby," to her, snatched the key and took off like a shot.

She sighed and settled in the rocking chair. "He's in for it now, girlie girl. We'll see how long he lasts in this parenting gig."

But part of her knew Kade McKay wasn't a short-term kind of guy. He was the type to stick around for the long haul.

That scared her far worse than him not being around at all.

Chapter Four

Twenty miles from Moorcroft, Kade turned off the main highway onto a gravel road. He motored past the gigantic steel building, noticing an open gate to the parking lot. Being a lifelong rancher, leaving gates open drove him crazy.

He passed through another wide-open gate, which separated the Sky Blue factory from Skylar's private residence. The old ranch house was blocked from view by a row of scraggly trees.

Unlike most Wyoming residents, her front door was locked. Kade set his bags next to the staircase in the cool, dark foyer. He looked at the pictures lining the hallway, a mish-mash of snapshots, artwork, formal studio poses and old-time sepia-toned groups of photos from a century past.

The items on the opposite wall were hand-stitched family samplers. Mini-quilts, needlepoint, delicate doilies; all fussy female handiwork encased in glass and gilded frames. He wouldn't have pegged Skylar's decorating taste as old-fashioned, Western and homey.

He didn't snoop beyond checking out the rooms on the main floor. Baby stuff had overtaken the antique dining room table. Didn't look like Skylar did much entertaining, which filled him with an odd sense of relief.

The formal feeling of the front room—matching floral couches, heavy velvet drapes, tasseled pillows, elaborately carved antique end tables—was completely overpowered by more baby paraphernalia. A swing. A stroller. A half-barrel-shaped thing camouflaged with a lace canopy. Piles of pastel-colored clothes were stacked on the coffee table next to every baby book imaginable.

Kade cringed when he finally caught sight of the tiny TV shoved in the corner by the dust-covered piano. After a year of no television, a big screen would be his first contribution to the household.

On impulse he picked up a pink, fuzzy one-piece outfit with snaps from the top down to the feet holes. The scent of soap and baby powder wafted up and his stomach clenched. It smelled like Eliza, clean, soft and powdery sweet. As much as he'd loved just holding her, he couldn't wait to do all the corny things like count her fingers and toes, blow raspberries on her stomach and rock her to sleep.

His cell phone trilled in his shirt pocket. No big mystery who was pestering him. "Hiya, Grama. Look, I know you wanna see Eliza, but you hafta give Skylar and me time to work some things out first." He held the phone away to keep it from blistering his ear.

"No, I don't know how long. I'll be drivin' to and from the ranch everyday startin' on Monday. Absolutely not. Kane and Dad can handle it for a couple days without me. Because I've been gone a year and they've done fine. Three more days ain't gonna make a difference. I'll keep in touch." He clicked the phone off. She'd be too busy bragging about her granddaughter to everyone in Crook County to call him back, for at least a day, and sad to say, few others had his new number.

He glanced at the grandfather clock. Skylar and Eliza would be home in roughly two hours. Picking up a stray blanket, he returned to the kitchen.

Kade unfolded the blanket on the table and placed the twenty-pound bag of russet potatoes in the center. He stared at it for a good long time before he sighed and wrapped the fleece around it. "Goddamn I hope nobody sees me doin' this."

The potato baby didn't answer.

Gently, Kade picked up the bundle and tucked it in the crook of his arm. He paced the first floor from room to room, keeping hold of the spud baby, bouncing it, rocking it. Performing all the motions he'd seen women doing with their infants—short of crooning a lullaby. He felt like a darn fool, slinking around, hugging a plastic bag that smelled like dirt, but he was determined Skylar wouldn't know just how much of a greenhorn he was when it came to holding babies.

A loud crash out by the barn startled him. He tripped on the rug in the foyer and right before he hit the ground, his "baby" squirted out of his arms like a slippery bar of soap. The bag busted open and potatoes flew everywhere.

Damn. That didn't bode well. His face burned with shame as he gathered up the potatoes. First thing he'd do was confess his ineptitude in the baby arena rather than risk hurting Eliza because of his stupid pride.

An hour later the front door slammed. Thundering footsteps echoed down the hallway. Before he turned around, an angry female voice demanded, "What the fuck are you doing in my sister's house?"

Kade tossed in a can of beans in the enamel pot. "I'm makin' supper."

"You think that's funny?"

He shrugged.

"Who the hell are you?"

Kade spun, giving his accuser a once over. Definitely a stunning woman, despite her unnaturally colored scarlet-tipped black hair. Despite her irate posture and the angry tapping of a combat-booted foot. The motion rattled the chains attached to her purple leather mini-skirt. His gaze swept her colorful arms. Whoa. Was that tattoo circling her wrist a flesh-colored snake? Or a very large, very erect cock?

"Eyes off the ink, buddy. Who are you?"

He met her angry gaze head-on. "I'm Kade McKay."

She actually stumbled back a step. "Holy shit. You're Eliza's father."

He nodded, noticing the woman's arched eyebrow was pierced, as was her nose and her lower lip. Both ears were weighted with a variety of sparkly stones and shiny hoop earrings.

"She looks just like you."

"I know. I saw her today for the first time."

"For the first time? She's over three months old!"

"Yeah, I heard."

"You *heard*? How could you abandon my pregnant sister, you worthless piece of shit?"

"First off, no more name callin'." He soldiered on despite the woman's mulish look. "Secondly, who are *you*?"

"Skylar's sister, India." India crossed her arms over her chest. "Sky knows you're here?"

"Who do you think gave me a key?" Kade's eyes narrowed. "Do *you* live here?"

"Not anymore. I did while Sky was expecting, since the jerk-off loser who impregnated her vanished and someone needed to keep an eye on her out here in the middle of nowhere."

"Before you keep rippin' on my character, let me assure you that I didn't know Skylar was pregnant. If I had known, no way would I've left her. No. Way."

"So where've you been that she couldn't call you up and tell you the news about her bun in the oven?" With mock sweetness, she asked, "Prison?"

"Funny."

"No, really, what were you doing?"

India was a nosy thing, but Kade appreciated she was protecting Skylar. "Ranchin'. We bought new grazin' lands about forty miles northwest of our place. Rugged country. No phone, no Internet, no satellite TV. Don't have electricity in the cabin half the time. Closest town is sixty miles further north up into the mountains, and the road leadin' to it is damn near impassable from the end of October to the end of March. I volunteered to stay to see if it was viable to keep a year-round cattle operation up there. I returned home two days ago after havin' been gone for a year. Today I find out that Skylar and me have a baby girl."

India stared at him for the longest time. "You said your last name is McKay?"

"Yeah."

"You related to all the McKays living around Sundance?"

He resisted the urge to deny it. "Yeah."

"Those McKay men have reputations as wild men and womanizers, boozers and brawlers and I cannot believe my straight-laced sister would get mixed up with one of them."

Story of his life. "I've been out of the loop, so I have no earthly idea what some of my rowdier cousins might've been doin'."

India cocked her head. "My first thought when Sky became an unwed mother, was that she was embarrassed by who knocked her up, so that's why she didn't want anyone to know."

Very evenly, Kade said, "Did you ask her who the father was?"

"Repeatedly. Can't say I blamed her on keeping mum. I made no secret I'd planned on tracking down the lowlife to beat him within an inch of his life."

"There you go with the name callin' again."

"If the spur fits." She smiled nastily. "Far as I know, she didn't tell anybody else either. I didn't even know she'd been seeing anyone, so her pregnancy was a complete shock."

"Hell, I didn't even have time to get used to the pregnancy; I gotta wrap my head around my baby." Kade sighed. "And like you said, my family has quite the reputation. Maybe she was embarrassed. Can't say as I blame her since I wasn't around."

"What really happened between you two?" India shifted from boot to boot.

Her nervous energy set Kade on edge. "I did a dumb thing, she broke it off when she found out, wouldn't let me explain, and I ended up leavin' because of it. I wasn't happy, but she'd left me no choice but to let her be."

"She's good at pushing people away."

"I sorta figured that out," Kade said dryly.

"Tell me this. If the misunderstanding between you two would've been cleared up, would you have left?" He shook his head. "Does she know that?"

"Not yet."

"When do you plan on telling her?"

"When the time is right."

"You play your cards pretty close to the vest, McKay."

Kade thought that was better than wearing his heart on his sleeve.

An uncomfortable moment followed.

"Fine." India threw up her hands. "Pull that strong, silent cowboy crap. So what happens now?"

"If you're askin' if my intentions toward your sister are honorable, I asked her to marry me today."

"She immediately said no, didn't she?"

He frowned. "Yeah. How did you know?"

"Because she's been..." India shook her head. "Because I don't think she has a spontaneous bone in her body. She's always been that way. So, in addition to her all-pro status of pushing people away, Skylar excels at taking an eternity to make a decision, any decision. She's meticulous. She weighs every opinion, thought, word, action and deed from every conceivable angle before she really gets down to the nitty-gritty of making a final determination on a course of action."

"Great." He squinted at her and challenged, "Doesn't sound like you like her much."

India's blue eyes nearly turned black with anger. "I worship her, I'd do anything in the world for her, and I'm thinking about punching you in the mouth for suggesting I don't, McKay."

Kade held up his hands. "Sorry."

"Skylar and I are polar opposites, but that doesn't change the fact she's the greatest person in the world and she's a wonderful mother."

"Which is all good and well, even if she won't agree to become my wife, I am movin' in to help care for Eliza."

"You are?"

He nodded.

Another pause hung in the air. Then India smiled like a loon. "That's hysterical. She won't marry you, so you just bulled your way into being her roommate?"

"Pretty much."

"Surprises me she allowed it."

"Me too. Sky might be all kinds of reserved, but I am damn determined to have my way on this, India."

"I can see that. Since I've already given you the 4-1-1 on her, I should also warn you Skylar is used to being in charge of everything."

"So am I."

"Yeah? Then it oughta be interesting to see if she'll even let you be a father to Eliza."

"*Let* me? I *am* Eliza's father. I ain't givin' her a choice. I'm here for good. Eliza better get used to it. Sky'd better get used to it." Kade sent Skylar's sister a half-menacing smile. "You'd better get used to it too."

"Please. You don't scare me, cowboy. I deal with drunks and druggies and bikers all damn day. But one thing my sister and I do have in common? We're both fighters. Hardheaded. You determined to get your way is not gonna be easy. For either of you."

He didn't rise to the bait. Nor would he back down. "Nothin' worthwhile ever is."

India considered him without malice. "No pain, no gain, huh?"

"Not the phrase I'd choose, but yeah, I suppose that fits."

"Good luck, because, man, are you gonna need it."

Kade grinned. "Oh, I don't need luck. I've got something even better."

"What's that?"

"A strong set of ropes, an iron will, and all the patience in the world."

Chapter Five

The spicy aroma of tomato and chili powder greeted Skylar at the front door. She half wondered if she'd stumbled into the wrong house, especially when a gorgeous man strolled down the hallway with a grin a mile wide. A grin aimed at her.

"And here I was hopin' you'd yell, 'Hey honey, I'm home'."

"Sorry to disappoint you."

"Maybe next time. Lemme take her." He plucked the baby carrier from her arm like it weighed nothing.

"Thanks." Skylar kicked off her sandals and noticed Kade was barefoot. She also noticed he'd changed out of his usual cowboy attire. Instead of Wranglers and a long-sleeved shirt, he wore faded black sweatpant shorts and a gray tank top, which showed off his muscular arms and broad chest.

"Supper's done whenever you're ready." He headed for the living room.

She followed him and bit back a groan. The view from the rear was just as good as the front view. His wide shoulders tapered into a narrow waist, ending with an ass so round and tight she could've bounced a quarter off it. Or sunk her teeth into it to double-check if it was as firm and yummy as it looked.

Get control of yourself, Sky.

Why was she having this physical reaction to him again? Strictly hormonal on a biological level because he was the father of her child?

No. You're reacting this way because that man—your new roommate—is smoking hot.

He set the car seat on the floor. "You wanna show me how

to get her outta this contraption?"

"Sure. Push the red button, move the handle up until it locks. Then unfasten the seatbelt. Just like that. See? Easy."

Eliza's eyes blinked open and she stared at Kade as he lifted her out.

"Well, aren't you a bright-eyed little thing?"

Skylar watched him, chattering away to his daughter like it was an everyday occurrence. Her emotions shifted from jealousy to relief to flat-out amusement. The man was a goner for Miss Eliza Belle. He'd taken to her faster than Sky ever imagined.

"Is she always this good?"

"No." Sky glanced at the clock. "Give her an hour. She gets really fussy around dinnertime. And then right before bed."

"I'll keep her entertained if you wanna eat."

"She does have a baby bouncer. You don't have to hold her all the time."

Kade's eyes met hers. "I wanna hold her. You're gonna have a devil of a time gettin' her away from me." When Skylar balked, he amended, "That didn't come out right. What I meant was...I'm just pretty much stunned by her. Not only that I didn't know she existed, but if it'll ever sink in that she's really mine. And I'm responsible for her for the rest of her life."

"It's a daunting concept, isn't it?"

"Yeah. I really haven't been around babies all that much, if you wanna know the truth, so I'm gonna need your help."

Skylar expected gruffness, not Kade to act as bewildered and awestruck as she'd been. She touched his forearm, offering him reassurance "Give yourself more than a day to process it all, Kade. I had six months to get used to the idea of a baby, while she was growing inside me. You've had six hours. The more time you spend with her, the easier it'll get."

"You trust me with her?"

"You wouldn't be here if I didn't. Besides, I didn't know all that much about babies either. To some extent, it is instinctive. Only way to learn is by doing."

Sky sidestepped him and wandered to the kitchen, shocked at how easy it was to leave Kade with their daughter.

He'd cleaned the counters and washed dishes. A pot of chili

simmered on the stove. A round bakery box with a chocolate frosted cake sat in the middle of the table. She sagged against the doorway. He'd remembered her favorite dessert.

Dammit. It'd be easier to keep this situation impersonal if he was a complete dickhead.

Impersonal. Right. A little too late for that. They had a child. The man had proposed to her not four hours ago. Apparently, he'd moved in. And apparently, she didn't mind. She expelled a heavy sigh and muttered, "Maybe I should've just said yes."

"The offer still stands, Skylar."

His deep voice next to her ear sent a shiver through her. "You scared me."

"I know."

Did he mean he knew sneaking up on her scared her? Or was he talking about his marriage proposal? Rather than dig herself into a hole, she bit back the demand for clarification.

During dinner she shared the abbreviated version of her pregnancy and Eliza's birth while Kade pored over the pictures and information in the baby book. When Eliza began to fuss, Skylar taught him how to mix formula, how to warm a cold bottle and how to test the temperature. After he finished feeding Eliza, Sky tossed him a spit-up rag and instructed him on burping.

Kade listened so attentively Skylar half-expected him to whip out a notebook and jot down notes. It didn't faze him when Eliza barfed all over him. Changing a diaper didn't make him turn green. He walked the floor until Eliza fell asleep in his arms, and he still wouldn't relinquish his hold on her.

"Seriously. Put her in the bassinet. She'll nap for an hour and then she'll want to eat again before she's out for the night. Or part of the night. She still doesn't sleep straight through."

Reluctantly, Kade laid Eliza on her back in the bassinet, tucked a blanket around her and flopped on the opposite end of the couch.

He expelled a long slow breath. "We need to talk."

She waited, half-afraid/half-curious about how this'd play out.

A beat passed. "First off, I wouldn't have taken the job if I woulda known you were pregnant."

"What would you have done? I didn't find out until the end of November. By then I was a little more than three months along. And I did call your parents' house to talk to you. I had no idea what I should do when your brother said you'd be out of touch until the following summer."

He scowled. "You talked to Kane?"

"Briefly. I wasn't comfortable having him pass on the message about your impending fatherhood."

"So you kept the information to yourself?"

"What other choice did I have?"

"What choice did *you* have? Jesus, Sky, that's the problem. You seem to think you get to make all the choices and keep all the control in this relationship. You have since day one." Kade shoved a hand through his hair. "I'll admit I made a mistake in not tellin' you I wasn't Kane. But you cut me off without lettin' me explain my side of things."

She bristled. "You pretended to be someone else. I slept with you thinking you were Kane. How is that my fault?"

"It isn't."

"At least we agree on that point."

Kade sighed. "Skylar. I don't wanna fight with you."

When it occurred to her he'd used the word *relationship*, she looked at him oddly.

He stared right back, completely nonplussed. "Does anyone ever mix you up with your sister?"

"No. Even before India became the tattooed woman we weren't hard to tell apart. Different eye color, facial structure, body type." India was lean and muscular and sometimes Skylar resented that she'd been cursed with a rounder, womanly physique, but they were easily distinguishable from one another.

"This ain't an excuse, but you don't have any idea how that feels. Not only am I saddled with an identical twin, but we also look just like our other McKay cousins in three counties. Some folks act as if we're all interchangeable. So I've heard 'one of them McKay twins' or 'one of those wild McKay boys' my whole life. Seems I don't have an identity beyond my last name.

"Might sound stupid, but I'd convinced myself that for once, the name I had, the name you knew me by, didn't matter, because you were interested in the man inside. Yeah, I realize it was dumb. But I didn't have any idea on how to go about making it right back then."

She waited, unsure of where he was going with this and unsure of how she'd respond.

Kade reached for her hand. "Except I can make it right now. Let's start over."

"It's too late."

"It's never too late. Come on. I'll go first." He formally shook her hand. "Howdy, little lady. I'm Kade McKay."

Skylar laughed.

"You shore are purty. Anyone ever told you that you have a beautiful laugh? Like bluebells in springtime."

"Kade."

"You maybe wanna go out with me sometime?" He grinned and gave her an exaggerated wiggle of his eyebrows. "Or do you just wanna skip all that normal datin' stuff and have my baby?"

She laughed again. It'd been a long time since she'd made that carefree sound. She'd forgotten how Kade had tried to cajole her out of a mood during their dates, if she'd had a stressful day at the office. Not only was he sweet, he was the rare person who could make her laugh. She squeezed their joined hands. "You goof-ball."

"C'mere." He tugged her until she fell across his lap. His arms came around her, keeping her close. "You looked like you could use a hug."

She twisted her neck to gape at him. "You remember that?"

"I remember everything. I had nothin' but time to think about it. All of it."

Even when her mouth said, "This isn't a good idea," Sky's attempt to squirm away was half-hearted at best.

"Relax. I ain't gonna maul you. We'll be less apt to argue if we're close like this. Plus, if I have hold of your hand, you won't be tempted to take a swing at me, since rumor has it you're a fighter."

She wondered where he'd heard that. Did she have a reputation around town as a hard-nosed business woman? Cold, efficient and emotionless? No matter, for now, she'd let him soothe her with simple human contact, just for a minute or two.

"You take Eliza to work with you every day?"

"Yeah. She's usually pretty good and it helps I can set my own hours. I try to keep us both on a daily schedule. If I have to be on a conference call, or meet with salespeople and distributors, I can leave her with the onsite daycare."

"You have onsite daycare at Sky Blue?"

"It's the one thing I insisted on. The women working for me all have kids. Since a large chunk of their paychecks would go for childcare, I set up an area onsite and have them care for each other's children so they can keep every penny they earn."

"Smart. But how's that work?"

"I opted to have all employees rotate all positions. It cuts down on training time, since they are trained on every job. Every six days they rotate from the factory into the daycare. So even if someone is sick, we won't get behind on production because another employee can step in and do her job. Plus, it is a load off their minds that their kids are close by, and well-cared for, which in the long run means steady productivity and happier employees."

"How many people work for you?"

"I have six full-time employees in the factory. One woman who helps me with office work."

"I'll bet you have a waitin' list a mile long for potential employees, if any one of those women would be foolish enough to quit workin' for you."

"Now that I'm a mother, I know I made the right decision in setting up the business the way I did."

Kade was quiet. "So when it rolls around to quittin' time, you drive up the road and spend your nights carin' for Eliza? After bein' with her all day?"

"Eliza isn't a burden, Kade, she's everything to me. I never knew I could...love someone that much." Her voice dropped. "Sometimes I'm so overwhelmed by her, by what a perfect little being she is and how much she's become my life..." Sky was still stunned every day by how much Eliza's birth changed her as a person. Now Kade was here, giving her the opportunity to bare all the emotions she'd kept inside about how their miracle "oops" was the best thing that'd ever happened to her.

Would he understand? Or did it just make her seem pathetic that she had no one else to talk to? Especially when she knew he had support from his huge family?

Sure, Sky could spill her guts to India; God knew she'd listened to India's issues for years. But India had already provided tons of emotional support during Sky's pregnancy and Eliza's birth. It seemed cruel to wax poetic about the sheer joys of motherhood and her beautiful baby considering the heartbreak India had suffered through a few years back. As much as Sky appreciated and genuinely liked her employees, there was a line of propriety between worker and boss she didn't feel comfortable crossing. Between setting up her business and birthing Eliza, she hadn't had much opportunity to get to know other women in the community or to make friends.

Did she just want friendship from Kade McKay?

"Skylar? What's goin' on in that pretty head?" he murmured.

Emotional soup. Wanna bite? Sometimes it's hot; sometimes it's cold.

Kade turned her around to face him. "Hey."

"It's not like I had a choice."

"You do now." He caressed her cheek. "I'll be here every night as soon as I finish up on the ranch. I ain't gonna let you do this alone any more."

Might make her a fool, but she wanted to believe him. She wanted to throw herself in his arms and weep with gratitude. But blind faith had caused more problems in her life than self-reliance, so she kept her shield of skepticism intact. "Just like that? No arguing? You're just accepting this? Accepting her?"

"Yeah." His thumb traced the dark circles she knew were visible beneath her eyes. "No doubt Eliza is my child. She's my responsibility. In my mind, that means you are, too. Believe me, that isn't a burden either."

Rational thought vanished when he touched her. His

sweetly spoken, heartfelt words, his gentle caress, the warmth in his eyes packed an emotional punch and she didn't attempt to dodge the blow.

Then the look in Kade's eyes changed from comfort to pure male sexual power. His thumb moved down and swept across her bottom lip. Over and over. Making it softer. Wetter. He didn't say a word; he didn't have to.

Her mind screamed retreat. She felt the shift in him and tried to stop her body from answering in kind. His breath fanned across her cheek in an erotic stroke of heat. No man had ever looked at her the way he did. It scared the living crap out of her; it always had.

She tried to scramble away, but he clamped his hand around her upper thigh.

"Let me speak my piece before you run off. This isn't what I came here for. But there's been a hot spark between us since the day we met. I'll be damned if I'm gonna deny it's happenin' again."

"Denial would be easier."

"Maybe for you. Not for me. Never for me. I pretended with you once. I won't do it again. Ever." Then he released her, and walked out of the room.

Nice going, McKay. Tell her you're not going to maul her and what's the first thing you do?

Growl and go all Big Bad Wolf on her.

Christ. He was an idiot. One touch, one hopeful, coquettish look from Sky and he morphed into a horny toad. Kade inhaled several deep breaths and stared out the window above the sink.

His feelings for Skylar hadn't changed. Things had gone to hell between them last summer before he'd mustered up the guts to confess he'd fallen for her. Hard. And judging by the way she was acting, she wouldn't welcome any declaration of his feelings or his intent. At least not right now. Seemed he had no choice but to hang back and let this play out at her pace, not his. Luckily he was a patient man.

Calmer, Kade grabbed a bottle from the refrigerator. Eliza would be up soon, he may as well get ready to feed her.

Soft footsteps stopped behind him.

Kade spun around. "Look. I'm sorry. I touched you like I had a right to. I don't. The last thing I want is to make you uncomfortable in your own house."

"Let's forget it, okay? Chalk it up to being a stressful day. I'm going upstairs to get your room ready. Eliza is still down here in the bassinet. Will you listen for her to wake up?"

"Sure. Where am I sleepin'?"

"In the guest bedroom."

"Where does Eliza usually sleep?"

"In my room."

"That's gonna be a problem when I get up with her in the middle of the night."

"No it won't be. I'll just deal with the night feedings and get up with her like I always do."

"The hell you will. I'm here to care for our child. That means day and night. If she sleeps in your room, so do I."

Skylar looked petrified for a moment before she regained her composure. "Funny, McKay. You had me going there for a second."

"I ain't kiddin'." He crossed his arms over his chest, knew it looked belligerent and didn't care. "I'd be fine if you moved her crib into the guest bedroom with me."

"But all her stuff is in my room. I hadn't planned to decorate and put her into her own room for at least another month."

"Then it'd be smart to keep her right where she is, wouldn't it?"

She blinked with the same owl-eyed expression Eliza had earlier. "So what you're saying, is..."

"It appears you and I are gonna be roomies, darlin'."

"Oh no."

"Oh *yes*. You stay on your side of the bed. I'll stay on mine."

"So we're sharing a bed strictly as parenting partners?"

"Yep."

"You'll be a perfect gentleman?"

"If that's what you want. Besides, you'll probably be so glad to get a full night's sleep that you won't even notice I'm there."

"But—"

"But, it's only for a few weeks, until you put her in her own room, right?"

"Ah. Right."

"So, how hard can it be?"

The look on Skylar's face was priceless. He knew she wasn't convinced it'd be no big deal having him in her bed.

And that's exactly what Kade was counting on.

Chapter Six

Two weeks later...

"Wah. Wah. Wah." Pause. "Waaaaaaaaaaaaaaaaaaa."

Skylar groaned and rolled toward the edge of the bed. "Hang on, baby. I'm coming."

Kade placed his hand on her shoulder. "Stay put. I'll get her. Go back to sleep."

She mumbled, "Thanks." The minute he was out of bed, she sprawled in the middle of the mattress and snagged his pillow.

What a bed hog.

"Wah. Wah. Wah."

"Good Lord, child. Them lungs work fine at four in the mornin', don't they?" Kade murmured, scooping Eliza out of her crib. He skirted the footboard and snuck out of the room.

Downstairs in the kitchen, he kept the lights dimmed as he reheated a bottle. Eliza rooted against his chest, making angry snuffing sounds. He brushed his lips across the top of her head, inhaling her sweet baby scent, rocking her back and forth. "I know. Poor starvin' girl."

The timer dinged. Kade plucked the bottle from the pan, tested the temperature, shifted Eliza into the crook of his arm and popped the nipple in her mouth. Greedy sucking noises echoed in the quiet house as he headed for the rocking chair in the dark living room.

After he set the rocker in motion, he closed his eyes. He was tired. The third time he'd been up with their fussy baby in so many hours. Usually he and Sky took turns, but the last two nights Eliza hadn't slept for more than an hour at a stretch. Didn't help Sky said Eliza wasn't napping during the day. She screamed bloody murder any time Skylar wasn't holding her, so Skylar had fallen behind at work.

When Kade returned from a long day at the ranch, Sky passed Eliza off to him and snuck back to the office for a few hours. He'd gotten into the habit of dozing when Eliza did, as it was his only chance for a little rest. How had Sky done this by herself for three months?

No matter. The important thing was Sky trusted him with Eliza. His darling Eliza's immediate and unconditional acceptance of him was damn humbling too. It filled him with pride that both mother and daughter had begun to rely on him, to need him, and it amazed him how quickly he, Sky and Eliza created a family routine.

So as exhausting as the past two weeks had proven, Kade didn't remember ever being so content.

He sure as hell didn't remember ever being so horny.

Damn. If he wasn't thinking about formula and diapers, or wondering how loud his daughter could howl, or what he wouldn't give for a full night's sleep, his thoughts focused on sex. Hot sex. Slow sex. Fast sex. Nasty, dirty, raunchy sex. Sweet vanilla sex. Any type of sex, really. He'd gone for long stretches without it in the past. When he tired of his own fist as a partner, he'd find a willing woman to scratch the itch. Problem solved.

Now the problem was Kade couldn't fathom having sex with anyone besides Skylar. Fearful of her rejection, he hadn't the balls to make the first move.

What the fuck had he been thinking, promising that gentleman crap? He didn't want to be her goddamn "parenting partner"—he wanted to be her lover. The sexiest woman on the planet lay beside him, mere inches away, every night. Warming the sheets with her body heat. Surrounding him with her alluring scent so he couldn't breathe without thinking of her. And to make his descent into lust complete, the standoffish Skylar had started...snuggling up to him in her sleep.

Oh, she wasn't aware of spooning her body to his. She wasn't aware she hummed contentedly before drifting off. But he was aware. Acutely aware. Painfully aware.

Still, Kade never touched her. His hands ached from squeezing them into tight fists. Some nights his cock was so hard he couldn't sleep, yet he couldn't force himself away. He'd close his eyes and breathe her in.

On those rare occasions Eliza let them rest for a few hours, Kade imagined waking Skylar with hot kisses. Peeling away the baby doll pajamas she favored. Running his hands down her long, slender throat, between her full breasts and over her belly, until his fingers brushed the curls covering her sex.

She'd dreamily whisper, "Please," in the darkness as she opened her legs for his touch. With his mouth busy on her neck, or his tongue tasting her nipples, his fingers grew damp and sticky from her arousal. He'd slide in and out of that sweet heat, deeper, faster, sweeping the pad of his thumb over her clit, building her excitement. When he sent her soaring over the edge, he'd clamp his mouth over hers and swallow her cries as he mounted her.

He'd stare into her eyes, pushing his cock into her, an inch at a time while she was still coming. Kade would fuck her with painstaking precision, keeping her teetering on the brink of another orgasm. She'd whimper for more; he'd deny her, keeping her body pinned beneath his. When he allowed her to climax, she'd moan his name. He'd ram into her, coming hard enough to leave them both gasping, sweaty, fucking her so completely she'd never mix him up with another man again.

Tame, as far as fantasies went, but damn perfect in his mind.

He glanced at Eliza. She'd finally crashed. He removed the bottle from her milk-slackened mouth and carefully repositioned her on his shoulder. Two pats on her back and she belched.

Wearily, Kade rose out of the rocking chair and climbed the stairs.

The bed dipped and Skylar rolled to her side.

"She asleep?"

"Yeah."

"You're a good daddy."

"Mmm. I'm good at a lot of other things too."

The next thing she knew, the bedcovers were flung back and his hot, naked body was pressed against hers.

"Kade, I don't think—"

He sank his teeth into the curve of her shoulder and her whole body shuddered. "Then don't. I'm dyin' to touch you, Sky."

"But, Eliza—"

"Is sleepin'. We're not. Maybe we oughta take advantage of that fact."

Rough hands skated from her collarbone down to her hip. His warm mouth left a trail of kisses up the back of her neck and his breath stirred her hair, making her shiver. Making her realize how long it'd been since she'd felt this rush of need.

"Lemme make you feel good."

"Kade—"

"Ssh." Then he shifted so she was lying on top of him. Her back plastered to his immense chest. Her legs layered over his, the coarse hair and rougher skin of his thighs tickled the backside of her knees. Her arms were stretched high above her head. He'd nestled his erect cock in the crack of her ass, lengthwise between her butt cheeks. A low, sexy chuckle burned her ear. "Kinda like a hot dog fittin' into a bun, huh?"

She groaned softly at his strangely voiced observation and gave up any pretense of resistance. His callused hands traced her arms from her wrists, down past her elbows, over her biceps until his big palms cupped her breasts. He strummed her nipples with the pads of his thumbs while kissing the slope of her shoulder.

"I love your tits. So soft and round. Perfect for my hands and mouth. For buryin' my face in. Suckin' 'em for hours until you come."

Skylar turned her head to try and kiss him.

"Ah-ah-ah." Kade flattened his hands and dragged them oh-so-slowly down her belly to her hips. The first two fingers on his right hand breached her curls, and slipped down her slit to plunge inside her sex.

She hissed.

He stroked her several times, each thrust deeper, each thrust bypassed her clit.

"Touch me."

"I am." He sucked on the spot behind her ear that made her head swim. "Maybe you oughta point out exactly where you want me touchin' you." Kade reached for her right arm, placing his palm over the top of her hand, gliding their joined hands down her torso to rest on the top of her pubic bone. "Show me."

Skylar pushed their joined fingers inside her pussy, pumping in and out, coating all four digits with her wetness. "You do that," she said, leaving his fingers. She slid her hand up, placing her middle finger on her clit, rubbing in circles, making sure he could feel her every movement. "While I do this." Sky never remembered being so bold. So brazen. So confident with her sexuality.

Kade created a rhythm, setting her whole body tingling with anticipation. Then he tilted his pelvis slightly and his cock slid in her crack as he fucked her pussy with his fingers.

"Oh. That feels...good. Really good." She rubbed her finger faster over that engorged nub. Sweat made their bodies slippery. The room was filled with the sounds of skin scraping on fabric, heavy breathing and a slight squeak of the bedframe.

"Clench your cheeks." Kade's beard rasped over her arched neck as he drove his fingers deeper and rolled his hips. "Come on, darlin', bear down. Squeeze me hard."

Her internal muscles clamped around his thrusting fingers. Her butt cheeks tightening around his cock set off an orgasmic chain reaction, traveling from her pussy to the top of her ass crack and she moaned, "Yes, like that. Please, deeper."

The tip of his cock jerked, coating the small of her back with sticky warmth, and he swore a blue streak in her ear.

She flung her arm over her eyes, rocking into him, slowing the strokes on her clit to prolong the moment. The blast of pleasure roared in her head, blocking out all sound but her stuttered gasps of orgasmic bliss.

Kade heard Skylar thrashing around in bed before he opened the door to peek inside. It took a second for his head to decipher the images his eyes were relaying.

Skylar was in the middle of the bed. Pajama bottoms off. Her left forearm draped across her eyes. Her right hand stroking madly between her legs as she climaxed.

Holy shit.

He waited. If he burst in now she'd probably die of embarrassment. But Kade realized Skylar wasn't aware of what she'd been doing; she'd been dreaming.

Jesus. Must've been some damn good dream. What would he've done if he'd been in bed next to her when she indulged in a little self-love?

Woken her up and fucked her like a madman, convincing himself it was his way of making her dreams come true.

Kade paced the hallway a few more minutes before he snuck in and tucked Eliza in her crib. He stared at Skylar's half-naked body lolling on his side of the bed, in the ultimate pin-up girl pose. The ultimate temptation. No way could he crawl in there and not touch her. No way.

The clock blinked five a.m. Sun'd be up soon. Might as well get an early start on his day. Right after he grabbed a shower.

A very cold shower.

Skylar was freezing. Disoriented, she sat up. At some point in the night she'd whipped off the covers along with her pajama bottoms. Her gaze landed on Kade's empty side of the bed. Huh. She squinted at the crib and saw Eliza's dark head. Vaguely she remembered Kade getting up with the baby.

When?

And why in the world was she half-undressed? Carnal images bombarded her. Kade. Stretching her out on top of him. Touching her. Bringing them both to a shuddering orgasm.

It hadn't been a dream...had it?

The old pipes rattled, signaling Kade was in the shower. Why was he up so early?

Probably washing up after he came all over your back and his belly.

Her hand flew to the base of her spine. Dry. Not sticky. She patted the bed behind her. Warm. Not wet.

Not real. A dream.

Why did disappointment jab her in the gut?

Because you're too much of a chickenshit to admit Kade McKay turns you on beyond reason. And the last thing you want is a gentleman in your bed; you'd prefer a wild man.

Not her first raunchy dream starring the hot rancher. She still remembered the hot dream from last week where he'd stripped her naked, shoved her to her knees, and bound her wrists behind her back with a soft leather strap. Then Kade's hands impatiently twisted in her hair as his cock shuttled in and out of her mouth. Saliva poured down her chin, between her bared breasts, trickling down her belly to mix with the wetness glazing her inner thighs.

Kade recited a play-by-play in that husky voice of how sexy that she was submissive before him, never allowing her a choice of what he expected from her. But even in the dream she'd been greedy, lost in the slick feel of his cock rubbing over her tongue, scraping against the roof of her mouth, stretching her lips as she sucked hard enough to make him lose his mind.

And rather than give her the prize she'd earned, he denied her his taste, pulling out as he climaxed, coming on her chest in long creamy spurts. His eyes glittered with satisfaction as his seed dripped off her hard nipples.

In the next dreamscape, she was blindfolded, straddling his thighs on a kitchen chair—he'd immobilized her hands with a thick rope. Kade fucked her slowly, sucking and biting her nipples, driving her insane with the heat and wetness of his mouth. Sky was on track to the most explosive orgasm of her life when she woke up.

Maddening. How sad was it that not only was she sexually frustrated in real life, but in her dreams too? And what was up with her kinky bondage fantasies?

She'd never get back to sleep now. She shimmied into her pajama bottoms and scooted off the bed. After checking on Eliza, she crept down the hallway.

The bathroom door was ajar. Odd. Kade always closed it. Maybe she should see if he was okay.

See if he wants coffee.

See if he's naked.

See if he needs a towel.

Screw the towel. See if he needs you to lick the moisture off every square inch of his wet, ripped body.

Sky eased the door open. Rather than startle him by shouting over the sounds of running water, she'd wait until he shut off the taps.

The clear shower curtain, dotted with red umbrellas and yellow ducks, offered very little coverage. Thank the shower curtain gods for that bit of foresight.

Speaking of gods... Man. She'd never seen Kade completely bare-assed. She'd seen him half-dressed in cut-offs and tight T-shirts. Lately he'd strolled around bare-chested. But she'd never witnessed him wearing nothing but his skin.

Which was a damn crying shame.

He'd braced his left forearm on the wall below the showerhead. Water streamed over his dark hair, dripping on the chiseled lines of his face. Rivulets trickled down the back of his neck, disappearing into the indentation of his spine. A few water droplets beaded on his muscular shoulders. Soapy drops flew off his wrist and splattered against the shower curtain.

Her gaze was drawn downward as his hips pushed forward. The muscles on his right side were strung tight, bunching and flexing with each movement of his arm. The long, thick muscle between his legs was clutched in his fist. His hand moved rapidly. Rhythmically.

Oh wow. Kade was jacking off. Right in front of her. He was so intent on the task at hand he hadn't noticed her.

Yet.

She should leave, sneak out, forget she'd stumbled upon such an intimate moment. But she couldn't tear her eyes away from him, lost in self-pleasure. It was the sexiest thing she'd ever witnessed, the contour of his brawny body tensed in anticipation. Hearing his indecipherable mutters as his hand flew faster and faster over his cock.

Her heartbeat spiked. Blood pulsed in her throat, and her nipples, but mostly between her legs.

The scent of lemon sage soap and steam and Kade swirled around her until she was dizzy with want. Why couldn't she climb in with him and finish the job? Using her hands, her body, her mouth to bring him over the edge?

Just as she'd decided to doff her pajamas, Kade's neck arched. A low grunt bounced off the tiled walls and his movement slowed. Water beat on his face as he stilled and savored his orgasm.

Talk about sexy. But not nearly as sexy as when Kade said her name. Startled, her eyes zoomed back to his profile, expecting to be busted for her voyeurism. But Kade's eyes were squeezed shut. He'd said her name, not because he's seen her, but because he'd been thinking of her as he'd masturbated.

Sexual need like she'd never experienced dimmed her vision and thickened her blood.

Maybe the gentleman was a wild man.

Maybe he's exactly the kind of man you need.

Maybe you should quit dreaming and supposing and just flat-out ask him.

Skylar slipped out as quietly as possible.

Chapter Seven

"You ain't complainin' about bein' tied down with a kid and all that shit now?"

Tied down. As if. Eliza had turned his world upside down, but she hung the moon and the stars as far as Kade was concerned. He was absolutely head over heels for his little Miz Eliza Belle Ellison McKay. Thinking about her sweet face, big inquisitive eyes, toothless grin and plump cheeks filled him with so much pride and love, he was damn close to bursting out in song.

"No complaints," Kade said.

"Really? So how's diaper duty?"

"Ain't any worse than shovelin' hot cow shit."

Kane snorted. "If you say so."

His brother's sarcastic comments about Eliza were getting tiresome. Kade rested his forearm across the posthole digger handle and tried to rein in his temper. "What's that supposed to mean?"

"Nothin'."

"I'm serious. Why you always sayin' shit like that, Kane?"

"Maybe you oughta be askin' why you're so touchy about it. I can't say nothin' lately without you bitin' off my head, bro." Kane continued to fiddle with the coil of barbed wire and wouldn't look at him.

"Yeah? Maybe I am a little touchy 'cause my only brother can't be bothered to drive sixty miles down the road to meet my baby daughter."

"I ain't good with babies," he said softly. "You know that."

Kade hadn't been either up until about two weeks ago. "Look. I ain't gonna make you change her diaper."

Kane's mouth twitched.

"But I would like you to see her. Next to her mama, she's the prettiest thing in the whole world."

"I reckon she probably is. But you ever think it might not be the best idea for me to see her? Or for her to see me?"

"Didja hit yourself in the head with a hammer?"

"Why you say that?"

"'Cause you ain't makin' a lick of sense."

Kane squinted at him. "Yeah? Did it escape your notice in the year you've been gone that we're identical twins? That havin' two men who both look like daddy might be confusin' to her?"

Hell. That hadn't occurred to him.

"I know you're bondin' with her, or whatever you wanna call it, and it'd be just my luck if I'd fuck it up somehow. I done that once with you and her mama. I ain't lookin' to do it again."

Kade had no idea how to answer. For once his brother had brought up a valid point. "I appreciate your honesty. But it wasn't your fault I never came clean with Skylar about me not bein' you. I pissed away my chances to tell her and I gotta live with my stupidity."

A couple of minutes passed where the only sounds were bugs and birds and the grinding chink of tools against hard-packed soil.

A heartfelt sigh drifted up from where Kane worked in the dirt. "Didja ever wonder why Ma named us Kane and Kade? Jesus. It ain't bad enough hardly anyone can tell us apart? We gotta have names that are damn close to identical?"

"Yeah, I wondered that. But neither of us has balls enough to ask the blonde tornado just what she was thinkin' when she popped out a matched set," Kade said wryly.

"True. Dad'd skin us alive if we upset the queen bee, even now." Kane twisted the wire cutters. "Anyway, I'm thinkin' about changin' my name."

Kade laughed. "Right."

"I'm serious. Something that don't start with a 'K' or a 'C' like everyone in this damn family."

"How about...Dick?"

"How about you fuck off, smartass?"

Kade grinned. "So whatcha thinkin'? Bubba? Spud? Deuce? Fred? Ethyl?"

"I think Bennett's datin' a woman from Thermopolis named Ethyl."

"No kiddin'?"

"Yeah, I'm kiddin'. Goddamn you're easy to tease, Kade."

"Give me a break. I ain't had to make small talk besides with the cattle for the last year. Good thing Eliza ain't expectin' me to be a brilliant talker."

Kane clipped a section of wire. "What about Skylar? Does she expect that from you?"

"Who the hell knows?" Frustrated, Kade pounded his foot against the metal jaws of the posthole digger. "We don't talk about nothin' except Eliza."

"That's to be expected, ain't it?"

"Probably. But it's been a few weeks since I moved in. I thought since I was up with the baby last night that Sky would be rested and we could talk about something else this mornin'. But after I got out of the shower, she'd already made up the bed. When I tried—"

"Whoa whoa whoa." Kane held up a gloved hand. "You said she made the bed? As in—you're sharin' a bed with her?"

"Uh. Yeah."

"So, man, why are you worried about talkin' if you're already nailin' her?"

"Because I'm not."

"Not what?"

"I'm not nailin' her, okay?"

A stunned look crossed Kane's face and then he laughed so hard he fell over on the ground.

When Kade suffered enough of his brother's hysterics, he said, "It ain't funny."

"Yeah, it is. Jesus, Kade. The last year turned you into a Wyoming monk? You've been sleepin' in the same damn bed with Skylar, the woman you have a child with, the woman you've been crazy in love with for over a year, and you haven't tried to get busy with her? Not even once?"

"No."

"Does the thought of screwin' her with the baby in the room...give you performance anxiety or something?"

"What the fuck do you mean, *performance anxiety*? No. I don't have any problem gettin' it up."

"Does havin' the baby listenin' to you squeakin' the bedframe freak her out?"

"I don't know!"

"That is just plain sad, man. Sad."

"No shit."

"I'm assumin' you still want her?"

"Like you wouldn't fuckin' believe."

"So why would you throw in the towel so soon?"

"I haven't." Kade kicked a clod of dirt into the ditch. "I promised Sky I'd be a gentleman. At first I needed to be in her room to learn how to take care of Eliza. I thought maybe after Sky got used to me bein' around and I rebuilt her trust, things might change. We'd use the bed for more than sleepin'. Nothin's changed. I'm waitin' on her to give me some kinda damn sign."

"There's your problem. Waitin' on her. Actin' like a lap dog, happy for scraps." Kane stood and jammed the wire cutters in his back pocket. "See, women tell you they want a gentleman, when in reality, they want a man to take charge. Sexually speakin'."

"What?"

"Hear me out. A woman wants a man who can't keep their hands offa them. A man who can make them feel feminine, sexy and needed. Desired, but not in a way that diminishes their independence outside the bedroom."

He stared at Kane with his mouth hanging open. What'd gotten into his brother? Kane was worse than him when it came to talking about touchy-feely relationship crap. Kane never thought about man/woman shit beyond the locker room trash-talking of, "I fucked her" or, "I wanna fuck her" or, "Is she any good with her mouth?"

Now Kane was channeling Dr. Phil? It shocked Kade to the point of speechlessness, leaving him no choice but to take note of his brother's opinion.

"Take a woman like Skylar, who's used to callin' all the shots in her life," Kane continued, oblivious to Kade's shock. "She's ambitious. She's convinced herself she always has to be in charge—of her business, of her family, and probably of her sexuality."

A strange sense of déjà vu surfaced. That described Skylar to a T.

"Maybe she's secretly lookin' for a man to render decisions in the bedroom. So, by you doin' nothin', she don't see you as a real man. She sees you as another person in her life she has to be responsible for."

Lord. He had a point. Sky'd been teaching him how to care for Eliza, much like how she'd taught her employees to do their jobs. Did she see him as just another project to finish? Get him up to speed in the parenting department and then merrily skip on to the next task?

Like hell.

"I think the only way you can combat Skylar's way of thinkin' is to prove to her otherwise."

"Who are you?"

Kane actually blushed. "What? Everybody in this family wants me to change and then when I do, I'm told I ain't allowed to? Or they don't believe I can?"

"Shit. Sorry. I just can't believe that Skylar would..." Want the man Kade used to be. That idea was just beyond bizarre.

But worth a shot since nothing else seemed to be working.

"Where did you pick all this up, Kane?"

"I've had a lot of time to reflect in the last year about what a first-class prick I've been to women." He bristled as if the admission stung. "Besides. It ain't all my fault. Blame my roommate."

"What's Colt got to do with it?"

"Since our cousin quit drinkin', he's been doin' some soul searchin'. Always bringin' home them self-help books. I ain't got nothin' better to do, so I've been readin' up. Hopin' if I meet a woman I really like, I won't be an idiot and blow it like you did."

"Gee. Thanks."

"Anytime." Kane punched him in the arm. Hard. "I missed you, you dumb fucker."

"Same goes." He followed Kane's lead and punched him in the arm. Hard. "So what do I owe ya for the advice? A buck?"

"Buck." Kane rubbed the back of his glove under his chin. "You know, that's a downright good name. Real cowboy. Real different from yours. That's whatcha can call me from now on."

"Buck?"

"Yep. Now let's get this fence fixed so you can go home early and fix your love life so I don't gotta hear about it any more."

Every woman in the factory stopped when Kade McKay sauntered into Sky Blue.

Didn't matter his boots were muddy, his Wranglers were dusty, his chambray shirt had dirt smears across the chest, or his hat looked as if he'd sat on it before he'd placed it on his head. The man took total command of the place.

Dee and Bonita checked their reflections in the metal vats, but Kade only had eyes for her.

Skylar forced herself to stay put as he meandered over. When he hit her with that sexy smile, her stomach cartwheeled.

"Hey, boss lady. How's it goin'?"

"Good. You're off the ranch early."

He shrugged. "A rare slow day. What about you? What time you callin' it quits?"

"Another hour."

"You need any help?"

"With what?"

"Anything." He moved closer. "Anything at all I can do for you?"

For me? Or to me? Oh yeah, cowboy. Go to the house. Strip out of those dirty clothes and wait for me in bed. Naked. With a piece of straw between your teeth and that wicked I-wanna-bend-you-over-the-closest-haybale grin.

"Skylar?" he murmured.

She stared up at him. Lord. He was so tall. So big and broad. So intent. So thoughtful. So freakin' hot. So...here.

"You okay, sweetheart?"

"I-I don't really know."

Kade ran the knuckle of his index finger down her jawline. "You feel fine to me—very, very fine, but maybe you oughta be in bed."

Her mouth went dry as powdered milk.

"Let me take you to bed and take care of you."

Yes! "Ah. Okay."

"What say we get out of here?" His voice dropped to a sexy growl. "Now?"

Before Skylar could drag him home, forcing him to fulfill the promises darkening his eyes, Annie shouted from the office. "Sky. Yellow Wheel Promotions. Line two."

She backed up so fast Kade's hand shot out to steady her. "Easy. Didn't mean to spook you."

"You didn't." *Liar, liar.* "I-I have to take that call."

"I'll just wait and have a look around. Do you mind?"

"Not at all."

Then Dee was right there. Grinning and batting her fake eyelashes. "I'd be happy to take you on a tour."

"That's not—"

"It'd be my pleasure, yes-sirree, a real pleasure. You look awful familiar to me, honey," Dee cooed. "Have we met?"

"No, ma'am."

"He looks familiar, Dee, because his daughter looks just like him."

Kade shot her a startled glance.

Skylar couldn't withhold a smirk. "This is Eliza's father, Kade McKay. Kade, Dee Bancroft."

"Nice to meetcha, Miz Bancroft."

When Annie yelled, "Sky. Did you hear me? Line two,"

Skylar had no choice but to dump him with Dee.

Ten minutes later, she found Kade and Dee chatting in the herb-drying room. He turned around at her approach. His heated I-wanna-eat-you-up look made her nipples hard and her belly clench. Then his handsome face lit up when he noticed Eliza was in her arms.

"There's my sweet girl."

At the sound of his voice, Eliza's tiny feet kicked.

His grin widened. "Didja miss me, baby? You been behavin' for your mama today?"

"Your sweet girl hasn't slept for more than fifteen minutes at a time all day."

"Maybe that means she'll sleep all night for a change." He nuzzled Eliza's pudgy neck. "Which ain't fair because it's your night to be up with her."

"My night? I thought we were taking turns?"

"Me too, sweetheart. But I took all the turns last night. You didn't move when I got out of bed. At midnight. At two. And at four."

Dee chuckled. "Oh. I get it now." Still smiling, she said, "Nadia wants to talk to you before you leave. She says it's important." Dee disappeared around the corner.

Skylar withheld a groan. She liked Nadia. She liked that Nadia wasn't afraid to talk to her when she kept her distance from everyone else. She liked that Nadia wasn't a drama queen. But it bugged the heck out of her Nadia was so fickle, and Sky didn't have to guess what Nadia wanted to talk to her about. Again.

"Lemme take Eliza home so you can get back to work." Kade lifted her from Skylar's arms. "Come on, girlie. You and me gotta date with a warm bottle and a hot bath."

"Do you want to drive my car? Or just take the car seat out of it?"

He frowned. "I have a car seat in my truck."

"Since when?"

"Since the day after I moved in. I bought one, figurin' it'd be easier if we had two."

"I didn't know."

"You didn't ask. You assumed. I'm findin' you do that a lot with me, Skylar." His eyes met hers. "See you at home."

Why was everyone acting so weird today?

The second Sky returned to her office, Annie, a forty-something, no-nonsense native Wyoming cowgirl, descended on her like a rabid coyote. "So Eliza wasn't an immaculate conception as you'd led all of us to believe?"

Sky snorted.

"Granted, that spectacular hunk of a man is pretty damn close to god-like."

No argument here.

"Not that he had eyes for anyone but you. Lord, with the hot way he was eatin' you up, we all thought he was gonna nail you right there in the main room next to the coffee pot."

Her cheeks heated.

"Eliza's daddy is living with you, and you couldn't mention it to me? For godsake, you're *sleeping* with him and you've kept it to yourself?"

Damn. News traveled fast around here. "It's not what you think."

"No?"

"No."

"Then you are an idiot, Sky. A freakin' idiot." Annie tossed up her hands and stormed out.

What was wrong with everybody today?

Thirty minutes later Nadia knocked and Skylar motioned her in.

Dark-haired, dark-eyed Nadia was a refugee from Bosnia who'd immigrated to the United States through a local church.

Last year during the interview process, Nadia had referred to herself as the perfect peasant. Ugly, stick-thin, strong as an ox, uneducated, and an "eyes forward, no-talking" kind of worker. The description haunted Skylar, as did the occasional evidence of physical abuse on Nadia's arms and face.

Despite repeated attempts of her coworkers to convince Nadia to ditch her husband, and Nadia's promises to follow through with it, Nadia stayed with the abusive man. A sad fact of life in rural America. With the lack of financial and social resources, many women didn't have a choice but to stay in a bad relationship.

The whole situation worried Skylar, and quite frankly, she'd nearly called the damn sheriff herself, but as Nadia's boss, she couldn't interfere. The one time she'd approached Nadia to offer whatever support she'd needed, the woman tearily told her to mind her own business. And as much as it pained her, Skylar had done as Nadia asked.

So far, Nadia's son, four-year-old Anton, hadn't shown signs of abuse and was a well-adjusted little boy who played well with the other kids in the daycare program.

Instead of standing in front of the desk like she was facing a firing squad as she usually did, Nadia paced. "What's up, Nadia? Dee said it was important."

"It is." She paced to the far wall and back. "I like working here. It is good for Anton, it is good for me."

"I like having you here. I'm not flattering you when I say you are a great employee."

"Thank you." Nadia stopped and looked at Skylar with haunted eyes. "When I'm here I work hard." She clenched her hands at her sides. "I need to ask you a favor."

"Okay, I'm listening."

"If my husband calls, I'd like you to tell him I'm not here."

A thick silence hung in the air.

Sky's stomach churned. How many times in the last year had Nadia asked for this favor? A dozen, probably. The very next day Nadia would recant her request, claim she'd been stressed out or tired and she hadn't meant it. Then she'd vehemently deny her husband had anything to do with her decision. Skylar had suffered through this type of wishy-washy behavior before with her sister. India promising to get clean. To get sober. To stop using and abusing her body and take control of her life.

Nadia was in the same holding pattern. It might be cynical, but Sky didn't think this was the time Nadia would stick to her declaration either and she tried damn hard to keep the doubt out of her voice. "I know you're a private person, Nadia, but honesty is necessary for me to understand what's going on.

Why should I lie to Rex?"

"Because I'm leaving him. For real this time. A friend is letting us stay with her. I need this job and this is the first place he'll try to find me."

"As happy as I am that you're taking a positive step, do you think he'll believe you just up and left town? Especially when he knows how much you like working here?"

"He thinks I hate this job."

That was a new twist. "Excuse me?"

Nadia thrust out her chin. "It's not true. I lied to him. In the last couple of weeks I started complaining to him about this place and how bad it'd gotten. How I hated everyone who worked here. I even hinted I was looking around for something else and I'd found another daycare for Anton."

Smart woman, laying the groundwork, but it made Sky absolutely sick that Nadia had to go to this much trouble to get out of a horrid, unsafe situation.

"When he realizes we're gone, hopefully he'll think I've moved to Denver. I told him I have cousins there."

"Do you?"

"No. I don't have any friends there either, so there's no way he can trace me. Except through here."

Skylar stayed calm and professional even as she wanted to ask more detailed questions on why Nadia was convinced this outlandish ruse would work. She tapped the pen on her calculator, contemplating issues Nadia might not have considered, but ones that affected everyone in her employ. "Is the woman who's hiding you out another employee?"

"No. I'd never ask that of someone or put such a burden on you. You've been very good to me, which is why I hate to ask such a big thing. Again."

Helpless to say no, Sky said, "Okay. I'll inform Annie since she fields most of the phone calls. But you have to promise me one thing, Nadia."

"What?"

"If anything changes, if you decide to return home, or if he threatens you, you have to tell me right away. I can't be flying blind in this situation when I have a business to run and other employees—including children—to consider."

"I promise. But this time it's for real."

Sky wanted to ask what'd happened to force the change. She wanted to know if Nadia had enough money. If Anton had his favorite toys. If Nadia was scared. However, Sky did none of that. It'd make Nadia even more self-conscious and might make her reconsider her plan if Sky questioned it.

She pretended to squint at the clock when she was trying to hold it together and follow Nadia's lead, remaining brusque and businesslike. "Ten minutes until quitting time. Maybe you'd better fill in your coworkers on what's going on before you take off."

Nadia nodded.

Just as Skylar took a breath and dropped the mask of hard-ass boss lady, Nadia stopped at the door and turned around.

"That man who was here earlier? Is he Eliza's father?"

"Yes."

"Why wasn't he around before, when you were pregnant?"

Wow. That was an intensely personal question from mind-your-own-business Nadia. "That's a long story and one I'd rather not get into. Why do you ask?"

"Because he reminds me of my husband. A stubborn cowboy. A big man who'll use his fists to prove himself."

"Kade is not like that."

"Don't kid yourself. They're *all* like that," Nadia said, and slipped out the door, leaving Skylar in stunned silence.

An hour later, Skylar entered the quiet house. No sign of Eliza or Kade in the living room. Maybe they were napping upstairs.

She rooted around in the freezer and threw a boxed casserole in the microwave. She set the plates and silverware on the ruffled placemats and poured two glasses of tea.

The stairs creaked and a freshly showered Kade entered the

kitchen with an empty bottle. "She's scrubbed, fed and sleepin'. I ain't gonna claim sleepin' like a baby, 'cause I've learned that sayin' is a total lie. But she's out."

"Great timing. Dinner's done."

"Good. That looks mighty tasty. Thanks for cookin'."

"You're welcome." Weren't they civilized and polite? What happened to the heated looks and his suggestion of taking her to bed? Why didn't he suggest they skip supper and head straight for dessert?

Why don't you take a chance and tell him what's really on your mind?

Kade shoveled in a forkful of rice and chewed. "This is good. What's the spice?"

"I added fresh savory."

"Mmm. That it is."

He ate. She ate. They finished the meal in uncomfortable silence.

She started to clean up the dishes and declined his offer to help.

Finally, he said, "You gonna tell me what's wrong?"

She slammed the cupboard door. "I don't know."

"Could you at least give me the courtesy of lookin' at me when we're talkin', sweetheart?"

Skylar wheeled around. "We aren't talking, Kade."

"Is that the problem?"

"Maybe."

"Only one way to rectify that, Skylar. If you have something to say to me, spit it out."

"Fine. For lack of a better term, we've been playing house for over two weeks."

"Playin' house? Is that what you think we're doin'?"

"Isn't it? And despite the fact you're living with me, you're in my bed, today you came into my plant and tried to charm the pants off me in front of my employees."

Kade lifted both brows. "Does that make you mad?"

"Yes, it does. I sound like a total idiot, but yeah, it makes me wonder why you don't use that silver tongue on me when we're alone."

"Where exactly do you want me to use my tongue on you, darlin'?"

Everywhere. "You know that's not what I meant. And it doesn't help my self-image when I realize we've been sleeping in the same damn bed for almost three weeks and..."

"And what?"

Just say it. Calmly. Confidently. With dignity. She blurted out, "And why haven't you so much as laid a single hand on me?"

He blinked several times. "Come again?"

"You heard me. You asked for honesty, there it is."

"Yeah? Well, I asked you to marry me, remember?"

"And I said no. That doesn't answer my question."

Kade wiped a cloth napkin across his mouth with deliberate slowness. "The reason I haven't done anything more than sleep next to you in that bed is because I'm followin' your lead, Sky. You never indicated that's what you wanted."

"You haven't acted like you're interested, McKay."

"Wrong. I would've fucked you on the couch the first night I moved in. I would've spread you out on every goddamn surface in this kitchen morning, noon and night. I would've banged you on the concrete floor of your herb room until my knees bled the second I saw you today, in another one of them sexy-assed dresses you always wear.

"I want you like crazy. It don't matter to me where, but it sure as hell matters when, because I ain't gonna start nothin' with you until you're ready to get into an intensely physical relationship with me."

Skylar's belly flipped at the words *intensely physical relationship.* "Being a true cowboy gentleman, are you?"

"I'm sure as hell tryin', because that's what *you* told me you wanted from the get-go. It ain't easy as I thought it'd be."

Rather than admit she was wrong for demanding his stupid gentlemanly behavior, she taunted, "So is that why I caught you jacking off in the shower this morning?"

His eyes glittered. "Me jackin' off was in direct response to the show you were puttin' on in the middle of the damn bed about five minutes before that."

"What show?"

"I'm not supposed to react when you're diddlin' yourself in your sleep?" Kade leaned forward. "I watched you come. It was hot as the Fourth of July. Made me hard as a fuckin' brick. And rather than risk wakin' up Eliza and goin' all caveman on you, poundin' your luscious body clear through that mattress, I took matters into my own hands. Because sweetheart, I've had a lot of experience with that in the last year."

Kade thought her body was luscious? Skylar stared at him. Turned on, turned inside out. "You haven't been with anyone?"

"Not since you...not since the night Eliza was conceived in my truck in Ziggy's parking lot."

She whispered, "Me either."

Kade stood so fast the chair crashed to the floor.

"No one has touched me since that night." As he stalked her, she backed up until her lower back connected with the counter edge. "Well, I mean, I've been touched. I had to be when pregnant and giving birth, but no one...no man...except that one male nurse...oh God, I'm not making any sense am I?"

Her gentleman cowboy was right in her face. A sexy menace. A man out of patience. "Skylar."

"What?"

"Shut up."

And then he slammed his mouth down on hers and kissed her.

Chapter Eight

Kade kissed her as thoroughly as he'd been dying to.

His hands were buried in her soft hair; his body was pressed tightly to hers until not a sliver of daylight remained between them. He ate at her deliciously sweet mouth, nibbling, licking, leaving tiny love bites on her lips. Sucking on her tongue. Drawing the scent and the taste of her down his throat and into his lungs like food and air.

Skylar opened her mouth wider, attempting to swallow him whole. Her tongue grew hotter, wetter, more insistent. She clutched his shoulders. Her nails dug through his T-shirt and gouged his skin. Whimpering noises vibrated from her throat into his mouth and traveled down his torso to settle in his already hard cock. His prick damn near saluted when she'd confessed to spying on him as he'd whacked off in the shower.

His hands untangled from her hair and Kade went straight for her tits. Still kissing her, he made short work of the buttons on her dress.

Kade trailed his lips down her flawless neck. "You taste as smooth here as I remember. Way better than chocolate cake. Remember what I said I'd like to do with the frosting?"

"You always pick lousy times to have a conversation, McKay."

He chuckled. Her abundant breasts were straining against the fabric and he couldn't get them free. "Undo this damn bra for me, Sky, so I can put my mouth on you."

She batted away his fumbling fingers. Something snapped and those perfectly soft mounds fell into his waiting hands.

"Oh yeah. Gimme." Kade swept his thumbs across her rosy

nipples, placing open-mouthed kisses on the upper swells of her breasts. Rubbing his cheeks and lips and jaw against her bared flesh, feeling her whole body quiver in response. Watching her face, he closed his mouth over her left nipple and sucked. Hard.

Sky arched back and released a strangled moan.

He worshipped the tits he'd been fantasizing about for months. Teasing her, pleasing himself. He was in no mood to be rushed. He suckled her nipples softly, then with unrestrained zeal. Tweaked them with his fingertips. Nipped the tips with his teeth as he held the weight of them together. Squeezing and tonguing, imagining sliding his cock in the slippery valley of her cleavage. Kissing them, loving the fullness and her responsiveness to his every touch.

"Kade. Enough. I-I can't think."

"Good." He scattered kisses up to her lips and stared into her eyes, letting her see the hunger raging inside him.

Don't be a gentleman; be a real man. Tell her straight up.

"I wanna make love to you, Sky."

Make love? What the hell happened to "I wanna fuck your brains out, baby"?

"I want you too," she whispered against his mouth. "In a bed this time. Do you have a condom?"

Kade tasted the smooth skin of her jawline. "I have a whole goddamn box. Let's go."

He guided her upstairs. They stopped in front of the door to the bedroom where Eliza was sleeping. Skylar's nervousness was obvious and he softly touched her cheek. "How about we do this in the guest bedroom across the hall?"

She nodded.

"I'll grab the condoms. And if you ain't in there, make no mistake, I will rip this house apart lookin' for you." Kade sprinted to the bathroom. He dug through his shaving kit for the stash and was back at the door to heaven in under a minute.

With the shades drawn and the hall light off, the room was completely dark when he stepped inside. "Where's the light switch?"

"Doesn't matter. The bulb is burned out."

"Don't you have a lamp in here or something?"

"Kade, I'm in the middle of the bed completely naked. Do you really want to talk about the lack of lighting?"

"Nope." He stripped to skin. "But I'll admit I'd hoped to see more of you this time than last time."

"You can feel as much of me as you want."

He walked in a straight line until his shins hit solid wood. "Fuck. That hurt."

"Come up here and I'll kiss it and make it better."

"I'm holdin' you to that." He crawled on the bed to find Skylar was indeed, totally buck-ass bare and in her usual position—right smack dab in the center of the bed. "You do know you're a bed hog, right?"

"What are you talking about?"

"You. See, a week or so back, you started snugglin' into me in the dead of the night. At first I thought it was because you liked bein' close to me." Kade's fingers circled her ankle and he slid her right leg aside to crawl between her thighs. "I hoped that was your way of sayin' you wanted me." He kissed the top of her foot, jangling the bells on her ankle bracelet. "Then I realized you were used to havin' the bed to yourself and didn't wanna share. Snugglin' into me was your way of pushin' me out of your space."

The mattress shifted and Skylar sat up. "Why didn't you tell me?"

"Because I liked havin' you next to me, no matter what your motives were. Don't matter right now." He fluttered his fingertips up the inside of her thighs. "Spread your legs wider for me, sweetheart."

Kade caught a whiff of her arousal. Thick. Sweet. Warm. He wanted to taste her so damn bad his mouth was watering. Keeping his hands gripping her thighs, he leaned over and put his mouth on her belly button.

Her stomach muscles rippled beneath his lips.

He dipped his tongue into the indentation, then dragged it down to the top of her pubic bone. He blew softly across her damp curls.

Goose flesh broke out across her legs and she softly gasped.

"Any objections about me kissin' you down here?"

"Ah. No. Please."

Kade chuckled at her polite eagerness. After a couple of gentlemanly licks, he buried his face in her pussy, found her pulse with his tongue and began to suck her clit.

She moaned his name. *His.* Kade.

Oh yeah. This is what he wanted. Needed. Just Sky. Just like this. Pliant. Eager, and his.

Skylar's hands stripped the sheet from the mattress. She ground her wet sex into his face as she started to come, gasping, thrashing against him and the bed, trying to suppress the sounds of her orgasm. He kept sucking her sweet pussy until she sighed contentment and her legs stopped twitching.

"God, Kade, you make me crazy when you do that."

"I know." Grinning, Kade rose to his knees. He reached for the condoms, ripped open the box and tore a package free.

"Let me."

"I remember how to do this part, although Eliza's existence might convince you otherwise."

"I don't regret anything about her, Kade. Not a single thing."

That shocked him into stillness.

"I didn't get to touch you anywhere last time. Let me. Please."

Couldn't say no to that. He admired her silhouette as she opened the package with her teeth. Sky smoothed her left hand up his thigh and he withheld a shiver at her tender touch. Placing the latex over the head of his cock, she rolled it down to the root. She curled her hand around the girth and stroked.

His cock jerked hopefully in her hand.

"You were pulling pretty hard and fast in the shower. Doesn't that hurt?"

"No. Another time I'll teach you the secret to a great handjob. Right now, lay back."

As soon as she was horizontal, Kade levered himself over

her—his legs brushing inside hers, his palms flat by her shoulders, matched pelvis to pelvis.

Sky touched his face with the tips of her cool fingers and passed her palms over his chest like she was sculpting him from memory. "You have such an amazingly hard body."

"Some places are harder than others."

"Show me."

"It's been awhile. This probably ain't gonna last long."

"Been awhile for me too, cowboy." She whispered, "Kiss me. I love the way you kiss me. Like I'm the only thing in the world."

"When I'm kissin' you, sweetheart, you *are* the only thing in my world."

Poised at the entrance to her body, he eased in as he took her mouth. He lost his mind in the glove-tight feeling of her pussy closing around his cock from tip to root.

He broke the kiss. "Are you okay?"

"Yeah."

"That wasn't very convincin'." Kade noticed she wore a strange expression. "What? Am I hurtin' you?"

"No."

"Skylar, what's wrong?"

"This is going to sound so stupid. Embarrassing." In a rush, she said, "Does it feel different for you?"

"Different how?"

"You know. Looser?"

"Looser?"

"Well, I did push an eight pound baby out of there. And I've heard the vaginal walls loosen and it doesn't feel as tight for men afterward—"

"You are a fuckin' perfect fit." He pulled out and pushed back in. Three, four, five hard, deep thrusts that bumped her cervix and made her bow into him with absolute abandon. "Perfect in every way." He shortened his strokes. "Jesus. You feel so goddamn good."

"Not half as good as you feel to me."

"You pick lousy times to have a conversation, Sky," he teased.

She groaned, "I deserved that." Then she bit his earlobe.

A shudder worked through him. "I don't know if I can go slow."

Pressing her lips to the hollow of his throat, she said, "So don't. It's not like we haven't done this before."

"Not like this we haven't." Something akin to a snarl burst from his mouth as he hammered into her. Pounding hips, flesh pounding flesh, his heart matched the rhythm of it all.

Sky arched her back, tilting her pelvis, allowing him a deeper angle. "Yes. Like that."

With her nails digging into his ass and her mouth sucking at his neck, Kade shoved hard, stayed buried balls deep and came with a long groan, sending her into another orgasm.

Still breathing with difficulty, he lifted his head and reconnected their mouths for another slow kiss. Then he whispered in her hair, "Marry me, Skylar."

She whispered back, "No."

"It was worth a shot."

Chapter Nine

Somehow in the following week Eliza settled into a routine, which made Kade happy. He and Skylar settling into a routine didn't make Kade happy. Not one iota.

Wasn't that why he'd moved in? What he'd wanted?

No. Not like this. Every night was the same. They'd put Eliza down. Skylar would sneak into the guest bedroom, strip, and wait for him. They'd make careful love, only face to face, only in the absolute darkness, only on the bed.

While they were in the moment, it was damn good. But, afterward, when Skylar immediately got up and dressed, he questioned why she bothered with a sexual relationship with him. After they both got off, she'd disappear, leaving him...lonely. At bedtime she'd curl up on her side of the bed and he on his. They'd take turns getting up with Eliza. Business as usual. Sky probably saw nothing wrong with the way things were going between them.

As the week progressed Kade became frustrated with the situation with Skylar and his incompetence in changing it. Or in his ability to be completely honest with what he needed from her. He'd had enough empty sex in his life...well, to last a lifetime. He wanted more with her...for both of them.

For years, Kade had acted in the same manner as Sky did, confusing sex with intimacy. Now that he'd learned there was a difference, he'd hoped to take their relationship to the next level, beyond parenting partners and mattress monkeys.

So what was the problem?

From what he could tell, Skylar wasn't interested in them becoming more intimate on any level.

Had they taken advantage of Eliza's sleeping hours by spending time talking, beyond the basic chitchat? No. Had they cuddled up on the front porch swing to gaze at the stars and moon? No. Had they plopped on the sofa to watch TV? No. Hell, he'd've been happy as a pig in shit cleaning the damn house and folding laundry.

They did none of the normal couple things. She'd allow him to touch her body within certain parameters, but it never ventured beyond the surface.

At some point, Kade realized his brother hit the nail on the head with his observation about Skylar's behavior. He'd swallowed his embarrassment and asked to borrow the pop psychology book Buck had spoken of and it just confirmed his suspicions.

It was all about Sky's need for control. When it came to their relationship, she controlled the where, the when, and how much time they spent in the bedroom. And, she controlled the amount of time they spent *out* of the bedroom. She controlled...everything. That didn't surprise him so much because as a successful businesswoman everything in her life was laid out. Scheduled. He'd be damned if they'd schedule sex. If he was just another thing she'd mark off on her "to do" list.

In her tidy world was Eliza a constant reminder of the consequences of Sky throwing caution to the wind?

Maybe Kade could use that mindset to his advantage.

Eliza squeaked. She studied him somberly with those big blue eyes. His heart was a pile of mush when she looked at him like that. "You got me wrapped around your little finger, girlie, and you know it."

She blinked.

"Like mother, like daughter, eh?"

She appeared to be listening, so he kept talking.

"I won you over, and I'm gonna win over your mama too. It may take some doin'. Think Aunt Indy is right in the *no pain, no gain* school of thought? No? Me neither. But your mama ain't gonna like nothin' I do to force her hand, so I might as well start out balls to the wall. Desperate times call for desperate measures. And between us, sweet thang, I'm desperate to make that woman mine. Body, heart, and soul. Just to make it interestin', I do believe I'll start with her body first."

In the last week Kade had taken to dropping by the shop on his way to the house. Skylar found herself looking forward to hearing his gruff voice bouncing off the rafters.

Today he'd meandered in and flirted with Dee, played a quick game of tic-tac-toe with Josie and the daycare kids, talked horses with Bonita, and checked the alternator in Vickie's truck. He tried to engage Nadia in conversation, but she went out of her way to avoid him.

Kade was unfailingly polite with Skylar, never hinting that anything but a parental bond existed between them in front of her employees, which is what she'd wanted.

So why did she secretly wish for his public display of affection? For that hunky cowboy to swoop in and kiss her madly? Spirit her up to her office, sweep everything off the desk and screw her silly on her day planner?

Probably because she was suffering from sleep deprivation. Passion like that only happened in the movies. Real life for her was spreadsheets, diapers, sleepless nights and if she was lucky, a quick bout of nookie before the baby woke up.

She'd never had much of a sex life, so the fact she was getting some good lovin' on a regular basis should've made her swoon like a giggling maiden. So why did it bug the crap out of her that sex had turned...routine? And that was saying a lot, coming from someone like Skylar who thrived on routine. Not only was she too chicken to take a chance on initiating sex with Kade, she was afraid he'd balk at seeing her flab-ulous post-baby body and end all sexual contact. She kept all naked encounters in the dark, figuring so-so sex was better than no sex? Right?

Wrong. The niggling feeling that something was missing outside of the bedroom didn't help her frame of mind because she had no frame of reference for a situation like this—sexually or personally. For the first time in a long time, she had no plan of attack, no earthly idea on how to go about implementing changes.

Sky left the office and headed home. The big screen TV in the living room wasn't on. Kade wasn't sprawled on the couch. The baby wasn't in the bassinet. She tracked Kade to the kitchen where he was slouched against the back door and yakking on his cell phone.

"I don't know if that's such a good idea. Because it's been a long goddamn time since we done it together. Ah fuck you, I ain't forgot how to do it. Let's say, I've been doin' some practicin' on my own."

She froze. Who was he talking to? What kind of practicing was he referring to?

"Right. Nah, I guess I don't give a shit what people say about us either. So, tomorrow? Fine. I'll be there." *Click.*

Kade slipped the cell phone in his pocket and wheeled around with a guilty look. "Hey."

"Hey yourself." Her gaze scanned the kitchen. "Where's Eliza?"

His eyes widened in mock-horror. "Shit. I don't know. I guess I musta left her in the barn next to the bucket of rusty nails, the pissed off horse and the loaded shotgun."

"Funny."

"You wouldn't think so if it was me constantly askin' you where our daughter was."

Whoa. He was a little testy. "Sorry. Habit."

"One I wish you'd break." Kade dragged a hand through his hair and flopped in a chair. "Anyway, she's asleep. There's soup on the stove if you're hungry."

"You cooked?"

"No. Ma sent it home with me, so you know it's edible and it ain't chili. Again."

Really testy.

Skylar dished up. She sat across from him and ate in silence. As she rinsed her bowl, Kade wrapped an arm around her waist.

He removed the clip holding her messy mane and draped the waves across her shoulders, burying his face in her hair. "You always smell so damn good."

"I'm glad you think so."

"Your hair is beautiful. Don't ever cut it. I'd like to feel it draped across my body as you're ridin' me. Bet it feels like silk on my skin." He angled her head and kissed her neck.

Immediately tingles raced from that spot straight to her core.

"Skylar. I want you so damn bad. Let me have you."

The man made her wet with just words. "Let's go upstairs."

"No. Right here in the kitchen. Spread out on this counter so I can feast on you with the evenin' sun shinin' on your glossy hair."

"What's wrong with feasting on me in a bed?"

"Nothin'." Kade's hands curled around her hips. "Come on, sweetheart. Be spontaneous. Be adventurous. We're closer to the chocolate syrup here. I'd sure like to drizzle it on your sweet spot and make you my Tuesday sundae."

She wrapped her arms around his neck. "Maybe some other time. Take me to bed, cowboy."

"No." Kade stepped back, way back, letting her arms drop to her sides. "Why are you so insistent on me makin' love to you only in a bed?"

"Why are you being so insistent on doing me in the kitchen in broad daylight?"

"What's wrong with that? Knockin' the dishes to the floor and havin' my wicked way with you on the table?"

Her briefly liberating thought: *Hallelujah! A man who cares enough to figure out what I want,* was replaced with her usual paranoid thought: *No way! It's neon bright in here and you'd be disgusted with my cottage cheese thighs and jelly belly.*

"There's nothing wrong with it if you're into that sort of thing."

"And you're not?" he demanded. "Is makin' love only supposed to be done in the dark, at night, in missionary position?"

"Is that the issue? You're discovering I'm not sexually adventurous enough for you? Or spontaneous enough for you?"

His answering grin wasn't particularly pleasant. "No, the real issue ain't about me or what I want. The real issue is you're scared to death to lose control to *get* what you want, darlin'."

Her heart began to pound. Dammit. Did Kade really know her so well in such a short amount of time? When no other man bothered to really see her? To dig beneath the surface, to look beyond her dress size and the size of her bank account? To figure out her cool efficiency was a facade? "Kade—"

"I can see you're afraid to lose control to anyone, not just to me. See, I'm pretty sure you think about us screwin' on this table. Goin' at it on the living room floor until we're covered in rug burns. You think about gettin' on your knees and suckin' me off. Or me pinnin' you to the shower wall and fuckin' you mindless while we're wet and slippery. Or me bendin' you over the porch railin' and poundin' into you from behind. You think about doin' sixty-nine with me on the couch. Or how raunchy it'd feel to have me in your ass. Or usin' sex toys on you. Or me tyin' you up. You think about me fuckin' you in all the ways you've never let any other man fuck you."

With each accentuated phrase, Kade sidled closer.

"But know what I really think?"

She shook her head.

"You don't *wanna* think. You wish I'd take control of all sexual situations so you don't hafta worry about your response. You get to experience pure sexual satisfaction without guilt. You do what I tell you, knowin' full well that you'll love every damn minute of it. Because you know in your heart, I'd never do anything to hurt or humiliate you. In private or in public.

"You crave that out-of-control feelin', Sky. I can give it to you. I can give you everything you've ever wanted in bed and out of it. You gotta take a chance and trust me, sweetheart. You gotta take a chance and let go of your goddamned iron control and give yourself to me without boundaries."

Kade kissed her in a brutal show of male possession, of frustration, of absolute pure animal attraction, of a man choosing his mate and marking her his.

That raw power sucked her in like a drug. The ultimate aphrodisiac. Skylar kissed him with equal abandon, following his lead until he ripped his mouth free and backed away from her.

"Your days of controllin' our sexual encounters end now."

"But—"

"Ah-ah-ah. I ain't done. If you say yes to me havin' complete control over everything sex-wise, you don't get to change your mind. And you sure as hell don't get to say no, at any point, to anything I tell you to do once we start this."

"You're joking."

"No, ma'am, I've never been more serious in my life. I'm trying to prepare you for what bein' intimate with me means."

Skylar stared at him, almost as if she'd never seen him before. The Kade McKay she knew would never make demands like this.

Maybe you don't know him as well as you thought.

Maybe you don't know yourself as well as you thought if you're considering saying yes to this craziness for one single minute, Skylar Blue Ellison.

She wished the prim and proper voice in her head would take a hike. Yet, his demands scared her to pieces. Maybe she could get him to back down a little. Redefine his laundry list of suggestions. Promise to ease into fun and sex games. Not start out at super-kinky and progress to wilder sexual scenarios from there.

Softly, he said, "It won't work."

"What?"

"The deer in the headlights look. The puppy dog eyes. The female half-pout. There ain't no half-measures for either of us anymore, Sky. It's all or nothin'."

Semi-annoyed, she demanded, "So what? If I say no to being your sex slave you're leaving us?"

He was in her space, dark and dangerous, all pissed off primal male. "I'm not leavin'. Eliza is my daughter and I'm in her life. Period." He angled his head, letting his hot breath tease her ear. "And aren't you clever, tryin' to change my focus to something besides the fact you didn't deny you'd enjoy the hell out of bein' my sex slave?"

Holy crap. She hadn't denied it. And why did just the feel of his mouth so close to her skin make her weak-kneed and brain addled, wondering if she should invest in palm fronds, grapes and silken scarves?

"I don't expect you to decide changin' your whole approach

to intimacy right now. I'll give you a couple of days to think on it. Lettin' me know your answer by Saturday oughta be good enough."

When she didn't respond, he teased, "Disappointed I ain't bendin' you over and takin' what I want from you right now?"

Yes. "Just trying to understand why you bombarded me with raunchy images that leave me—" *craving what and who I could be with you* "—stunned and then Kade McKay, gentleman cowboy, tips his white hat at me as he rides away?"

"I never said I was gonna play fair."

"So am I just a game to you?"

Kade shook his head. "This is for real. This is for keeps, Skylar. Just so you know how serious I am, I moved my stuff out of your bedroom and into the guest room for the time bein'. I also put a new light bulb in the empty socket and in the lamps on the dressers."

Crap. She should've known he'd figure that out. It was a silly ploy anyway and she was surprised it'd worked as long as it did.

"I'll still get up with Eliza at night. I bought another baby monitor for my room so I can hear her. But you might wanna keep in mind I won't be back until late the next coupla nights."

Ask him where he's going.

Like hell. The old, stubborn Skylar asserted herself and pointed out they weren't married. Kade could do whatever he wanted and damn him for not being satisfied with her in bed or out of it. But wasn't that just the story of her life? "Anything else?"

"Nope." He pointed to the living room. "Unless you're up for watchin' a little TV with me now that we got that long overdue discussion outta the way?"

Frustrated with him, but mostly herself, she half-snarled, half-growled as she stormed up the stairs.

She heard Kade say, "I guess I can take that as a no."

Chapter Ten

"Hey, baby girl. Stop screaming. Ssh. It's okay. Mama's right here. Ssh."

Eliza kept right on wailing. For the fourth hour in a row. She wouldn't eat. She wouldn't sleep. She didn't have a dirty diaper. Or diaper rash. She didn't have a fever. She hadn't thrown up. She didn't have gas. She didn't have diarrhea. She was beyond fussy.

And Skylar didn't know why. Made her feel like an awful mother. She'd had to leave work before noon because Eliza wouldn't stop crying. She'd tried putting her in the swing. The baby bouncer. She'd tried rocking her and singing to her and reading to her. She'd strapped on the Snugli and walked up and down the driveway. She'd soaked her in a soothing bath steeped with calming herbs. She tried rubbing her tummy. Rubbing her back. Nothing worked.

On a whim, Sky packed Eliza in her car seat and headed for Sundance. Usually the rhythmic sounds of the tires clacking on the bumpy road put Eliza straight to sleep. Today it didn't matter. Eliza cried all the way into town. All thirty miles.

Sky parked in front of Sky Blue, juggling the baby carrier—complete with screaming, mad baby—the diaper bag, the Snugli, her purse and her sanity. She trudged inside. It was one of the only times she was thankful the store was empty.

Eliza shrieked as Skylar set the carrier on the floor.

India barreled around the corner. "What's wrong? Why are you here in the middle of a workday? Is Eliza sick?"

"I don't know. She won't stop crying." Sky unceremoniously dropped everything else where she stood. "I've done everything I can think of and I'm at my wit's end because nothing is helping."

"Well, aren't you a little banshee today, Miz Eliza Belle? How about if Auntie Indy takes over for a while, hmm? Mama's ears need a break?"

She watched as India lifted the angry baby out of the carrier and tried to calm her down.

Eliza was having none of it.

Her heart clenched at her baby's continued distress. "Maybe it is something serious. Should I take her to the doctor?"

"It's your call, Sis. She's your baby. You oughta know."

Skylar burst into tears. "But I don't! I'm the worst mother on the planet!" She knew it wasn't fair to bust in on poor India, making her deal with a hysterical mother and a screaming baby, but she had no one else to turn to.

What about Kade?

The thought of calling him, confessing her ineptitude with their daughter, letting him see how completely she'd lost it...well, she cried even harder at exposing that flaw, when he already thought she had plenty of other flaws.

That was the other thing. Why didn't Eliza fuss around him? Not that he'd been around the last two nights, and dammit she missed him. She sniffled and the sobs kept coming.

India was gently bouncing Eliza in her arms, eyeing Skylar warily.

"So what? I'm crying."

"You never cry."

"I never do a lot of things I should. I'm so tired of everybody thinking I'm some kind of robot. Of everyone thinking I can handle everything." She started bawling harder. "I can't! How do women have cranky babies and demanding jobs and confusing relationships and run a household by themselves without going insane?"

"I don't know, but I'm wondering if a stiff shot of whiskey wouldn't be the best thing for you right about now."

That caused Sky to laugh through her sobs and Eliza's wails. "Great advice coming from an alcoholic."

India smirked. "At least I didn't suggest you snort a line of coke or smoke a joint."

A loud pounding sounded on the door that separated the business spaces. A muffled voice inquired, "Indy? You okay?"

India walked over and twisted the lock. The door opened and AJ McKay stepped through. "I heard a baby crying."

"Crying is putting it mildly."

"Poor thing." AJ looked at Sky. "You okay?"

"Frustrated."

"I imagine. Mind if I hold her?"

"Knock yourself out. Or knock her out, whatever works," India muttered, and passed Eliza to her.

AJ placed one hand under Eliza's head and neck and the other on the baby's butt. "Such a mad face on such a pretty girl. What's wrong, cutie-pie? Just having a bad day?"

"I don't know what's wrong with her. I've tried everything. And I-I..." More tears fell. She wanted to scream in misery right along with Eliza.

"I'm sure you have." AJ nuzzled Eliza's cheek and cooed, "Yes, sweet baby, she's a great mama to you, isn't she?"

"She's not very happy with her mama today."

"Sometimes those people who make us the happiest can also make us the most mad," AJ said. "It's a trade off."

That observation startled Skylar.

India said, "Eliza's mad all right. Look at how hard she's shaking."

A thoughtful look crossed AJ's face. "Skylar, do you mind if I try something with her?"

Sky wiped her eyes and shook her head. "Please. If you can help her..."

"I'll see what I can do." AJ sat in a chair and stretched Eliza out on her lap, belly up. Holding her head with one hand, she rubbed her thumb from the base of the baby's skull to the bottom of her neck. She massaged the left side and right side, speaking softly to Eliza as she continued to gently rub and Eliza continued to shriek.

After several long minutes, which seemed a lifetime to

Skylar as her precious baby wailed, the cries tapered to whimpers. The whimpers ended with a hiccup. It became quiet enough they heard Eliza sigh deeply.

Skylar felt that sigh clear to the marrow of her bones.

India peered at the infant. "It's a miracle. What did you do?"

AJ blushed. "Nothing, really. Massaged her neck. We learned when babies are learning to hold up their heads, it can create extra pressure on the tendons in their neck. When they get all tense, they seize up, mostly in their neck, where their vocal cords are. They scream, it hurts and they scream more."

"Thank you." Skylar stared at the twisted Kleenex in her hand. "I feel like such an idiot. I didn't know that." Tears welled up again. "There's lots I don't know."

"Hey, I wouldn't have known if I hadn't gone to massage therapy school. Trust me, my sister had the same issues with all three of her kids, so it's not you."

Sweet words. AJ was the sweetest woman around.

AJ continued to rub Eliza's neck and the baby's long lashes fluttered closed. "As long as you're here...I have a bone to pick with you, Skylar Ellison." Those silver eyes locked on hers. "Why didn't you tell me Eliza was Kade's baby? All this time and I had no clue you were carrying a McKay?"

Ooh. Not so sweet now.

"Kade didn't even know," India pointed out.

"You bet your behind he didn't, because no way would Kade have let you go through pregnancy and childbirth alone. I've known him all my life and he is not that kind of man. Cord told me the only reason Kade took that job up in the north country was because he'd had a bad break up with a woman. I never imagined that woman was you."

Skylar bit back the retort, *I never imagined he'd pretend to be his twin brother and knock me up, either.*

"And if you'd bothered to tell any of us you were pregnant, we would've made sure he received the message."

"Am I going to be defending my decision to the entire McKay family for the rest of Eliza's life?"

"Probably." AJ straightened Eliza's jumper. "We're all

overjoyed because you birthed a girl McKay. Keely has been the only girl for four generations."

"Kimi mentioned that." Kade's mother had called a couple of times to chat after Kade had taken Eliza to see her grandma. Kimi was a real spitfire. She claimed she had to be tough to survive being married to a wild McKay man and raising two more McKay hellions. Sky developed an instant rapport with Kimi, even when Sky shied away from asking questions about Kade and his childhood, because she didn't want to seem nosy.

"My sisters-in-law have hope the next McKay out of the chute, so to speak," AJ grinned cheekily, "will be the stem-less variety."

"What about you, AJ? Since Channing and Macie have both birthed boys, you itching to be the one to break their streak?" India teased.

"God no. Ky is plenty for us to handle right now. Besides, Cord and I've only been married since December. We're breeding horses for the time being, not kids."

Footsteps echoed from the back room. A deep male voice asked, "India? You seen my wife?" Cord McKay crossed the threshold.

Skylar stared. Good God. Was every single one of the blasted McKay men so sinfully good looking? No question this man was related to Kade—same dark hair, same vivid blue eyes.

But Cord only had eyes for AJ. Hungry eyes. "Hey, baby doll. I was lookin' for you."

"And you found me."

"Appears you found your way to the babies again," he murmured and angled over her shoulder to examine Eliza.

"I can't help it. Isn't she the sweetest thing?"

"Yes, she is. Least that's what her daddy says." Cord's eyes met Skylar's, almost in challenge.

Sky's mocking look challenged him back. "Kade is a sucker. He's already promised to buy her a pony."

"I imagine so." He thrust out his hand. "I've seen you around, and I know India, but we've never been introduced. Cord McKay."

She shook his hand. "Skylar Ellison. Do all you McKay cousins and brothers look alike?"

"The wonder twins notwithstandin', I don't see the resemblance, but other folks do. I imagine we all oughta wear name tags tomorrow, so you don't get us mixed up."

"What's going on tomorrow?"

"The big rodeo. Kade and Colt are competin'. Everybody's talkin' about it. I figured you'd be there so Kade could show off the baby."

"He hasn't mentioned it, but he's been pretty scarce the last couple days."

An awkward moment followed.

"Well, I'm sure Kade'll tell you about it when he finds time." Cord set his hand on AJ's shoulder and squeezed. "I came to remind you we gotta get Ky pretty quick."

AJ stood and handed the sleeping baby to her mother. "Thanks for letting me have my baby fix. See you tomorrow."

The couple barely cleared the backroom when AJ gasped and a low masculine laugh answered. The connecting door slammed.

"Those two. I swear they're always doin' it in her studio. I think it's the only chance they have to be alone without rambunctious Ky underfoot."

"Kids do have a way of messing up the best-laid plans."

"Sounds like you have some experience with that?"

Rather than respond, Sky wandered. She was too restless to sit and half-afraid if she quit moving Eliza would wake up. Her thoughts wandered to Kade.

Why hadn't he told her about the rodeo? Because he expected come Saturday she'd pass on his intriguing offer and that part of their relationship would be over? They'd be friends, Eliza's parents and nothing more to each other? That thought made her sort of ill.

"Sky? You okay?"

"Not really. Something's been brought to my attention and I'm asking for your honest opinion."

"Shoot."

"Do you think I'm controlling?"

"Do you mean in control, or manipulative of others?"

"In control." Sky faced her sister.

"Yes, you are in total control, at all times, of all things."

"Is that bad?"

India shrugged. "Not necessarily. Unless you're unwilling to bend a little, to loosen up once in awhile. We both know that's not in your type-A personality, especially given your past association with jerk-off men. Why do you ask?"

"Kade mentioned he thinks I have control issues."

"He's right."

India's automatic agreement jarred Sky. "You're siding with him?"

"I'd never side against you, Sis. Never. I am really proud of you for being such a great mom, even if I'm surprised you aren't more controlling and psycho when it comes to Eliza."

"What?"

"I honestly was scared you'd become one of those mothers who obsesses over every little thing."

Sky's stomach pitched. "You saying I don't care?"

"No. You love Eliza fiercely, but it's not an insane I-need-to-control-every-minute-of-this-kid's-life kind of love that I expected from you."

"I'm really like that?"

"With most things, especially your business. Case in point: You've finally hired an office manager after I nagged you incessantly, but do you let her manage? No. You still do it all, which drives me batshit. How long will Annie have to work for you before you decide to give her more responsibility?"

"I—"

"Let me finish. I know you weigh pros and cons from every conceivable angle. You never jump headfirst into any situation." India cocked her head and challenged, "How many baby books did you read when you were pregnant?"

Forty. "Where is the relevance in that question?"

"You asked for an opinion, I'm giving you mine. So knowing how you are, how you've always been, it really blew my mind when Kade came back into the picture and you trusted him with Eliza from the start. No second-guessing his parenting abilities. No 'trial period' for him to prove himself to you or your daughter. You just flat-out accepted him."

That *was* an atypical reaction for her, and Sky admitted, "He's taken to fatherhood in a way I could only hope for. He is so great with her. Better than I am at times." Like today.

"So, how did the topic of you being controlling come up with Kade? Does it have to do with Eliza?"

"No. It's more...personal."

India's eyes narrowed. "Are you sleeping with him?"

"You mean sharing a bed? Or—"

"You know what I mean, Sky."

"Yes. I'm sleeping with him."

"Has he asked you to marry him again?"

Surprised, Sky said, "How did you know about that?"

"When I stopped in at your place, I ah...grilled him about a couple of things, he told me he asked you, and you said no."

"Well, the only reason he asks me is because of Eliza."

"*Asks?*" India repeated. "As in he's asked multiple times?"

Skylar nodded.

"You're one hundred percent certain that the only reason Kade McKay is with you is because of your daughter?"

"Most likely."

"Hah! I think you're wrong. And here's where I'm gonna piss you off. You're using Eliza as an excuse. After all the shit that's happened to you with men, you don't believe any man would want *you* without an ulterior motive."

Skylar snapped, "Excuse me, but that *has* been the case in every goddamned relationship I've ever been in."

"Does Kade know about Ted?"

"Do you really think I want to share that humiliation with him right off the bat?"

"No, but he needs to know." India softened her tone. "Would it really be so bad to open yourself up to Kade? To trust him? To let down your guard? And yes, let him have a little bit of control in your relationship?"

For the first time since Eliza's birth, Sky wondered if she'd ever be able to break that sheet of glass she kept between herself and the rest of the world. Why did the wall of defense she'd built feel like a prison rather than self-protection?

"Sis?" India prompted.

"It terrifies me to think of giving Kade control even temporarily. Part of me worries he'll keep it and I'll never get it back. I've been there, Indy. I'll never make that mistake again."

"But you're making another mistake, maybe a worse one, by not giving Kade a fair shot at proving he won't abuse your trust. By holding yourself back from what could be the best thing that ever happened to you." India pointed at Eliza and got in Skylar's face. "Oh, I know you say Eliza is the best thing that's ever happened to you, but without Kade, there wouldn't *be* an Eliza. So in my mind, that makes *him* the best thing that's happened to you. Think about it."

The chimes jingled out front and India left.

Chapter Eleven

The late afternoon sun burned across the dirt, reflecting off the metal fence at the back of the corral. Been an eternity since Kade spent time in the chutes and barn behind the Boars Nest. Seemed a lifetime ago he'd called this place home.

His brother and his cousin had been busy beavers in the last twelve months. Hauling away broken-down equipment, replacing fences, painting outbuildings. The old place looked like a ranch, rather than a rural slum.

"Getcha head in the game, cuz."

"Colt, we flat-out suck at this. Even another week of practice wouldn't help us none," Kade hollered over the stall.

"Kwitcher belly-achin'. Watch the barrier this time."

Kane—aka newly self-christened as Buck—whooped, "Gentlemen, start your horses!" and dropped the orange rope. The calf took off out of the chute in a red blur, Colt and Kade hot on its heels.

Dirt flew, saddles creaked, ropes twirled in the hot, dusty air. Both men let their ropes loose at the same time; Kade aimed for the head; Colt for the back feet.

Each rope hit the mark and the calf jerked to a stop. The horses knew the drill, backing up in opposite directions until the rope was pulled taut and the calf was stretched between them like a Chinese finger-pull.

Kade wiped his forehead as he waited the four seconds the calf had to be down for their time to even count.

"Time!"

Buck raced into the paddock and untied the calf. "Seven

point eight seconds. Not bad."

Colt coiled his rope after Buck released the calf. "Least we didn't break the barrier."

"Least we caught the goddamn thing," Kade said. "That piss-poor time ain't gonna win us a dime tomorrow."

"Ain't about money."

Kade squinted at Colt. "What the hell are we competin' for then?"

"Honor." Colt spit out a wad of chewing tobacco.

"For Christsake, Colt, that's the dumbest damn thing I ever heard. I'm a little old to be defendin' my honor, let alone yours."

"Kade's got a point."

"Shut the fuck up, Buck." Colt grinned. "I gotta admit I'm likin' the way your new name rhymes."

Buck gave him the finger.

"Maybe I didn't mean honor as much as I meant I don't wanna get shown up," Colt said.

"Shown up by who?"

"Quinn and Bennett are competin'."

"So? They been travelin' the circuit team ropin' on a regular basis?"

"Nah. But that don't mean they ain't been practicin' together down at the south end of the ranch when we've been up here workin' on our separate sections. If you'll remember, they whupped our butts but good last time."

"That was damn near seven years ago."

"Hey, ain't that the time Cam and Carter teamed up?" Buck asked.

"Yep. Folks were laughin' at my brothers' attempts at ropin' and wrestlin', instead of laughin' at the damn rodeo clown," Colt grumbled. "So it *is* about honor. The honor of kickin' our cousins' sorry butts in front of the whole county."

Kade loosened his grip on the reins and patted Colby's old rodeo horse on the neck. "Didja think that maybe folks'll be laughin' at us instead?"

"Nope, because we're gonna win and make 'em choke on our dust."

Buck snorted. "You know Trevor Glanzer and Cash Big Crow are competin'? And they were both professional rodeo cowboys. If any team's got a leg up, it's them. Or Dag's old partner, Jess Barton."

Silence cut through the dirty air. It'd be the first year without Dag or Uncle Harland.

"Like I said, it's about honor."

Kade realized Colt's insistence on participating was a tribute to their cousin. That put the whole thing in a different light. "Only way we're gonna beat them guys is if we keep practicin'."

"Works for me. Load up another calf, Buck." Colt spurred his horse back to the chutes and Kade returned to his side.

After the team roping practice, Buck nagged Kade into hazing for him while he attempted to steer wrestle. But none of the taunts from either of his crazy relatives would convince Kade to climb on the back of a bull at tomorrow's rodeo.

Two hours later, dusty, sore and tired, Kade, Buck and Colt were sitting on the tailgates of their trucks, drinking iced tea out of mason jars. The sun hung low in the purple sky.

Talk turned from rodeo competition to cattle to ranch business to women. The conversation wasn't nearly as raunchy as it'd been in years past. Kade didn't know whether it was because they weren't liquored up, or because they'd all grown up.

"You bringin' that baby of yours to the rodeo?"

"Yep."

"Ma says everybody's gonna be there."

"That don't surprise me." It occurred to him Skylar hadn't talked to him about anything the last couple days. Maybe she didn't want to hang out with his kin at the rodeo. After his I-control-all-the-sex-and-you'll-give-it-to-me-anyway-I-want-it ultimatum, maybe she didn't want to hang out with *him*.

His conscience piped up. *Can you blame her?*

He shoved aside that guilty thought. He was trying to help Skylar access a side of herself that scared her. He was trying to give them both a shot at real intimacy without barriers. He'd never do a blasted thing to hurt her and she knew it. She was just being stubborn. And controlling. Which brought him back to square one.

"Been a real baby explosion around here."

"The McKay name ain't gonna die out any time soon." He smiled. "Except for our line, bein's I have a girl."

"So what's it like, havin' a kid?" Colt asked.

"Weird. Cool. Cool as hell, actually. Eliza is a lot of fun. She's growin' every damn day, which is a kick to watch. But she's a lot of work, feedin' her, changin' her, and holdin' her all the time. Mostly it don't feel like work. I like doin' it. When she looks at me…it's like I want to do everything in my power to protect her and make her happy." Funny. That's how he felt about Skylar too. Still, at that honest admission, Kade braced himself for his brother and his cousin to rag on him about being baby-whipped, but they didn't make a smart ass remark.

In fact, Colt said, "We gonna be hearin' weddin' bells soon?"

"They ain't gonna be ringin' for me." He chugged the rest of his tea and passed the empty jar to Colt. "Later." He climbed in his truck and went home.

The house was quiet. Skylar didn't wait supper on him, although she'd left a plate in the refrigerator, which was so damn sweet it gave him a funny tickle in his chest. He ate the beef and mashed potatoes cold, barely tasting it. Damn lonely eating by himself. He'd gotten used to his family's company in the last three weeks.

Kade showered. Checked on the baby and wandered downstairs. Skylar dozed on the couch. The baby monitor sat on the coffee table and the TV droned in the background. For some reason, an odd sense of peace filled him at the domestic scene. He snagged the remote and settled on the floor, not wanting to disturb her rest.

An hour or so later Sky stirred behind him.

"Hey. How long have you been home?"

"Couple hours. Before you ask, she's fine. She's still sleepin'."

"I'm that predictable, huh?"

"No, you just think about her first. You're a good mama,

Sky."

"You wouldn't say that if you'd seen me earlier today."

Kade turned around. Sky's face was blotchy. Her usually sparkling eyes were red-rimmed and sad. "Why? What happened?"

"Eliza screamed. I mean she really screamed. Literally for hours. I didn't know what to do." Skylar explained in such detail Kade found himself wincing at her obvious anxiety. She finished with, "When I fed her right before I tucked her in bed, that sweet baby girl just looked at me with those big blue eyes, like she was...disappointed in me for being such a bad mom." A small hiccupping sob punctuated her distress.

"Ah, sweetheart. C'mere." He crawled next to her on the couch, bringing her into his arms. Skylar curled her body into his and cried softly. He let her, even when it broke his damn heart. After she'd calmed down, he brushed his lips across the crown of her head. "Sorry you had a rough day. I expect Eliza Belle will give us both more than a few of 'em."

She nodded against his chest.

As Kade ran his hands up and down her spine, he realized Skylar hadn't granted him much opportunity to just hold her. To soothe her. She hadn't shown her vulnerable side to him. Ever.

Now that she'd finally lowered her guard, his earlier demand of her total sexual submission made him feel like a fucking heel. Maybe if he didn't bring it up again, she'd forget about it, allowing him to gentle her like he'd do with a skittish horse. Oh, he still craved her succulent body nine-ways-'til-Sunday, no doubt about that, but he wanted her heart too.

And that took time.

Good thing Kade was a patient man.

He closed his eyes and breathed her in, matching his exhalations to hers and floating off to sleep.

Hours later a wailing cry startled them both. Skylar groaned.

"Stay put, I'll get her." Kade fed Eliza and rocked her back to sleep. He couldn't drum up the energy to climb the stairs so he nestled her in the bassinet. Then he snuggled behind Skylar on the couch, covering them with a blanket. He waited for Sky to wake up and protest, but she just burrowed deeper into his body and sighed.

Skylar woke with a start.

"Easy." The warm body next to hers shifted. The very hard, very warm male body.

"What...Kade?" She blinked at the sun peeping through the lace curtains. "Why are we in the living room?"

"Must've fallen asleep."

"You've—we've been here together? All night?"

"Mostly, yeah. I ain't surprised you don't remember. You were pretty wrung out last night when I got home."

No kidding. Sky remembered feeling alone and inept after returning from Sundance. Crying herself to sleep on the couch, missing Kade like crazy, wondering why she kept pushing the man away when she wanted him around.

When she'd woken up and saw Kade, she'd been so relieved, she'd blurted out every sordid detail of her bad day with Eliza. In the face of her complete meltdown, Kade had been amazingly sweet, not judgmental. He'd made her feel safe. And competent. And cared for. Sort of...loved.

So how had she repaid his kindness? By blubbering all over the poor man and clinging to him all night so he couldn't escape to his own bed.

Her cheeks heated and she tried to wiggle free.

"Hey now, what's the rush?" His voice was gravelly with sleep. "I gotta admit I like wakin' up with you in my arms, Sky. I've missed you the last couple of days."

A pregnant pause hung between them, as if he was waiting for something from her. The truth, probably.

After all this man has done for you, he deserves your honesty. Face it: You deserve to be honest with yourself.

She relaxed into him and simply said, "I missed you too." She felt him smile against the top of her head.

"Good to know."

They stayed embraced in easy silence for a good long time.

Kade's hand lazily traced her spine. "So what time you comin' to the rodeo today?"

"What rodeo?"

"The Devil's Tower Rodeo outside of Sundance. You know, the one me'n Colt are team ropin' in? Seems my whole family is gonna be there, and everyone is chompin' at the bit to meet Eliza. It's gotten to be some kinda crazy big deal with a family reunion."

"Then why is this the first I've heard of it, Kade McKay?"

His hand froze. "Shit. I didn't tell you?"

"Nope."

"You're sure?"

Skylar lifted up to look at him. "Positive. You haven't exactly been around the last couple days to tell me anything."

"Ah hell, Sky, I meant to. I'm so damn sorry."

"Me too." Could he read between the lines and understand she was sorry for so many things that'd gone wrong between them?

"I'd understand if you didn't want to come on such short notice."

His sheepish expression squashed her intent to keep teasing him. "Lucky thing Miz Eliza Belle and I don't have anything else to do so she can make her McKay family debut, huh?"

Relief swept his face. "Lucky indeed."

"Will you be around?"

"Some. Why?"

Sky could scarcely think over the clucking noises echoing in her head. Truth was, she might be totally confident when it came to running her business, but this social situation absolutely petrified her, especially when she'd heard rumors about the wild, boisterous McKay family. She also feared they'd circle the wagons around her, holding pitchforks, demanding an answer to the same question AJ McKay had posed: why hadn't she told Kade about her pregnancy?

"Sweetheart? What's wrong?"

That pesky "be honest" voice appeared again. "I'm nervous, okay? I don't know anything about big families and if you won't be there I'll probably freak out and then people will think I'm some kind of West Coast nutjob—"

Kade muffled her protests with a gentle kiss. "It'll be all right, I'll be around as much as I can. That said, I ain't gonna lie. My family is a bit overbearin'. They'll ask all sorts of personal questions that quite frankly, ain't none of their damn business. But I've seen you in action, Skylar. You can handle anything."

"Anything but you, it seems," she murmured. Without conscious thought, she traced the dark stubble on his jaw; her fingers detoured to outline his full lips. "You have such an intriguing mouth. Even when you're scowling at me."

"Yeah?"

"Yeah. I know you think you're just another one of those McKay men that populate three Wyoming counties, but you are different, Kade. From Kane. From your cousins. Even your standard issue McKay blue eyes are more compelling...they draw me in. Every damn time. Anyone who can't see the differences is a fool." *Why haven't I seen it? Why have I acted like such a fool?*

"Sky—"

Eliza squeaked once. Twice. Louder the third time.

"Oops, there's our alarm clock." Saved from further embarrassing admissions about his virtues, she rolled off the couch. Impulsively she leaned over and kissed Kade's forehead. "Thanks for last night."

She felt him staring as she cooed to their baby and got a jumpstart on the big day.

Chapter Twelve

"Skylar! You're here."

She bit back a smile at the sight of Kimi McKay nearly skipping toward her. "Don't you mean Eliza is here?"

"No, smarty. I'm just as happy to see you as I am my beautifully perfect granddaughter."

Kade didn't get all his sweet-talkin' ability from the McKays. Sky had no doubt Kimi could charm the bees from the flowers. "Here she is. All decked out for her first rodeo."

Kimi laughed with delight. "Where on earth did you find jeans that small? With rhinestones?"

"Aunt India. She goes a little insane buying Eliza clothes. Toys. Books."

"About that..." Kimi smiled. "I sorta went hog wild too, but that cute girlie stuff is impossible to resist, especially since I've never had the chance to buy it before. I keep reminding Kade to load it all up and take it to you. He keeps forgetting."

Casually, she asked, "Why don't you bring it over?"

"Really?"

"Sure. Pick a day. If you want, I'll even put you on babysitting duties while I'm at work and you can have Miz Eliza all to yourself. Of course, you'll have to hand her over when Kade gets home. He's a bit territorial when it comes to time with his girl."

Kimi made a frowning, blinking expression.

Had she said the wrong thing to Kade's mother? "I didn't mean to presume—"

"Presume? Lord, girl, you really don't know how much I

appreciate the invite."

It was Sky's turn to act surprised. "You don't need an invitation, Kimi. You're welcome any time."

"Really? I've been tickled the couple of times Kade has brought Eliza into Sundance so I could see her. But I haven't wanted to butt in and be a nuisance. Overstep my bounds. Meddle where I wasn't wanted."

"Seems we both have boundary issues," Sky murmured. "As far as meddling? You're Eliza's grandma. Actually, you're her only grandma." A tiny burst of sadness broke inside her, thinking about her own mother never knowing her child and she looked away before she refocused on Kimi's all-knowing eyes. "Just because Kade and I are...whatever we are, I didn't intend to keep Eliza away from him or any of her family."

"Then why didn't you tell anyone Kade is her father?"

"Because Kade deserved to know first." She glanced at their alert daughter. "The way the situation played out wasn't ideal for anyone. But the bottom line is, Kade's a really great dad. You should be proud of him."

"You don't have any idea how much that means to me. All of it." Kimi wiped a tear and laughed. "Lord. I'm leaking."

Sky was leaking a little too. Flustered, she handed the squirming baby to her grandma.

"What a little angel. Your mama did good, didn't she?"

Eliza cooed back her agreement.

Before Sky started leaking again, she said, "So I brought everything but the kitchen sink. Help me figure out what to load up."

Kimi eyed the pile in the back of the car. "Things sure have changed since my boys were babies. I would've loved to have one of them double strollers." She winked. "Maybe next time you and Kade will have a set of twins."

"Next time?"

"I'm greedy, aren't I? Cal and I always wanted to have more kids, but it never happened, so feel free to overfill my arms and life with grandbabies."

Rather than feel put on the spot, Skylar laughed. She and Kimi chatted easily as Sky pushed the empty stroller across the bumpy ground while Kimi walked beside her holding Eliza. Family friends would stop and admire the newest McKay baby, congratulating both mom and grandma, and Kade in absentia. Another pleasant revelation was so many people knew about the Sky Blue store and already considered her part of the community. It made Sky wonder if she was spending too much time at the manufacturing plant and not enough putting a face with her products. If she should take India's advice and let Annie have more responsibility so she could focus on local marketing.

When they reached the entrance, Kimi said, "I believe these tickets are for seats in the upper stands, but I didn't know how long you'd want to stay up there. Gets mighty hot and it'll be a while before Kade competes."

"What is he competing in?"

"Team ropin' for sure."

"Is that dangerous?"

"All rodeo events are dangerous, honey."

"Is there a chance he'll get hurt?"

"Yes."

Suddenly, the fun afternoon took on a more ominous slant. "Then why would he do it?" Sky couldn't fathom the idea of Kade purposely putting himself at risk. She couldn't stand it, dammit, it'd hurt her to watch the big, tough cowboy get injured.

"I don't know. I'm thankful neither he nor Kane were obsessed with being a rodeo star like some of his cousins. Kade dabbled in events. Nothing serious like Chase is doing now and Colby and Dag done." A stark look flashed in Kimi's eyes.

Skylar placed her hand on Kimi's arm. "Sometimes I have zero tact. I'm so sorry. I didn't mean to bring up painful memories."

"Thanks, sweetie, but it's unavoidable, especially on a day like today. Dag's death was hard on all of us. Then Dag's father, my brother Harland, died not a month later."

"Really? I didn't know. How awful for your family. That's so sad."

"It was a mess. Colt was in rehab. No one could get a hold

of Cam. Chase was competing in a special PBR event in Mexico and he couldn't get home. Kade had only been up north for two weeks so Kane had to drive up there to give him the bad news and bring him home for the service. Poor Chassie was a zombie. Everything between Dag's funeral and Harland's funeral was kind of a blur." She shook her head as if to clear it. "Been a really rough year for the Wests and McKays, which is just another reason we were all so tickled about Eliza.

"So to take the long way around answering your question, I suspect Kade is competing because Dag isn't here. Lots of Dag's rodeo friends are showing up today to lend support and engage in a little friendly competition." All at once an enormous grin lit up Kimi's face. "Speaking of...Chassie. Over here."

Skylar turned and watched as the woman sauntered toward them—saunter being the operative word. Her gait screamed one hundred percent cowgirl. So did her clothes, she was no rhinestone belt-wearing buckle bunny. She wore battered lace-up boots, skin-tight faded jeans and a long-sleeved T-shirt emblazoned with, "Real Cowgirls Do It Best in the Dirt". Dark brown hair as long and glossy as a horse's tail was plaited in a single, thick braid that fell past her butt. An angular face—apple cheekbones, pointed chin, broad forehead and a generous mouth that hinted of Native American ancestry.

"I tried calling you, but Uncle Cal said you were already gone. Is he coming?"

"I expect him any time now."

"Oh wow, is this who I think it is?"

"Yep. This is Eliza Belle. Isn't she a doll?"

"Absolutely precious." Chassie bent closer. "We girls are few and far between so we gotta stick together. Man. She does look like Kade. Bet he's struttin' around like cock of the walk."

"That he is."

Chassie straightened. Her liquid brown eyes sparkled, and her sweet, wide grin was infectious. "Ah. You'd be the vessel who brought forth the long-awaited McKay girl baby?"

Skylar smiled. "Aptly put."

"Skylar Ellison, this is my niece Chassie West."

"It's Chassie Glanzer now." She wiped her hand on her jeans before she offered it to Sky. "Nice to meetcha, Skylar.

Congrats on the wee one and welcome to the family."

"Thanks." Chassie wasn't much bigger than Kimi and Sky felt positively Amazonian next to the petite, skinny women.

"Chassie just got married in February. She and her husband Trevor took over Harland's ranch after he passed on. How you doin' today, honey?"

Chassie's smile faded. "It's weird being here without them. I keep expecting to see Dag hanging on the fence behind the chutes, waiting to ride. Or Daddy standing in line for a beer."

Her look of sadness prompted Sky to offer, "I'm so sorry for both your losses."

"I appreciate you sayin' so."

"What all is Trevor competing in today?" Kimi asked.

"Everything. Poor delusional man thinks he can win the all around title. I know he's doin' it in Dag's memory, which is unbelievably sweet, and yet stupid, because he's going up against hungry pups in their late teens."

"It's not like Trevor is old."

"True. And I ain't gonna complain about seein' him in tight chaps, sexy rodeo gear, swingin' a rope and buckin' hard." Her brilliant smile reappeared. "But they're still gonna kick Kade and Colt's ass in team roping."

"Yeah? Wanna bet?"

"I'd hate to take your money, Aunt Kimi, but I will. Twenty says Cash and Trevor win."

"You're on."

Chassie cocked an eyebrow at Skylar. "Not gonna bet on your man?"

Was Kade her man? A possessive little voice piped up with a firm *yes*, so Sky said, "Bring it. Twenty on the McKays."

Kimi whooped, "That's my girl."

"You heading to the reunion, Aunt K?"

"Yeah. We'll see you in there."

They wound their way through the crowd, stopping on the edge of the bleachers. Kimi passed Eliza back to her and fussed with the collar of Sky's shirt. Smoothed a flyway strand from her cheek. Acted very motherly, which just made her like Kimi

McKay all the more. "You are pretty as a picture. You ready?"

Skylar blushed. "Ready for what?"

"To meet the West family."

"But I thought we were meeting the McKay family?"

"That's later tonight and tomorrow. Lucky you gets a double whammy this weekend. This is my side of Kade's family, the West side. You'll probably recognize some McKay family members, since my sister Carolyn married Carson McKay, Calvin's brother, making our kids double cousins." She grinned. "Confused yet?"

"Yes. No wonder Cord said you should all wear name tags." Skylar squinted at the large cluster of people milling beneath a big tent. "Maybe you should point out which ones are family members."

"Honey, they're all family members."

There had to be at least fifty people in there. "Oh. My. God."

"Smile. And when Genevieve West starts talking about quilting, run like hell."

Talk about being in a fish bowl. Skylar wished Kade would've been there, helping her navigate the waters. Faces blurred. She'd never remember all their names. And this was only half of Kade's family.

After an hour passed, a feeling of panic started. A sense she was an interloper, even when everyone was friendly and went out of their way to include her. She and Kade and Eliza must've gotten fifteen invitations to dinner. Several women promised to check out her Sky Blue products. It was unusual in that no one thought it was strange to automatically embrace Skylar and Eliza as part of their family. Their immediate acceptance made her feel humbled. Grateful. Swamped by so many conflicting emotions, Sky feared she'd break down, and wouldn't that leave a great first impression? Instead, she reverted to her normal behavior, keeping a polite distance as her eyes searched for an escape route.

Then Kimi was by her side again, soothing her, rescuing her. "Looks like you could use some fresh air, sweets."

"Yes, I could. Thank you."

Outside, Kimi said, "What happened? Did Janet harangue you about you and Kade livin' in sin?"

"No. Nothing like that."

"Then what?"

Before she schooled her tongue to stay still, Sky blurted out, "I've never met so many genuinely nice people in my life and it was like they were happy to meet me, not giving me the evil eye wondering who the hell I was crashing their party."

Kimi chuckled. "Not used to that?"

"No. I'm used to people ignoring or sucking up because they want something from me."

"I can't imagine what it must've been like growing up, always questioning people's ulterior motives. Must make it hard to trust not only yourself, but everyone around you."

"It does."

"Whatcha see is what you get with us, honey." Kimi tucked a loose hair behind Skylar's ear and murmured, "I'll be damned. You are a little shy, aren't you?"

"About some things." She studied Kimi's kind eyes. "Is it obvious?"

"Only to me."

Skylar gave her a skeptical look and Kimi cracked.

"Okay, it's partially mother's instinct, and partially Kade making me promise to look out for you because he can't be with you. He's worried about leavin' you alone to deal with our crazy family."

That man embodied sweet and something undeniably warm moved through Sky.

Kimi squeezed Sky's shoulder. "Even knowing that, and as much fun as we're having, I'm afraid I've gotta leave you to your own devices for a bit. The rodeo is about to start. You better get settled and I'll meet you later."

Skylar climbed the stairs in the grandstand. Clouds covered the sun, blocking some of the heat. She secured her sleepy baby in the Snugli, strapping it to her chest, and stood next to the railing. The noise or the crowds didn't bother Eliza. Sky took a minute to breathe it all in. The scents, the sights, the sounds of rodeo. Nothing like it in the world.

Saddle bronc riding ended and the steer wrestling—bulldogging—was set to begin. She listened to the announcers extolling the qualities needed to be a great bulldogger, and couldn't fathom why any man would throw himself off a moving horse onto a moving horned animal.

"Skylar?"

Startled by someone calling out her name, she looked down and saw Chassie grinning up at her.

"Hey. You wanna come sit with us?" Chassie pointed to a small group of people by the bottom railing.

Yes. "Oh. I wouldn't want to impose."

"Nonsense. You're family and we'd love to have you." Chassie winked. "I'm always lookin' for a leg up on McKay gossip. Plus, it'll be fun. I promise. Nothing like the chaos in the tent at the West family reunion. You were lookin' a little goggle-eyed."

"I was." Sky followed Chassie and listened while she made introductions. "Everyone, this is Skylar Ellison, and the sleeping babe is the infamous Eliza Belle, who proud papa Kade's been braggin' on to everyone within spittin' distance. So who's next? Name and family affiliation to make it easier on Skylar since she's already been subjected to the West family today."

"I'm Macie McKay, we've met at your store a few times."

They had met, but for some reason Sky hadn't connected her to the McKay family. "You run Dewey's?"

"Oversee it since we live in Canyon River half the time."

"Cat does a great job. The food is wonderful and the place is so homey."

Macie beamed. "Thanks. Is India here?"

"No. She's holding down the fort. I hope we get lots of traffic because of the rodeo."

A long, lean man with McKay blue eyes and a riot of unruly curls waved. "Carter McKay of the Carson McKay branch. I'm Kade's cousin. Macie's my wife, and our son Thane is a couple months older than Eliza. They'll have a lot of fun growin' up together."

"Raising hell together you mean. Thane and my twins,

Rider and Ella, are napping in the camper under Velma's watchful eye." The older blonde woman, who appeared to be pregnant, thrust out her hand. "I'm Gemma Big Crow. No relation to these McKay yahoos, except by marriage. My husband Cash, is team roping with Chassie's husband Trevor, and sorry to say it, hon, but they're gonna kick some major butt today."

"You wish," Carter said. "Kade and Colt are on fire."

"Huh-uh. Dad and Trev rule."

Chassie leaned over. "FYI, Macie is Cash's daughter from a previous relationship. Carter is Colt's younger brother."

"I'm never going to keep all this straight."

"It takes time, but you will. Despite their surface similarities they've all got distinct personalities."

Sky thought of Kade's comment about feeling interchangeable with not only his twin, but his male McKay cousins and felt a punch of sympathy. If she didn't know him, she'd probably be like everyone else and lump him in with his family.

The announcer's voice boomed. "First up. Buck McKay. Not a McKay name I'm familiar with."

Carter laughed. "The SOB really did it. Said he was gonna do something drastic to set himself apart."

"Set himself apart from who?" Macie demanded.

"From Colt, but mostly from Kade. Kane—aka Buck—is determined to get his new nickname to stick. Aunt Kimi is appalled."

"Is Kade his hazer?" Gemma asked.

"Yep. Poor Kade got roped into all sorts of events," Carter said.

Sky leaned over and asked Chassie, "What in the world is a hazer?"

"The rider who keeps the steer in a straight line for the bulldogger is called a hazer."

The chute opened, a steer bolted into the arena and two horses raced after it.

Skylar didn't see Buck launch himself onto the steer and flip it over. She was too busy staring at Kade—all grace and control—atop the sleek and powerful horse. It was the first time she'd seen him duded up in full cowboy regalia. She was used to him coming home from work, dirty and tired, but she'd never seen him look like this.

Was chasing down cattle on horseback part of his daily routine? A guilty feeling twisted her gut when she realized she knew nothing about his life as a rancher. Talk about self-centered. He'd taken a big interest in her business, why hadn't she returned the favor?

"You're looking flushed." Gemma scooted over and thumped the bench. "Sit."

"Thanks." Skylar rubbed circles on Eliza's back as she dozed in the front pack. The normally soothing motion did nothing to soothe Skylar because she was wound tight as a spool of thread.

After a minute or so, Gemma said, "First time you've seen Kade in the arena?"

"First time I've seen him on a horse. Seeing how he moves and rides...I had no idea."

Gemma patted her leg. "We've all experienced that bowled over feeling."

"Even you?"

"Even me."

"That's good to know, because I feel like the world's biggest idiot for being ignorant to this part of Kade's life. He doesn't talk about it and I'm ashamed to say, dealing with Eliza and running my business I haven't even asked him."

"Aw, honey, don't beat yourself up. Most men are like that—especially cowboys. You've gotta pry information out of them."

Skylar nodded. It didn't help that Kade had to pry things out of her too.

Kade made a sharp turn on the horse, bumping up in the saddle, and she caught a glimpse of his tight ass, his long muscular legs hugging the horseflesh as he stretched taller in the stirrups. Add in the contestant number flapping on his broad back, the cowboy hat shading his handsome face, making him look mysterious and dominant, and Skylar let out a purely feminine sigh.

"I recognize that sound. There's something enormously appealing about a man who knows his way around ropes and reins and rides with confidence. But I think the attraction boils down to seeing a man control all that raw power of an animal, and the horse trusts him not to abuse it. Takes guts and finesse. Not an easy combination, but damn potent when it works."

"Damn potent," Sky muttered.

The steer wrestling ended and the team roping started.

"We have a great line up, folks. Only one go-round, which means only one chance for these cowboys to put a little jingle in their pockets today. On deck is a coupla brothers, ranchers from Weston County. Quinn and Bennett McKay."

More McKays?

The rope barrier fell, the calf ran out and two men on horseback thundered past. The ropes spun and snapped and hit their marks, head and heels. The crowd waited for the judge and the time. Eight point four seconds flashed on the scoreboard.

Carter said, "Not bad."

"Gonna have to do way better than that to beat our guys." Chassie and Gemma high-fived each other.

"Chass, you lookin' to up our bet? Fine. I'll take it."

Macie slapped her hand on Carter's butt to keep him from reaching for his wallet. "Wrong, moneybags. I'm not covering your bets when you lose."

"Darlin', I can't help it you're the breadwinner in our household."

The next competitors were announced. The header missed with his loop and the team received no time. The team after them broke the barrier and didn't score either.

"Next up another set of McKays, Colton and Kade, local ranchers from right here around Sundance." The audience whooped and Skylar held her breath.

Again the calf raced out and dirt flew as Kade ripped past, left hand on the horse reins, his rope twirling above his head, his focus absolute. Colt brought up the rear, posture identical to Kade's. They weren't pretty, but they looked fast. The ropes were released at different times but each loop managed to snag the intended target. The calf bawled as it was jerked to the ground.

The judge trotted into the arena and nodded.

"Folks, we have new leaders. Official time is seven point eight seconds."

Carter turned around and grinned at Skylar. "Slap me some skin, sistah."

Skylar couldn't believe her giddiness that Kade and Colt had done so well.

Luck had it that Trevor and Cash were the last to go.

"The crowd is in for a treat today. Our next team is comprised of two former professional rodeo cowboys. Trevor Glanzer and Cash Big Crow. Both these fine men have made it numerous times, not only to the Dodge Circuit Finals, but to the NFR. Let's hear a big Sundance welcome."

Gemma, Macie and Chassie let out enthusiastic yells and wolf whistles.

Same drill as before. The calf shot out, the cowboys tore past, Trevor in the header position, Cash as the heeler. Even as a novice Skylar could tell the difference between the pros and amateurs. The two men were flawless. Perfectly synchronized. The calf stayed down through the judge's inspection.

"Time recorded at four point two. Folks, give a hand to your team roping champions, Trevor Glanzer and Cash Big Crow."

They waved to the crowd and exited the arena.

As one, Macie, Chassie and Gemma held their palms out to Carter. "Pay up."

Skylar pulled a twenty out of the diaper bag and grumbled good-naturedly right along with Carter.

Eliza woke. "That's my cue. Thanks for letting me hang out with you guys. It was fun."

"Bring more money next time," Chassie teased.

Sky exited the stands with a grin on her face and moved the stroller to a shaded picnic area. She changed Eliza, hoping the bottle was warm enough not to upset her stomach.

A shadow fell over the stroller canopy. "Need a hand with that beautiful baby, little lady?"

Kade.

She straightened up and crashed right into him.

"Whoa." He curled his big hands around her biceps to keep her from stumbling. "Careful."

At that moment Skylar knew being careful with Kade McKay was no longer an option. She wanted a man who could soothe her with a simple smile. Inflame her with just one look. A man with guts enough to make the demand of complete sexual control over her, and with finesse enough to carry it off. A man who thought she was sexy. A man so freakin' hot that she was a fool for taking so long to come to her sexual senses.

She placed her palms on his chest. The cotton shirt was stiff and damp, the flesh beneath firm and warm. Lust surged through her.

"Sky? What's wrong?"

She met his concerned blue gaze and it steeled her resolve. "You gave me until Saturday to make my decision about things changing between us in regard to our—*my*—previous intimacy issues."

"About that—"

Sky briefly put her fingers over his lips. "My answer is yes."

Stunned silence.

"You're serious?"

"Never been more serious in my life, mister."

Then he said, "Prove it."

"Let's go home and I will."

"Huh-uh. Now."

"Now?"

"Yeah. Right now." He kissed her fingertips and closed the gap between their bodies. "No backin' out, Sky. Once you're mine, you're mine, exactly the way I want you, any time, any place. I'll make allowances for us takin' care of Eliza, but that's it. So, you're sure you understand all I'm demandin' of you?"

No. "Yes."

"Baby, that is good. So good." He teased his soft lips over hers. "Now, say no."

"No."

"Remember it, because that's the last time you get to say *no* to me." Kade smashed his mouth to hers. She clung to him just to remain upright in the wake of his possession.

Someone yelled, "Get a room."

Kade murmured against her mouth, "That's a damn fine idea."

Eliza chose that instant to remind them of her empty belly.

"Where's Grama? She's been wantin' time with her granddaughter, here's her chance." Kade whipped out his cell phone, his hot eyes locked on Skylar's. "Ma. You busy? You wanna watch Eliza for an hour so Sky and I can wander around? We're at a picnic area by the east entrance." He closed the phone. "She's on her way."

"Is there much to see around here?"

"Sweetheart, the only thing you're gonna see is my cock. Up close and personal."

Skylar didn't say a word. She couldn't, actually.

"Here's how it's gonna play out. Soon as Eliza is settled, we're takin' a walk. Straight to Colt's horse trailer. It has a sleepin' compartment with a real nice bed and a door that locks."

"I've never been in a horse trailer that has a bed."

"Oh, we ain't gonna be usin' the bed."

"We're not?"

"No. Because you are gonna be on your knees."

Chapter Thirteen

Skylar said yes.

Sure as hell not what Kade expected, but he wasn't about to look a gift horse in the mouth.

At best, he'd imagined her trying to negotiate a different scenario. At worst, well, it involved her seeking revenge by tying him up to the four-poster bed.

That fantasy had taken on a life of its own the last couple days. In his triple X version, Skylar wore PVC, blood red lipstick and a lewd smile as she disciplined him.

Both his folks showed up to watch Eliza. His dad wasn't the type to go gaga over kids. Kade doubted Calvin McKay had changed a diaper in his life. So it really shocked him when his gruff pops plopped down, eager to hold his granddaughter.

"Why you starin' at me, son?"

"Just wonderin'—"

"—if I know anything about babies?" His dad smiled. "Been awhile, but we did have two boys at once, so I've done my fair share of holdin' and rockin' and feedin' babies."

Kade hadn't considered that. "Well, call me on my cell if you need anything. We'll be back in an hour."

"Take your time," Kimi said. "Have fun, we'll be fine."

Skylar seemed reluctant to go.

Kade skimmed his hand down her arm, threading their fingers together. "I wouldn't leave her, or ask you to leave her if I thought there'd be a problem."

"I know."

"The clock is tickin'. I want you." He nuzzled her ear. "I want to feel your mouth on me." They wended their way through campers, horse trailers and trucks. For once he didn't run into anyone he knew, so he wasn't forced to make small talk.

Which was a good thing. His brain was stuck on the image of Skylar looking up at him with his cock deep in her throat.

At Colt's horse trailer, he lightly rapped on the door to the sleeping quarters. "Colt? You in there?"

No answer.

Kade removed the key and unlocked the door. Skylar stepped up first and he followed. After he pulled the shades and flipped the inside lock, he reached for her.

She melted into him, into the steamy kiss. He sensed a change in her, an acceptance. It'd be easy to back off and be the undemanding, patient lover he'd been in the past. But he wanted so much more. For both of them. And he didn't want to wait.

His lips slipped to her ear. "On your knees."

She didn't even hesitate. She used her hands on his body to support herself on her way down until she was kneeling.

"That's real good. Now undo my belt."

A couple of tugs and the heavy buckle hung by his right hip and the strap by his left hip. She started on the zipper without asking. If he really was a controlling bastard, he'd point out she hadn't followed his instructions. Instead he watched as she let her instincts take over.

Zipper undone, Kade peeled the Wranglers and boxers down his legs until they hit the tops of his boots. The tail of his long shirt covered his erection, and he hastily unbuttoned it so there were no barriers between them.

Skylar inhaled sharply at the sight of his hard cock slapping against his belly. "I'll warn you. I've never been very good at this."

"Let me decide that."

"Just don't judge me too harshly."

"I'd never judge." He tenderly brushed the hair from her forehead. "I'm gonna love everything you do to me. Touch me, sweetheart. Please."

She didn't grab the stiff rod, instead, she delicately cupped his balls. He groaned as she rolled the tight sac between her slender fingers like she was weighing dice. Then with deliberate care, she swept her thumb up the center of his dick, allowing her nail to gently scrape under the rim of the swollen cockhead.

His cock twitched shamelessly for her attention.

Sky feathered her thumb through the fluid leaking from the tip. Loosely curling her fingers around his girth, she started to stroke.

Kade palmed the side of her face, bringing her mouth closer. "No hands yet. Mouth first. Lick it."

That pink tongue shot out and lapped at the vein throbbing up the length of his cock, from his tight balls to the tip. And slowly back down. And back up. On the last, gradual, wet pass, she wrapped her lips around the cockhead and sucked.

"Oh yeah. More. Suck it in."

Her tentative hands inched up his thighs. He looked down to see her full lips separate to impart the intimate kiss. Bit by bit his cock disappeared into the warm haven of her mouth.

Kade hissed.

Encouraged by his moans, she took him deeper with each teasing wet glide, her movements more rhythmic, more confident. The tip of her tongue flicked the sweet spot below the slit as he pulled out, making his breath stutter and his head spin like an unbalanced tractor tire.

She offered him a secret smile, sucked intently and that wicked tongue flickered all over the good spots she'd discovered.

Tingles raced up the back of his thighs like a thousand electric fingers. If he closed his eyes, he'd fall on his ass. The sensation of her avid mouth, the scrape of her teeth, the curl of her tongue working his cock were mind blowing. Shutting his eyes meant not seeing this earthy, sexy woman learning to pleasure him. Watching her discover that pleasing her lover was as powerful and freeing as being on the receiving end of complete sexual attention.

His balls tightened. "You're keepin' me nice 'n wet. It's so fuckin' hot feelin' your mouth all warm and slippery. You like doin' this to me, doncha?"

Skylar nodded even as her head bobbed.

"See how deep you can take me."

She breathed through her nose as he eased in until her lips were pressed to his pelvis and he was buried in that beautiful throat.

"Yes." He withdrew. "Again." His damn knees shook with the need to come. He returned to shallow, quick strokes. Kade grabbed her right hand and circled it around his dick at the base. He lifted her chin so he could see her eyes. "Jesus. You should see the look on your face. So goddamn wanton you steal my breath, woman." He swept his thumb across the tantalizing line of her jawbone. "Stroke me with your hand while you're suckin' me."

"Like this?" She pumped his shaft from root halfway up the length a couple of times.

"Not so tight. There. Christ. Like that. Oh fuck, *exactly* like that."

When Sky brought her mouth into play with her hands, the hot, wet suctioning concentration on the sensitive cockhead, he began to bump his hips, needing this submission from her. He threaded his fingers into her soft hair and the cool scent of rain-soaked flowers, an aroma uniquely hers, filled his lungs.

"God your mouth is so... Almost there. Faster. Yeah. Come on come on come on. Shit. There it is, open, wider, ahh, yes. Suck. More. Harder." Kade resisted thrusting deep into her throat by releasing her hair and clenching his fists at his sides. His head fell back as liquid fire shot out of his balls and up his throbbing shaft. His cock spasmed in hot bursts on her tongue that slid down her throat as she gulped every spurt.

Sheer heaven.

After the last pulse tapered off, Skylar let him slip from her mouth. She nuzzled his thigh and kissed the vulnerable skin between his hipbones on her way to rub her cheek against the inside of his other leg.

"Skylar."

"Hmm."

He looked at her as she stared up at him. "You're beautiful."

Her lips were fuller, redder, and ripe for kissing. They were also curved into what resembled a smirk.

"Why you smirkin' at me?"

"Because I never liked doing that before. Never thought I was very good at it."

He murmured, "I beg to disagree."

"It was different with you, Kade."

"Why do you think that is, sweetheart?"

"Because you told me exactly what you wanted."

"Is that all?"

She thought about it and shook her head.

"You got nothin' to lose by bein' honest."

"The truth is, sucking you off, making you go a little crazy, knowing I was taking you there was as much of a turn on for me as it was for you."

Her admission made him grin like a loon. "You still turned on?"

"Unbelievably."

He lifted her to her feet. She insisted on helping him get redressed, not in a sexual way, but in a sweetly intimate way. Buttoning, smoothing, straightening his shirt across his chest. The kind of fussy motions a wife might perform for her husband.

Kade managed a husky, "C'mere." He clamped his hands on her ass to make sure she stayed put. He took his time kissing her, loving the way she unconsciously rubbed and arched into him. After indulging himself with a thorough taste of her too-tempting neck, he whispered, "I want you imaginin' all the places I'm gonna touch you tonight when we get home. However I please. Wherever I please. As long as I please. You wonderin' where I'll start?"

"Yes."

"Could be I'll spread you across the back of the couch and lick you from here—" Kade ran his thumbs from her tailbone up to her nape, "—to here."

She shivered and released a tiny moan.

"Maybe I'll start with bitin' your toes. Or maybe I'll be so

129

crazy to feel your pretty snatch grippin' my cock that I'll pin you to the floor in the hallway and fuck your brains out. Right there on that flowered rug." He blew in her ear. "No matter what scenario I choose, Skylar, remember *I* get to decide when you come. Not you."

"Oh."

"I can tell you want to come right now. Can't you almost feel my fingers strokin' your wet pussy? One, then two pushin' deep? You ridin' my hand so my palm is teasin' your clit? Your moans are urgin' me to go faster, to press harder, to sink deeper?" His teeth lightly scored the outside of her ear. "Are you throbbin' between your legs?"

"God. Kade. Please."

"Soon. But don't be sneakin' into the bathroom to get yourself off because I'll know. And I will not be a happy camper, darlin', because I want you to be primed for everything I can give you tonight. Promise me."

Skylar panted against his neck. He heard her swallow hard. "I promise."

"Good enough."

Skylar's skin was so hypersensitive she feared a single touch, even an accidental brush of Kade's callused finger on her hand, would send her careening into an orgasm. In public.

Her first thought was to put distance between them. Get Eliza and come up with an excuse to leave. Since Kade had to unload the horses at Colt's before he came home, she'd have time to find a semblance of composure before the man set to breaking it down again.

"Skylar?"

She blinked. "What?"

"You wanna wander around and wait for the presentation of the buckles and awards? Colt and I did finish in the money."

Her neck flushed in memory of Kade on a horse. Of Kade with a rope. His power, grace, concentration and speed. She could not wait to have all of that completely focused on her. "I never said congratulations on second place. You've gotta be happy."

"Not bad for two ranchers who haven't team roped for years."

"You guys looked damn good. Although, I did lose twenty bucks to your cousin Chassie."

Kade's eyes widened. "You bet on me?"

"I wasn't gonna bet against you."

"That's so damn sweet." He smiled. "C'mere and give me some sugar."

"Huh-uh. We don't need any additional rumors flying about us."

"What rumors?"

"Besides the one we're living in sin?"

"Which is your fault, sweetheart, 'cause I've asked you to marry me. More than once. Try again."

Crap. Good thing she hadn't said, *living with their secret love child.* She'd never live that down. She took a different, flirty tack, which felt damn good. "With the hot and bothered way you've left me? I can't guarantee I won't jump you, or sneak off to touch myself, earning myself a whole passel of trouble for doing either, without your permission, if I simply hold your hand."

"There's part that's hopin' the 'jumpin' on me' school of thought wins out."

Outside the horse trailer, Skylar started toward the picnic area where Eliza was and Kade snagged her elbow. "I thought we were gonna wander around."

"Don't you want your parents to see the presentation? Beings that you placed and all?"

"Shoot. I hadn't thought of that. I'll tell them to meet us by the north end." After he made the call, he said, "Been a while since I've had a beer and I sure could use one, how about you?"

Now that Sky thought about it, she hadn't seen Kade touch a drop of alcohol since he'd moved in. "Sure. I'm curious, didn't you drink when we went out last year?"

"Used to. Don't so much any more." They walked in silence until they were through the parking lot and standing in front of the beer tent. He paid for two drafts, gesturing for her to precede him into the seating area.

"Thanks."

"No problem." Kade sipped the foamy goodness, licked his lips and sighed.

"Just so you know, if you want to keep beer in the fridge, I'm fine with that. I'm sure Eliza wouldn't mind if you had the occasional beer either."

His eyebrows drew together. "You think the reason I'm not drinkin' is because of Eliza? It's not. It's 'cause of Colt. And it ain't just about the drinkin' entirely. Other issues surfaced because of it, things that'd been simmerin' for years." His thumb rubbed the lip on the plastic cup, as he seemed to struggle for the right words. "I'm talkin' about family stuff, fistfights, hard words, unspoken resentment that was pittin' brother against brother. I wondered if any of us was ever gonna be able to work together on the ranch again. I was glad to get out of there. Last year was the ugliest, lowest point of my life."

She didn't interrupt.

"Colt's been sober for a year. I'm proud of him and I respect his sobriety enough that I don't drink around him. I haven't been drinkin' at all in the last year anyway."

"Not many honky-tonks up in the north forty?"

"No. Funny thing is, Colt was supposed to head up the cattle grazin' experiment, not me. But after all that'd gone down with Dag, and me messin' up so bad with you, and dealin' with the rest of the McKay/West family shit, I volunteered. I needed time to get my head on straight. Kane says Colt's had a rough go, mendin' fences with his brothers. Guess we all learned some things take time to heal."

Skylar let her fingers drift down Kade's arm and she covered his hand with hers. "I'm sorry and I'm not blowing smoke up your chaps when I say I understand what you've been through. My sister is a recovering alcoholic and a former drug addict. The last time they pumped her stomach? She coded twice. I thought I'd lost her. And the worst part at the time? My guilty feeling of relief. My life had revolved around middle of the night phone calls—from the hospital, or her scary drug dealer boyfriend, or the police, or trying to scrounge up cash for the bond agency, because she was in jail. Again. With our parents dead, I was all she had. I had to witness her ruining her life and nothing I could say or do would change her behavior. Fortunately, India wised up. She's been clean for five years."

Neither said anything, they sipped beer in the stuffy tent, lost in thought.

Finally Kade said, "Ain't I just a barrel of fun? Maybe we could talk about something else? When's Eliza's next doctor's appointment?"

"Much as I love our darlin' baby girl," she grinned when he looked up at her mimicking his vernacular, "I don't wanna talk about her."

"Then what?"

Sex. Tell me what's in store for tonight. In detail. Maybe with a hands-on preview.

"We're supposed to be getting to know each other, right? So, tell me about your day-to-day ranch duties."

Kade lifted both brows. "Why? You lookin' to take a nap?"

"No, I'm serious. I saw you on the horse today and I realized I don't have any idea what it takes to raise cows."

"Money. Stupidity. Stubbornness." He sipped his beer. "Sorry. What we do depends on the season. Right now, we gotta make sure the cattle have water where they're grazin'. The cows have been pregnancy tested. The calves have had their vaccinations and aren't ready to wean quite yet. We start cuttin' hay in another week, that's long, hard work, pretty much sunup to sundown. Something's always broken, equipment wise. Then there's the fences. Lord. I could hire a crew of twenty and send them out seven days a week for the next year and never get all the damn fence mendin' done."

"Wow. You must have a lot of land."

He gave her a sardonic look. "Or a lotta bad fences."

"Funny. So do you ride horses every day?"

"No. Wish I could, but it's faster to take the truck or the four-wheeler. I keep my horse at my folks' place. He's an old work horse, not a rodeo horse like Colby's." He took another sip. "What about you? Do you ride?"

"I can ride, not very well. And I do like it, but I don't have a horse."

"Seems a shame. You have a sweet setup with that big barn

and the corrals."

"Maybe someday, when life isn't so chaotic, I'll get a gentle horse. What do you do for fun when you're not working on the ranch?"

"Been so long, I don't remember. I used to like to do a little dancin' at the Golden Boot. Do you two-step?"

"I've never been very good at dancing."

He angled over the table, a mere kiss away. "You said the same thing about blowjobs and you proved yourself wrong there, so I'm thinkin' I'd like to prove you wrong on the dance floor. There's something mighty enticin' about the thought of holdin' you in my arms in public, Sky, holdin' you without apology."

The molten heat in Kade's eyes made her knees quake.

The loudspeaker boomed with news of the presentations. He eased back, drained his remaining beer and stood. "Better get a move on."

Kade kept his hand pressed in the small of her back as they crossed the grounds to the stands. Several young women studied him with blatant sexual interest, from the tips of his boots to the brim of his cowboy hat, lingering on the fit of his Wranglers and the size of his belt buckle. A couple of brave rhinestone cowgirls were so happy to see him back in action, they approached him to offer to make up for lost time, in whatever capacity he chose. Suggestions were tossed out, without shame.

Not one of the pouty-faced women called him Kade. Every single one called him Kane. And Kade didn't correct their assumptions. He'd probably gotten so used to it, he either didn't notice, or it didn't bother him.

It bothered the crap out of Skylar. Kade wasn't interchangeable. Kade was unique. And dammit, these buckle bunnies could kiss her butt. Kade McKay was hers.

When an older brunette, with over-teased hair and an overbite, slid her fingers up the buttons on Kade's shirt, Sky wondered if she were somehow invisible. Would these same "ride-me-cowboy" buckle bunnies be so eager to throw themselves at him if he held Eliza?

Probably. Kade was damn fine looking and one of the most

eligible bachelors in three counties. His obvious physical attributes were a bonus, as far as Sky was concerned. What made him irresistible to her these days? He wasn't afraid to show he loved his child to distraction. He rolled out of bed in the middle of the night so Sky could sleep. It was all the sweet, thoughtful, just plain nice things he did for her and Eliza, simply because he was that type of man and he enjoyed doing it, not because he had to or it was expected.

Throughout the conversations, Kade remained polite to his admirers. Skylar also noticed his warm hand remained firmly planted on her back. Even after they'd made their escape.

She spied Kimi and Eliza. Kade ambled up. Eliza took one look at him and her feet churned with glee. He grinned, stealing her from Kimi's arms. "There's my girl. Didja miss us, sweet thang?" He bussed the top of her bonneted head.

"She was an absolute angel," Kimi said. "Skylar Ellison, meet my sister Carolyn McKay. She had to skip out on the West reunion earlier because her daughter-in-law Channing got sick."

As they shook hands Skylar asked, "Your last name is McKay too?"

"Yep. We're sisters who married brothers. Long story we'll no doubt bore you with at some point. Anyway, I just wanted to tell you how much I love your Sky Blue products. Kimi has me hooked."

"I always love to hear that."

"You must not work at the shop in Sundance much?"

Sky shook her head. "I trust it to India while I'm running the manufacturing plant outside of Moorcroft."

Kade moved to block the sun from Sky's eyes. "You oughta see her setup. It's something. Way beyond anything else goin' around here." He rattled off a bunch of things that Sky was surprised he remembered from the brief tour. And he almost sounded...proud of her.

Carolyn whistled. "Kade, are you driving from Moorcroft to the ranch? Every day?"

"Yep. Ain't no big deal."

"Sixty miles is quite a stretch, especially when you're tired from working."

He rolled his eyes. "You sound just like Ma, Aunt C."

"I worry about all my family members, Kade, not just the ones I gave birth to."

"You'd say the same thing to Colby or Cord?"

"If they were driving one hundred and twenty miles round trip every day, I'd ask them to be careful too."

Skylar got right in his face. "You're driving that many miles? Every day?"

"Yeah."

"Why didn't you tell me?" Bewildered, she could only stare at him and feel more guilty. "I didn't know. No wonder you're so tired. You shouldn't have to—"

"*Have to* don't enter into it at all." He lowered his voice so only she heard him. "Because it don't matter. I want to. I'd drive twice that to be with you and Eliza every night."

She melted and only managed a humble, "Oh."

"Yeah, *oh*. This ain't a temporary thing for me, so I figured I'd better get used to it early on."

This ain't a temporary thing for me.

The announcer listed the program order and team-roping trophies were second on the list. Kade passed Eliza to Sky. "I've gotta help Colt, then I'll be right home."

"But there's a get-together at Colby and Channing's place tonight," Kimi said. "Everyone in the family is gonna be there."

"Everyone except us." Kade exchanged a hot look with Skylar and a wave of anticipation flowed through her. "Eliza's had enough excitement today. She's had a rough week and she needs an early bedtime."

"Fair enough. But you are comin' to the brunch at Carolyn and Carson's tomorrow?"

"Yes, ma'am." Kade winked at her. "Later, sweetheart."

Kimi and Carolyn moved closer to the action, while Sky watched from the fence.

She swallowed her jealousy at the legions of women who surrounded Kade and Colt. Strange thing was, neither man seemed particularly interested in any of them.

Cash Big Crow and Trevor Glanzer hammed it up for the

crowd. After the all-around title was announced, with Trevor as the winner, Trevor and Chassie took the stage. A buzz filled the air.

Trevor commandeered the microphone. "Last year due to an accident, my wife lost her brother, Dag West, and I lost a good buddy. Dag left behind many family members and friends. So in honor of Dag, his love of rodeo, and his love of this community, the Devil's Tower Rodeo Association has created an annual award in Dag West's memory."

Murmurs of approval and a smattering of applause.

"Every year this award will go to the cowboy or cowgirl who's shown heart, guts, and a whole lotta try at this event and others around the area. Someone who's overcome obstacles and still embodies the ideals and western way of life."

More buzz reverberated through the crowd as folks speculated who'd win.

"Chassie and I are happy to announce that this year's winner is a man well-versed in the cowboy way, a man who has thrived in spite of it." Trevor paused for the laughter to die down. "The First Annual Dag West Memorial Award goes to...Colton McKay."

Happy whoops rent the air. Colt lumbered across the dirt, the tattered fringe on his chaps flapping, clearly in shock. He hugged Chassie, clapped Trevor on the back, and studied the award. After a second or so, he faced the audience and raised it above his head. He seemed too choked up to speak.

The crowd went wild. A lump rose in Skylar's throat when the McKays and the Wests ran across the arena to celebrate with Colt. Maybe Kade would rather be with his family tonight, instead of sixty miles away.

She loaded Eliza in her car and headed home.

Chapter Fourteen

The rodeo didn't wear Eliza out. Skylar'd just put the baby down a few hours later when Kade's truck pulled up.

Perfect timing.

Thump sounded on the porch as Kade removed his dirty boots, like he always did. The man was so thoughtful. The door squeaked open and shut. He paused on the rug, after hanging up his jacket and saw her standing in the hallway.

"Hey. Got done and got gone as quick as I could."

"I thought you might call and say you were hanging out with your family tonight."

Silence.

In two strides he had her face cupped in his rough hands and was kissing her like he planned to eat her alive. After several minutes of tongue-tangling kisses that left her bare toes curling into the wooden floor, he broke his mouth free. "Does that seem like I'd rather be with anyone besides you?"

"Ah. No."

"Good. Hang tight. I need to wash the grime off. I shouldna been touchin' you."

"I didn't mind."

"Is Eliza sleepin'?"

"Down for the count. She's in her crib."

"I'll poke my head in and check on her."

"Do you want me to come upstairs?"

"No. Go on into the living room. I'll be down lickety-split."

Sky heard the shower turn on. She tried to sit but that lasted all of thirty seconds before she was up and pacing again. Her emotions ranged from nervous to excited, back to nervous.

The day's events played in her mind. Kade taking control. Dictating to her. Not by humiliating her, but teaching her with not-so-gentle determination. And it was sexy as all get out, being in the position of giving him pleasure, watching the ecstasy on his gorgeous face, bringing that violent response to his body. She hadn't been angling for false praise when she'd admitted her inadequacies regarding oral sex. But Kade acted as if she was a blowjob master and she couldn't wait to do it again.

The stairs creaked. She saw Kade striding toward her buck-ass nekkid.

She was so staggered all she could do was stand and stare. And drool. Oh man. Broad. Muscled. Big. Everywhere. Kade McKay was a perfect male specimen.

What would he think when he saw her? With her less-than-perfect body?

Again, he brought his mouth down on hers, intoxicating her with another bone-melting kiss. He murmured, "I wanna see you, Sky. All of you. I'm settin' the nekkid rule in place right now."

"The naked rule?"

"Yep. I say 'get nekkid' and you do it. That's the rule."

"Simple."

"I thought so."

Kade nibbled at her lips and jaw as he unbuttoned her lace blouse. Once it was completely undone, he peeled it down her arms and it fluttered to the floor.

Her stomach fluttered in response.

His callused hands slid down the sides of her body to rest on her hips. Work-roughened fingertips traced the skin beneath the waistband of her skirt to the zipper in the back. *Zzzz* sounded as her skirt hit the rug, leaving her standing in a pair of turquoise bikini panties and a plain white sports bra, which she realized didn't match the panties at all.

Skylar wanted to protest her near nakedness, to hide her

body against his, but Kade was having none of it.

"Lose the bra."

She eased away and lifted it over her head. Soon as she finished, her chin dropped to her chest and her hair fell over her face.

"Look at me."

It took all her courage to meet his gaze.

"Don't you know you're gorgeous? Ripe and lush and beautiful?"

"I don't feel beautiful, Kade. I've always been a little too round, a little too soft, a little too womanly. It just got worse after Eliza was born and now I'm still carrying around this extra baby weight…"

"I didn't notice."

Sky couldn't help it; she snorted.

He smoothed a section of hair from her hot cheek. "Is that why we've been makin' love in the dark?"

She nodded. "I didn't want you to see me naked. I thought you'd…"

"What? Jump on you like a horny toad?"

"No. I thought you'd be disappointed."

"Wrong. I've been dyin' to see you completely nekkid since the first time you barreled up to me wearin' them wicked purple heels. I thought about you standin' in front of me, wearin' nothin' but them sexy-ass shoes and a big ol' smile." He kissed her so sweetly tears prickled behind her lids. "Trust me, the last thing I am is disappointed. The last thing I'm gonna do is spend time talkin' when I could be touchin' you. Or tastin' you." He put his mouth against her ear. "You been thinkin' about this afternoon?"

"Yes."

"It was amazingly fuckin' hot to see you goin' down on me. Did you like makin' me weak-kneed and at your mercy?"

"Yes."

"Did you touch yourself while you were thinkin' about what I might be doin' to you tonight?"

"No."

"Good answer. Turn around slowly, darlin'."

Skylar complied.

"Keep your eyes open. No more hidin' from me. Ever." Kade punctuated his last command with a nip to her earlobe.

He dropped to his knees behind her and tapped her ankles. "Wider. Like that."

She held her breath, even as her heart raced, and her blood pumped faster. She was pretty sure her face was the same color as a tomato. Kade's magic fingertips danced up the back of her calves to stroke the vulnerable area behind her knees. Her trembles increased when his warm mouth followed the same path, first up her right calf, from the tight tendons above her heel, to bestow a teasing lick to that sensitive crease. She gasped. He chuckled and repeated the erotic process on the other side.

When he started in on butterfly flicks of his tongue across the backs of her thighs, especially the line where her legs met the lower curve of her ass, her knees buckled.

Kade latched onto her hips to keep her from falling. "Easy." He stood. His thumbs rubbed back and forth across the dimples at the base of her spine.

"Never woulda pegged you as the tattoo type."

"I'm not. It was India's doing. She needed a guinea pig for her Celtic scroll designs and she volunteered my skin."

"You're braver than I am, because I hate needles."

"Really?"

"Yeah, but this sure is pretty." More tantalizing stroking over the design with the edges of his rough thumbs. "Sexy as hell. Can't wait to run my tongue across it."

Heat radiated from his skin, making her crave more contact. Like the rasp of his chest hair on her bare shoulder blades. Or the bump of his erection against the crack of her ass. Or his big palms covering her breasts. But the only place his body touched hers was where his hands clutched her hips.

He didn't budge for the longest time. The tension inside her coiled tighter, driving her desire higher. Her panties were soaked to the point she smelled her own arousal. She was pretty sure Kade had gotten a whiff too.

"Kade—"

"Patience, sweetheart." His breath on the curve of her shoulder was the only warning before his firm lips landed on the spot and gently sucked.

Tingles shot down her arm. "Oh."

"You like that?"

"Uh. Yeah."

"You anxious for more?"

"Uh-huh."

"Mmm. No rush, 'cause I'm *so* enjoyin' the view." Those warm, soft lips brushed the exact same damp spot. Twice more.

Then he backed off slightly and his wet tongue slid up the arc of her spine, from the tattoo above her butt to the base of her skull. Even as another round of tremors rolled through her, Kade lightly sank his teeth into the tender spot on her neck.

Skylar nearly came unglued.

"Face me."

She spun around so fast she became dizzy.

Kade had retreated a few steps. His hands were at his sides clenched into fists. His eyes. God. His blue eyes were ablaze.

"Watch me lookin' at you. Don't move."

And again, Kade took his sweet time dragging his gaze across every inch of her body. It was exciting, witnessing his arousal. His high cheekbones were flushed a soft pink. His bare chest rose and fell rapidly from his erratic breathing. He licked his lips. Repeatedly.

Then there was his cock. Fully erect, the head shiny red, the tip jerked against his belly, leaving behind a slick kiss. Finally his eyes met hers again.

"Take off your panties."

Did he mean in a slow, sexy strip tease? Or in one passionate rip? Oh, who the hell cared as long as they were off? Skylar hooked a finger in each side and shimmied them down her legs, kicking them away.

The second she was unencumbered, Kade dropped to his knees. He grabbed her hands, placing them on her mound, demanding, "Hold yourself open for me. I wanna taste you inside and out. I wanna bury my face in your pussy and feel you come against my mouth."

Desire warred with her natural embarrassment. But she wanted his tongue burrowing inside her. She wanted his mouth suctioned to her clit. She wanted his lips and teeth and tongue everywhere, all at once, until she exploded in a burst of pure pleasure. She wanted to surrender to this man.

Skylar spread her legs and used her fingers to bare every inch of her weeping sex to his hungry gaze.

With something akin to a growl, Kade dove right in. He clamped his hands to her butt cheeks, pulling her closer yet as his mouth fastened to her sex. His tongue lapped and licked and plunged deep. He suckled the swollen pink folds until his groans of approval reverberated into her tissues, zinging through her blood, heightening her need for release.

"Oh. It's so close..."

"Come for me, baby. This is gonna be the first of many."

Many? She didn't know if she'd survive.

Her legs shook as he fucked her with his tongue. He held her tighter, pushed her closer to the edge. That heated melting sensation swirled in her belly and she whimpered.

Kade pressed his mouth to the top of her pubic bone and sucked her clit between his lips. The hard rhythmic pulls against his teeth and tongue sent her from almost there, right into a full-blown orgasm that left her stunned, throbbing, gasping his name even as she forgot her own.

Once she'd regained some semblance of sanity, she felt Kade rubbing his face over her belly.

He looked up at her. "You are so fuckin' sexy, Sky. You make me crazy with wantin' you." He rolled back on the balls of his feet and stood. "Stay right there." Thirty seconds later he returned with a box of condoms. Without a word, he led her to the couch and sprawled in the middle. He removed a single foil pack from the box, opened it and slipped it on.

"C'mere." Kade reached for her hands.

"Wait. What are we—"

"No questions, remember? Straddle me on your knees."

Skylar carefully positioned herself, keeping her focus on his cock. Just as she was about to impale herself, Kade stilled her motion and tipped her chin up with a finger.

"Did I say you could do that?"

"No. But I thought—"

"Ain't your job to think, it's mine. Now relax and sit on my lap, not on my dick."

Her protest, "But I'll break your legs," earned her a sharp smack on the ass.

"Don't ever let me hear you say nothin' like that again."

It was her nature to act indignant. To question him. She did neither. She waited. And watched him.

"Good girl." With their gazes locked, Kade's hands smoothed up her thighs. Paused on her hips. Traced the contour of her belly. Lingered on the swell of her breasts, finally cradling her face. "Gimme this mouth." He tugged her until their lips met.

The kiss was urgent. His tongue danced against hers, he angled her head to where he wanted it, taking her to a whole new level of soul kissing. His chest was firm and hot beneath her palms. As his mouth shifted, she tasted her own musk, a hint of mint, and the heady, masculine flavor she recognized as wholly his.

When she'd started to relax into the kiss, he pulled away and licked a path to the valley of her cleavage. "Offer these big beauties to me. Like you did with that pretty pussy. Hold 'em up so I can taste 'em as long as it suits me."

Her heart thumped as she cupped her palms under her breasts, pushed them together and lifted for his perusal.

"Look at you. So obedient." Kade's hands were braced on her upper back and he angled her closer, so he could suck both nipples. One right after the other. A very low, very satisfied male noise rumbled across her flesh and she trembled.

Every wet pull of his mouth reawakened the buzzing tingle between her thighs. Sky found herself rocking into him, searching for any friction as his sex rubbed against hers. Not that the man could take a hint. He ignored her subtle signals and did as he pleased, which if Sky was completely honest, pleased *her* to no appreciable end.

But still, she was dying for him to progress to the next stage of this drawn-out seduction. She must've made a disgruntled noise because he muttered, "Impatient?" as he nibbled the ticklish curve by her left armpit.

"Yes. Please. More."

"Who's in control, Sky?"

"You are."

"Remember that. Next time I ain't gonna be so nice about remindin' you."

Oh wow. She had the tiniest desire to disobey him just to see what type of "reminder" he employed.

Kade suckled her nipples deep and hard, using his teeth to skirt the edge of pain that bordered on bliss. He'd back off and nuzzle the fleshy mounds, gently lapping at the reddened peaks, blowing a soft stream of air over the damp tips to see them constrict. Then he'd begin again.

It was the most delicious torture she'd ever experienced.

He placed her hands to his shoulders and pressed his forehead to hers as he scooted her hips forward. "Take me in slowly. I want you watchin' as my cock sinks inside you."

Skylar looked down as Kade thumbed his erection away from his belly. She saw the thick head circle her opening, and become slippery with her arousal. After the first couple inches she couldn't see anything so she closed her eyes and lost herself in the feeling of all that thick male hardness filling her.

"Just a little more. Goddamn that feels good," he panted against her throat. "You're so wet. It's a fuckin' turn on."

This verbally explicit side of gentleman cowboy Kade McKay turned her on to epic levels.

She paused when he was fully seated inside her, tilting her pelvis to grind against his. Perspiration coated her skin. Her pulse pounded in her throat, in her nipples, between her legs. A single bead of sweat trickled down the side of Kade's neck and she dipped her head to catch the droplet on her tongue. Mmm. Salty. She licked the wet trail back up to his ear. "Tell me what to do, Kade."

"Ride me, baby."

"Always thinking like a cowboy."

"Can't help what I am. Oh yeah. I like that."

"See? I don't need a horse when I have you around to ride."

His chuckle turned into a groan when she began to lift and lower faster. Kade's mouth sought hers, as his hands seemed determined to touch every millimeter of her damp skin.

Time stopped as they moved together. Two lovers locked in passion. Fast. Frantic. Needy.

Kade's hips thrust up on her every downstroke. Her clit vibrated and pulsed in response to the grinding motion. "Yes. Oh yes. Don't stop." She barely withheld a scream as the climax knocked her sideways.

He groaned against her throat. "I'm right behind you. Come on, baby, squeeze me tight with your cunt muscles. That's it. That's *so* it."

With their bodies plastered together, she reveled in the slick feel of his rougher skin scraping on her softer curves. The urgency of his pumping hips.

"Fuck." His head dropped back on the couch cushion. His cock throbbed and jerked inside her. She swore she could feel his heat through the latex as he came. She shamelessly watched the concentrated look on his face morph to satisfaction.

After his last drawn-out groan, Sky buried her face in the curve of his neck, letting her lips travel along the strained muscles, tasting the sweat on his skin.

"Yeah. See, makin' love on the couch ain't so bad."

"True."

"I'm likin' this nekkid rule. A lot."

"Mmm."

"That was a damn content mmm."

"Mmm."

He whispered, "Skylar. Marry me."

She whispered back, "No."

A pause lingered and he sighed. "Give me a reason why you're always sayin' no?"

Should she deflect? Lie? Or buck up and admit the truth?

"See? Even you can't think of one good reason."

"Wrong." Skylar lifted her head and looked him straight in the eye. "I keep saying no, because I've been married before."

Chapter Fifteen

Kade looked at the embarrassment and truth warring in Skylar's eyes. "You've been married before?"

"Yes."

"When?"

"Years ago."

"Why didn't you tell me?"

"Because it wasn't the happiest time in my life, okay? I swore I'd never dwell...forget it." Skylar tried to maneuver off him, but he clamped his hands on her hips, keeping her in place, keeping his cock imbedded in her.

"No fuckin' way. You don't get to blurt out something like that and then run off like a scared bunny, Sky."

"I'm not scared." In response, she looked down at her hands braced on his chest, as if she'd just realized she was pushing him away.

"Then talk to me."

"Please. Let me go."

He inhaled a deep breath. "If I let you up, will you promise to stay here and tell me about it?" His hand slid up her arm to her shoulder. He twined his fingers in a section of her silky hair. "You gotta know nothin' you tell me is gonna make me change my opinion of you. And you can trust me to keep my mouth shut. Lord, I seem to be well versed in keepin' secrets."

"I guess I never have heard you talking trash about anyone. Not even your family."

"See? It's because I'm trustworthy."

Skylar didn't look up. "Would you have a glass of wine if I opened a bottle?"

"Sure. I'd like that."

"Let me climb off this ride, cowboy, before we get permanently stuck together."

"I sure wouldn't complain about that, sweetheart."

Sky lifted off his softened cock. She scooted back and stood between his legs.

Kade snagged her hand before she ran off. "Just so you don't get any ideas about puttin' them clothes back on, the nekkid rule still applies. Even while we're talkin'."

"We're drinking wine in the living room...nude?"

"Yep. And I wouldn't mind if you walked into the kitchen nice and slow, so I can get all hot and bothered starin' at your luscious ass."

She blushed before she headed out of the room.

"Oh yeah, baby, that's what I'm talkin' about. Shake it a little more. Mmm. Mmm. Damn, Sky, you are one smokin' hot mama."

She gifted him with a "come and get me" grin over her left shoulder.

"You're gonna pay for that look, woman."

"I can't wait."

Kade ditched the condom and tried to wrap his head around Skylar's unmentioned marriage. These days it wasn't a big deal to be divorced. They'd gone out a dozen times last year; it should've come up in conversation at least once. So why hadn't she told him?

Why didn't you tell her you were Kade, not Kane?

Shit. He hadn't thought of that. Man, it seemed they were both good at telling half-truths. Haunted by memories they'd rather push aside than openly discuss.

It wasn't the happiest time in my life.

He understood the desire to move on from the past. He'd done it, sending himself on a sabbatical to straighten out the mess his life had become. During the time away from family and friends, he decided he wasn't going to live his life full of regret for time and opportunities lost. Nor would he wait around for happiness to float into his life. He was going after it like a rodeo junkie chases the gold buckle: full throttle.

Watching his cousins living the life of home and hearth, the life Kade had always wanted, made him more determined to make that happen for himself. On his terms. Yeah, he knew exactly what he wanted. And she walked in the room stark naked holding a bottle of wine and two glasses.

"What are you smiling at, Kade?"

"You. What a pretty picture you make completely buck-ass nekkid."

She poured the glasses full of ruby-colored liquid, then sat on the opposite end of the couch with her knees tucked under her.

He didn't comment when she downed nearly half the contents in one long swallow.

A couple of minutes passed before she spoke. "You know I grew up in California. Graduated top of my college class. I scored a primo job at an ad agency in LA right out of college. Big money. Lots of prestige. I had my career all planned out. It never bothered me to be one of those women who are really successful in their work, but a total failure when it came to personal relationships.

"At a party I met this older guy named Ted. He was a real laid-back kind of guy, which was very appealing to me. We'd been dating for a month when my dad was diagnosed with advanced prostate cancer. Doctors told us he had less than three months to live. I'd always dreamed of my dad walking me down the aisle, and I was about to lose the chance forever. When Ted suggested we get married right away, I agreed." She laughed bitterly. "It was the only impulsive thing I'd ever done in my life."

Had she loved Ted? It tied a knot in his gut to think she'd married for less than the total love and adoration she deserved.

"Turns out my dad had less time. He died three weeks after the wedding."

"Sky. I'm sorry."

She knocked back a mouthful of wine. "Anyway, my mother went into a deep depression and decided to 'find herself' at a monastery on some damn island."

"You're shittin' me."

"Nope."

"People really do that?"

"My mom was a bit of a free-spirit, hippie type. She could do pretty much whatever struck her fancy because my father had left us well off." Her troubled gaze met his. "Very well off. She vanished and I didn't hear a word from her for two years."

Kade cringed. He'd essentially done the same thing, disappeared without a word. No wonder Skylar had sported the attitude that he might not care about Eliza's existence. Or that he intended to become a permanent part of her life.

"At the time, India was a drug addict and a drunk, in and out of rehab. I'd used my grief to bury myself in work and advanced to the level of vice president. Ted had a fairly low-stress job so he handled everything."

"Everything?"

"Yes." Skylar closed her eyes. "All the finances, all the household stuff. Some nights I'd come home from the office an emotional basket case and he took care of me too. I trusted him. I let him have total control of every single thing in my life." Her voice dropped to a whisper. "And he fucked me over. Big time. I didn't know he wasn't who he said he was. Ted wasn't a real estate developer as much as he was a con man."

No wonder she'd freaked out so badly about him pretending to be Kane. No wonder she was taking her time on deciding whether she'd marry him.

"I also didn't know he'd taken half of the inheritance from my father and squirreled it away somewhere. I didn't know he'd helped himself to half my earnings over a two-year period. I only found out when he hit me with divorce papers. There were very little liquid assets, where we should've been drowning in them.

"California is a community property state, which entitled Ted to fifty percent of what I had. My house, my cars, my pension, my assets—assets that had dwindled to damn near nothing in the time we were married. Everything I'd worked for, all the money my dad left me...gone."

"Oh baby, c'mere." Kade put their wine glasses on the coffee table and enfolded her in his arms. She didn't cry, this tough, independent woman who'd had every man in her life let her down. She just melted into him. That broke his damn heart. He didn't speak, partially because he didn't know what to say, but mostly because he now understood her need for absolute control.

"It was the most humiliating thing that's ever happened to me. So yeah, I have some issues with trust."

"I imagine so. Hell, I would too."

An unwieldy pause lingered.

Finally, he said, "Can you tell me the rest of it?"

"When we were at the end of the divorce proceedings, my mother returned. I moved into her new place, which ended up being a good thing because not four months later she was diagnosed with uterine cancer."

"Jesus. Are you serious?"

Sky nodded. "Sounds like a soap opera, doesn't it? Of course, my mom had let her health insurance lapse while she was in seclusion, so all the payments to the hospital and doctors came out of her pocket. India actually cleaned up her act for a while and helped me care for Mom. My grandma, my mom's mother, Elizabeth, came to help."

A warm feeing unfurled in his chest. "Eliza was named after her, wasn't she?"

"Yeah. She was a remarkable woman. It fascinated me she was part Cheyenne since my mother had never mentioned that part of our background. Grandma mixed up herb ointments for my mother that actually worked. When I asked her about them, she gave me the basics until she realized I had more than just a passing interest. We created batches of new soaps and lotions made from all-natural ingredients. I decided someday I would start my own company using her formulas. After she passed on and left us this land, I knew this was where I was supposed to be. Everything had come full circle."

"Well, you've done her right proud, sweetheart."

"You think so?"

"I know so. Know what else I know?"

"What?"

Kade brushed his mouth over her ear and was

tremendously pleased when Sky trembled. "That Eliza has a long line of strong women behind her to look up to. She's a lucky girl."

"You're so sweet, Kade, you're going to make me cry and I swore I wouldn't, not ever again. Not over him or what he did to me or anything from that awful part of my life."

"Go ahead and cry, baby, I gotcha."

Skylar didn't sob, but she allowed him to hold her and settle her, stroke her wherever he wanted. Her arms. Her breasts. Her belly. Up and down her thighs. Her breathing had become erratic, even as she relaxed against him.

Time to make his move.

"Thanks for tellin' me the truth. You gotta know I wouldn't ever do what that bastard done to you."

"Pretend to be someone else? Take something from me? Use me? No offense, but I've heard that line before, from every single man who's been in my life."

"I ain't like them."

"You sure? Would you be here with me if it weren't for Eliza? Especially since she's the rare McKay girl child?"

When Kade paused, she assumed it was a guilty pause. "I didn't think so."

"You're wrong, but it don't change a damn thing."

"Change what?"

"That I still wanna marry you. I'm gonna keep askin' until you're so sick of it that you'll say yes just to get some peace."

She smiled slightly. "Not happening, McKay. Once burned, twice shy."

"We'll see. I'm not Ted. I'll never be the man who wants more from you than you're willin' to give. But I'd be lyin' if I told you I didn't want it all." He turned her around so he could kiss her full on. He loved the way their mouths fit together, hunger fed sweetness. The kiss changed from slow and easy to hot and heavy.

Kade traced the line of her body from her neck to her knee. His fingers inched up the inside of her thigh until they reached that warm wetness between her legs.

Skylar made a soft moan when his first two fingers pushed

inside.

He rocked them in and out in a steady rhythm. She began to undulate and whimper, clenching and unclenching her thighs, kissing him with more force. Kade twisted his wrist so the heel of his hand rested on her clit. As he plunged his fingers in, he pressed on the swollen bit of flesh.

She jerked her mouth away, placing her own hand on top of his. "Move side-to-side."

Encouraging, that Sky'd become willing to teach him how to satisfy her. "Like this?"

"Yes. Exactly like that. Oh. Don't stop." She threw back her head and came on a low, throaty moan.

It was hot as hell, the way she looked, the sounds drifting from her beautiful throat when she let go. The fact she'd let go with him only made him want more of the same.

While Skylar was still tingling from orgasmic aftershocks, Kade reached for a condom and put it on. "Come on."

He led her to the hallway. Specifically to the antique armoire with a wooden bench seat located above the compartment used for storage. Metal coat hooks decorated the ornately carved top and both sides. What made the piece unique was the full-length mirror along the back.

They stopped in front of the mirror. Once Sky caught sight of her naked reflection, she immediately tensed up and tried to turn around. "What—"

"Ever done it in front of a mirror?"

"No!" She tried to twist away.

"Don't move."

"But—"

"That ain't a request," he growled, holding her against his body at a sideways angle. "Watch." Kade reached for her right hand, and brought it up, placing it behind his neck. "Look at you. See the way your body curves here?" He trailed his fingers from the outside of her thigh up to her hip. "And here." He flattened his palm, gradually dragging it up the bend in her waist, his fingers barely brushing her quivering belly.

He stopped at the bottom of her rib cage and moved his lips closer to the arch of her neck. "Look how havin' your arm lifted like this draws attention to the swell of your breast. One exquisite curve flowin' from bottom to top, creatin' this long sexy line. A sexy line just beggin' for my touch." His fingertips followed the inside of her biceps up to her elbow. "You have a gorgeous body, Sky. Can't you see that?"

She shook her head.

"Then look at your face. Your cheeks are flushed, your eyes are bright. Your lips are fuller, a little redder from kissin' me. See how fast you're breathin', makin' your chest rise and fall so my eyes are drawn to your breasts? See how hard and tight your nipples are, makin' my mouth water to taste them? If I touch you like this—" he dragged a fingertip from hipbone to hipbone, "—your belly quivers. Makes me crazy, rememberin' how you quiver when I'm balls deep inside you."

"Why are you doing this?"

"Because I can." He zigzagged his tongue up the column of her throat and blew softly on the wetness just to have her trembling in his arms. "Because you are as temptin' as sin. Because you're beautiful. Because this is how I see you. In my head. In the dark. In the flesh. So when I fuck you every way my sex-addled brain can dream up, you'll know I wasn't kiddin' about how hot you can make me burn."

She closed her eyes and turned her head to kiss his chin. And his throat. Kade allowed it, sensing her surrender.

He nuzzled the inside of her arm and gave a love bite on the tender flesh. She yipped and opened her eyes. "Bend over and hold onto the back of the bench." Sky appeared to be weighing her options, of which she had none. He said, "Do it. Now."

In a sensuous move that made his cock harder yet, she untangled from him and angled forward, sticking her backside in the air, letting her tits swing free.

He couldn't take his eyes off the roundness of her ass, the wavering line of her spine, the way her long hair hung past her shoulders. Mostly how her gaze locked on his.

"Tilt your pelvis up. That's good." Kade dipped his upper body and licked Sky from her tattoo up to the nape of her neck, layering his chest to her back. He breathed in the sweet scent of her hair. "I'm gonna fuck you hard and I want you to watch me. Watch me enjoyin' every damn second of you and your body.

155

Don't look away."

Kade snapped upright, latched onto her hips and plunged inside her.

Skylar gasped.

"Like that?"

"Yes. Do it again."

He withdrew and slammed in. Over and over. Hard and deep. Glorying in the pleasure on her face, feeling the welcoming wetness of her pussy with each thrust. His legs shook, sweat trickled down the side of his face, but he never once looked away from her passion-darkened eyes.

When she rocked her hips back to meet his thrusts, he said, "Can you come like this?"

"Faster."

He thrust four times more, prolonging her pleasure and their intimate connection.

"Yes." She threw her head back and came apart.

He hissed when he felt her pussy muscles clamping down on him. His last thread of control snapped. A surge of heat flashed and Kade hammered into her, his balls damn near crawled inside his body and his cock jerked as pulse after pulse of hot seed shot out.

When the primal roaring in Kade's head lessened, he met her gaze.

She murmured, "I'm never gonna look at this mirror the same way again."

Once again, he was at an utter loss for what to say. Sky deserved some kind of sweetly romantic words, but his brain was lazy, his body sated, and it took every ounce of control for him not to yawn.

Kade smoothed his hands up her back, past her shoulders and curled his hands around hers on the bench. He nestled his face next to hers as they both struggled for breath. He kissed her temple and slipped out of her body, helping her upright. She faced him, twining her arms around his neck. He was dying to know what was going through her mind, but he didn't ask. He just held onto her and was grateful she hadn't bolted in a fit of modesty.

A loud screech sounded from the baby monitor in the living room. Immediately Skylar pulled back. "I'd hoped she'd sleep all night."

"Go on and get her. I'll get the bottle ready and bring it up."

"Am I allowed to get dressed?"

"Depends."

"On?"

"Whether you're wearin' silky pajamas?"

"No."

"Then them eye-poppin' baby doll ones will do just fine."

She blinked with surprise. "You like those?"

"Yep." His fingertip journeyed from the dimple in her chin over the tip of her right nipple to the shallow dent in her navel. "But I like you in no pajamas much better."

Another loud screech echoed.

"I'm coming." Without turning around, Skylar said, "You're staring at my ass again, aren't you?"

"It's a damn fine ass."

"Yeah? I'm gonna kick yours if you don't get that bottle ready."

"I'm goin'." Kade cleaned up in the bathroom and grabbed a pair of sweatpants from the laundry room as he waited for the bottle to heat.

Upstairs, the small lamp in the corner of Skylar's room was on. She sat against the headboard with Eliza in her arms. He passed her the bottle and climbed next to her on the bed.

"How's our girl?"

"Surprisingly alert."

Kade leaned over and grinned at their owl-eyed baby. "Whatcha thinkin' about? Wonderin' what Mama and Daddy have been doin'? Tryin' to keep us from makin' a brother or sister for you?"

"Bite your tongue, Kade McKay."

"What? It's possible."

"Not when I'm on the pill and we've been using condoms every time." Immediately, she chattered at Eliza while fussing with her blanket.

So, the little sneak neglected to tell him she was on the pill. Interesting. Her nondisclosure was another layer of control. Being covered on the birth control front opened up a whole new realm of possibilities in teaching Sky about spontaneity.

Kade reached for Eliza's bare foot poking out of the blanket. "Her toes are so tiny. Her ears too. She has your cute little turned-up nose."

"You think so?"

"I'm hopin' she gets your freckles too. And your laugh. I love your laugh. When she wraps those little fingers around mine, I know I'm the one who's wrapped around hers. Sometimes when I'm feedin' her I just stare at her because she is so amazin'."

"That she is."

It was one of the most perfect moments of Kade's life. Contentment filled him, cuddled into Skylar as they admired their creation.

Eliza finished the bottle and Sky handed her to Kade. She was fully awake even after he burped her.

"What are we gonna do with you, sweet girlie? You ain't gonna go to sleep anytime soon, are ya?" He looked at Sky. "If you wanna get some shut-eye I'll take her downstairs and keep her entertained until she falls asleep."

"I'm not tired. You're the one who's had a tough day with all that roping, riding and rodeoing. I'd understand if you want to crash."

"I'm feelin' energized if you wanna know the real truth."

Sky blushed.

"We could watch TV or something in the livin' room?"

The look on Skylar's face indicated she was thinking about the "or something" activities they'd been involved in on the couch just a little while ago. Her clothes were still scattered everywhere. The wineglasses were on the coffee table. Would those reminders make her uncomfortable? Or have the opposite effect and make her as crazy to have him again as he was crazy to have her?

When she didn't answer, he scooted off the bed. "I'm takin'

her downstairs. Get some sleep."

"Hang on. I'm coming with you guys. Might as well pick a movie since we have that ridiculously large big screen TV. I'll make popcorn."

We. Kade loved the sound of that. He leaned down and kissed her square on the mouth. "Sounds like a plan."

Chapter Sixteen

The McKay family was overwhelming, to say the least. Add in the two dozen or so West aunts/uncles/cousins and Skylar didn't know if she'd ever remember anyone's name. It didn't help that Kade had deserted her.

He promised he'd come back. He did not desert you, her inner romantic chastised.

Good Lord, with all the voices in her head clamoring for attention and offering advice, her mother would've been better served naming her Sybil, rather than Skylar.

Late morning was surprisingly cool for the beginning of September. Wispy white clouds covered the big Wyoming sky. The aroma of barbecue smoke and the occasional whiff of the barnyard overpowered the ever-present scent of sage.

Skylar shifted in the wicker rocker. She'd attempted to hide in the house, but Kimi insisted on setting her up under a small white tent. One of the three tents needed to house the vast numbers of McKays. Clusters of people filled the other tents. The one she and Eliza inhabited was devoid of activity and Skylar didn't know whether to be thankful or embarrassed about that fact.

Horseshoes clinked in the background, competing with the twang of country music drifting from a boom box. Males shouting, females laughing, babies crying, doors slamming, vehicles zooming up the driveway in a cloud of dust—Sky fought off a full-blown panic attack.

She should've invited her sister along. No one would've noticed another body among the throng of cowboys and cowgirls. Then again, with India being the tattooed and pierced lady, she'd stick out like a circus performer.

Eliza squirmed. Sky adjusted her so she lay across her lap, loosening the blanket to keep her from overheating. When she looked up, a little boy around the age of four stared at her curiously. Black hair, vivid blue eyes. His genetics were obvious.

"Which McKay are you?"

"Kyler. Is that really a girl?"

"Really and truly."

He peeped at Eliza, practically nose to nose. "So she's my cousin? 'Cause I ain't ever had a girl cousin before."

"How many cousins do you have?"

"About a billion."

"Really?"

"Nah. Just kiddin'. Thane and Gib are both babies. Well, Gib is walkin' now so he's kinda cool, but Thane don't do nothin' but drool. Kinda borin' if you ask me, I don't see the big deal about babies. And Grama is all excited because we're gonna have another baby in the family."

"I think all babies are pretty cool."

He shrugged. "Know what I think are cool?"

"What?"

"Horses. Do you got a horse?"

"No. Do you?"

"Uh-huh. A pony *and* a horse. And a BB gun. I'm a good shot." He studied her. "Uncle Kade'd probably buy you a horse if you asked him real nice. Her too."

Skylar bit her cheek to keep from laughing. "You think?"

"Yep. He used to come over all the time and ride horses and shoot. How come you don't let him come over no more?"

"Kyler McKay, I've been looking for you!"

The boy muttered, "Crap," under his breath.

AJ strode toward them.

"Hiya, Mom. You sure smell good."

"Charm isn't gonna work, buster. And you're only saying that because I smell like cookies." She smiled indulgently and ruffled the dark hair on Kyler's head. "Didn't you tell Grama you'd pick green beans this morning?"

"Yeah. But I—"

"No excuses. Get going, she's waiting. There's a bucket hanging on the fence post by the garden gate."

The boy crawled under the bottom of the tent and disappeared.

"I hope he wasn't a pest."

"No. I was grateful for the company. He's an entertaining kid. He was looking for Kade. Have you seen him?"

"He and Colt and Blake were headed for the barn. Why? Do you need me to track him down for you?"

"If it wouldn't be too much trouble."

"Sheesh. It's no trouble at all."

"AJ. There you are." Macie loped toward them, a dark-haired, brown-eyed baby boy planted on her hip. "Can you take Thane? Carter and his dad are off somewhere and I need to lay down before I throw up again."

"Sure." AJ cocked Thane on her hip. "Are you doing too much?"

"I'm done cooking for now. I'll be fine if I can just close my eyes for a bit." Macie looked at Skylar and Eliza. "Don't worry, it's nothing contagious. Carter knocked me up again. I swear that damn virile man intends to keep me barefoot and pregnant for our entire marriage."

"Or he's competing with Cash," AJ said. "Have you met Macie's dad, Cash Big Crow and his wife, Gemma?"

Skylar nodded.

"Their twins are fifteen months and Gemma is pregnant again. Damn, maybe it *is* contagious."

"Channing would be happy about that."

AJ grinned. "I take it Channing is still going through with the plan to seduce Colby?"

At Skylar's blank look, Macie said, "Channing had sort of a rough pregnancy with Gib, so Colby is gun-shy about her getting pregnant again so soon."

"How old is Gib?"

"Nine months."

"Why would Channing want to get pregnant again when she already has a baby?"

"Like me, she wants to have kids close together. Besides, once you have a baby, your life is chaos, how much harder could it be to add one more?"

Skylar hadn't thought of it that way.

"Anyway, since Channing is nursing and can't take the pill, Colby is adamant about using condoms. We all know how...insistent these McKay men are," Macie said dryly. "She's managed to hold out on him for the last week. So the next couple of nights she's pulling out all stops to drive him wild and into having sex without a condom."

"If they haven't had sex for a week, he's toast," AJ said.

"No kidding."

Skylar froze. Not only were these women confiding something incredibly personal in her, neither of them realized Eliza's existence was due to lack of a condom. Which meant Kade hadn't told anyone the down and dirty details about their initial encounter.

"Oh, crap." Macie clapped a hand over her mouth and raced out of the tent.

"Poor thing. I'll see if I can't track Kade down for you," AJ said.

Skylar's respite was short lived. A gorgeous woman with legs up to her armpits, sporting the dark McKay hair and sparkling blue eyes approached her.

"This is the girl muscling in on my territory."

"Excuse me?"

"Can I hold her?"

"Maybe you oughta introduce yourself first," Chassie suggested from behind her.

"Oh. I'm Keely McKay."

"Ah. The prodigal McKay daughter," Skylar said. "I've heard about you."

"Don't believe any of it. All lies perpetrated by my brothers and cousins to distract everyone from their wild ways."

163

Skylar handed Eliza to her and Keely cradled the baby like a pro.

"Oh, lookit you, beautiful girlie-poo. Whoa, she really looks like Kade." Keely displayed a dazzling smile. "No offense."

"None taken."

"So, Skylar, you own Sky Blue? I love that store, especially the essential oils. I always stop and load up whenever I'm in town. I never see you in there."

"I'm usually at the manufacturing plant in Moorcroft."

"Well, India rocks. She is amazingly talented to boot."

Talented was always the tip-off. "Where'd she tattoo you?"

"On my butt." Keely mock-whispered, "Don't tell. My mother would have a cow if she heard about the big red lips tattooed on my derrière."

"Your secret is safe with me."

"Cool. Don't mention the McKay brand inked on my hip either."

Sky motioned zipping her lip. "You said whenever you're in town. You don't live here?"

"No. Right now I live on the road. Middle of September I'll be back in Denver to finish my sports medicine degree."

"Sports medicine? What kind?"

"I'm specializing in physical therapy for cowboys who participate in the various pro rodeo tours."

"Which means Keely is in her glory, surrounded twenty-four/seven by hot bull riders, bronc busters, and cowboys wickedly good with ropes. And she gets to put her greedy hands all over their sweat-slicked, muscled, half-naked bodies all the time. Bitch," Chassie added good-naturedly.

"Oh, that's rich, Chass, coming from the woman who's married to one of the hottest guys in the world. Now that he's off the market I'll never get to do him."

"Keely!"

"Puh-lease. You know I've had it bad for Trevor my whole life, since he's best buds with Colby. And you had to go and marry him. So now he's essentially my cousin, and I'll never know firsthand whether he's as good at ridin' out of the saddle as he's rumored to be."

"Trust me, the rumors don't do him justice."

"Bitch," Keely shot back.

Chassie laughed. "Now lemme hold her."

Skylar's head spun. She didn't know whether to laugh or run. How would she ever get a handle on this family's dynamics? It seemed they were in each other's business all the time. Talk about boisterous. And nosy. Did any of these people hold back any personal emotions or thoughts? Or was everything common knowledge?

Kade isn't blabbing near and far about the two of you, a prim voice reminded her.

And if she was totally honest, she was utterly charmed by this wild, crazy and fiercely loyal family.

"So when are you and Kade getting married?" Keely asked.

"Um. I-I—"

"I know he's asked you."

Skylar's eyes narrowed. "How?"

"Because he's Kade. He's never brought a woman to a McKay family function before. He's Mr. 'Do The Right Thing' more so than any of my brothers, well, except for Cam. Plus, he's been waiting for the right woman to settle down with for years. He's always wanted a family of his own. If anyone deserves it, Kade does."

What makes you think I'm the right woman? Would I be here if not for Eliza?

A man sauntered in, garnering Keely's attention, keeping his back to Skylar. "Way to ditch me, babe."

"My brothers giving you a hard time again?"

"Ya think? Started out with arm wrestlin'. Then I hadta prove my skill with a rope, and a horse, and a rifle, a pistol, and a shotgun. This was all *after* I did crack of dawn chores with Cord, Colby, Colt, *and* your dad."

"Poor baby." Keely kissed him. "Carter cut you some slack?"

"Only because he's friends with Jack, who'd happily kick his butt for messin' with me."

"Yeah? My money is on Carter. Your brother Jack is such a know-it-all, pompous, self-righteous, jerkwad, asshat."

"Hey, now, that's my kin."

"At least I didn't call him Jack-*off* like I usually do."

Skylar couldn't help but grin. Keely reminded Sky of India, that same in-your-face personality laced with a rapid-fire wit.

The man pointed at the baby in Keely's arms. "Whose kid is that one?"

"My cousin Kade's. This is Eliza's mother, Skylar. Skylar, my boyfriend, Justin Donohue. He's suffering through the McKay family dramas for the first time too."

"Pleased to meet you, ma'am."

Skylar didn't know if she was more taken aback by his chivalrous hat tip, or that the cowboy was one of the best-looking men she'd ever seen. Blond-haired, green-eyed, with a smile to rival the devil's. Chiseled features that would be the envy of the Marlboro man, and a muscular frame that'd make a body builder jealous.

When Keely saw Skylar's thoroughly justified inspection of Justin, she waggled her eyebrows and gave a thumbs up behind Justin's back.

Chassie rolled her eyes.

Sky withheld a chuckle. "Where are you from, Justin?"

"South Dakota, originally. Now I spend my time in Texas when I'm not on the tour."

Tour? Was this guy a musician? He sure looked like he'd be at home on the stage in front of thousands of adoring female fans. "Which tour?"

"The Professional Bull Riders tour."

"Oh. Really?"

"Justin is a bull rider, ranked twenty-three in the world standings. He's my cousin Chase's traveling partner. We met when I did my stint with the PBR and I worked on his injured shoulder."

"Keely saved my season. I'd be out if not for her. Except, I suspect her brothers are tryin' their damndest to kill me, not just re-aggravate my injury."

"Better not mention me sneaking out to see you in the bunkhouse last night, huh? They'd really be putting the boots to your very fine ass."

Justin hissed, "Will you keep it down? They have loaded guns. And I know they ain't afraid to use me as target practice."

Keely balanced on the tips of her funky cowboy boots decorated with flames and rhinestones, to whisper something in Justin's ear. His face burned beet red. He grabbed her hand and hauled her outside.

"Before you ask, yes, she's every bit as wild as you've heard."

"Chass, hon, you have a minute?" Trevor yelled into the tent.

"Hang on." Chassie passed Eliza back to Skylar. "Duty calls. See you later."

Skylar was alone again. It was a bizarre feeling to consider these people were Eliza's family; yet, they weren't Sky's family.

They could be if you'd say yes to Kade's proposal.

She had been thinking about it, but like India had pointed out, Sky never did anything impulsively. And what was the hurry? They were already living together. She meandered into the yard and saw groups clustered everywhere. A few she recognized—Kade's father and his uncles. Older women. A few guys a decade younger than Kade with the same coloring who had to be more cousins she hadn't met yet.

"Amazing, isn't it? All these good-looking men. Most of them still single. Makes you wonder what's wrong with them, doesn't it? Besides the fact they're ornery cowboys."

Sky turned. The woman was as plain looking as she was plainspoken. Stick-straight mousy brown hair nearly hid her heart-shaped face. She wasn't tall; she wasn't short. She wasn't fat; she wasn't skinny. She was sturdy. A woman who'd blend into the background. The typical Wyoming ranch wife. "Have we met?"

"No, but I've heard all about you. I'm Libby McKay. Quinn is my husband. I'd introduce you to him, but he abandoned me like he always does."

"Kade disappeared too."

"Better get used to it. Then again, you've proven your worth by popping one out, and a girl McKay at that. Wow. Quite an accomplishment."

Skylar didn't know how to respond. It made her wonder if she'd acted aloof when talking to Kade's assorted family members. Was constantly searching for Kade's familiar face considered rude? Is that why this woman felt she'd found a kindred spirit? Or was there another reason behind her bitterness?

"Sorry. That was totally uncalled for. I don't know what's gotten into me lately. Quinn always complains that I wouldn't say shit if I had a mouthful." Libby smiled and it was genuinely sweet. "Congratulations on your baby. She's gorgeous. You must be thrilled."

"I am, thank you. Do you have children?"

"No. Probably why I'm so defensive about it, huh?"

Again, Sky kept quiet.

"I'll fill you in, since I see the questions in your eyes but you're too polite to ask, which will change once you're firmly in the bosom of the buttinsky McKays. Quinn and I have been married the longest of any of his cousins and we're the only ones without kids. So at family functions I hear that question over and over, until I snap at perfect strangers." She smiled again. "Ignore me. Everyone else does." Her eyes focused on an object over Skylar's shoulder. "Well, well, speak of the ignorant devil. There's my darling husband now. I'll head him off at the pass and spare you from our marital spat."

Libby met a stocky man with his hat pulled down so low Sky couldn't see his face. They fought. Not loudly, but body language spoke more than words anyway. The fight didn't last long. Libby stomped off and her husband didn't chase her down. He just watched her go. Didn't appear airing family grievances was better than keeping them bottled up for Quinn and Libby. The scene bothered Sky enough that she knew she'd forego her usual none-of-your-business mantra and ask Kade about his cousin's situation later.

At loose ends, she spied Carolyn and Kimi taping down tablecloths on the long picnic tables and headed that direction. "Need help?"

"Nope. Soon as I finish I'm gonna take my granddaughter off your hands."

"Sounds good."

Kimi's smile died when she looked at Carolyn, who'd gone absolutely still.

"Caro? What's wrong?"

Carolyn took off like a bat out of hell and ran across the yard.

All conversation everywhere ended abruptly.

A lone figure loped down the driveway. The duffel bag in his hand dropped to the dirt as Carolyn launched herself at him. He spun her around and she was sobbing so loudly they all heard her.

Kimi gasped softly. "Oh my God. That's Cam."

Carson hurried past. Keely shrieked and she was running down the driveway.

"Who's Cam?" Skylar asked.

"Cameron McKay. Carolyn and Carson's son who's been in Iraq."

"They didn't know he was coming?"

"No."

Carter, Colby, Cord and Colt hustled by. As soon as the group finished their private reunion, the remaining family members rushed to meet him.

Although it made her feel like a voyeur, it was one of the most poignant scenes Sky had ever witnessed and she turned away in embarrassment to hide her tear-stained face. Damn hormones.

But Sky also realized that no matter what happened between her and Kade, Eliza would always be welcomed with open arms in this loving, tight-knit family.

Chapter Seventeen

Kimi bounded back to the seating area where Skylar hung on the periphery. "It's good to see Cam home in one piece, even if it is only for a few days. Every time he's gotten leave in the last few years, something awful happens over there and it's cancelled."

Skylar searched the McKay crowd for Kade. "That's too bad."

"Sweetie, I know that look."

"What look?"

"The, 'I'm a new mother and I'm always exhausted' look. The 'who in the heck are all these people' look. The 'where did my man wander off to' look."

Even through her melancholy, Sky was mightily amused by Kade's mother. "You recognize all those looks on me already, Kimi?"

"Yep, and this time Kade had nothing to do with it. Here, lemme take Eliza for a bit. Why don't you sneak into the house where it's quiet?"

Touched that Kimi seemed to be looking out for her once again, she said, "Thanks. I do feel a little lost in the crowd today."

"It's them durn hormones. Having a baby messes you up physically and emotionally for months afterward." She shook her head. "I don't know how you young women do it all these days."

"You had two babies at the same time. I don't know how *you* did it."

"To tell you the truth, I don't either." She laughed. "It's sort of a blur."

"Tell me about it."

Kimi made a shooing motion. "Now go on, scat. Eliza and Grama have serious showin' off to do."

Inside the big, old farmhouse, Sky wandered upstairs. Although the styles were the same, this one was much bigger than her house. Six bedrooms ringed a long, wide hallway. At the end opposite the staircase was a small bathroom. She snuck inside and shut the door, half-wishing she, Kade and Eliza could just go home.

Home. This area was Kade's home. She'd bet this house was as familiar to Kade as the house he'd grown up in. She stared out the window at the shadowed ridge of mountains in the distance. The hilly prairie, heavy with tall, dry grass, clumps of scrub cedar. Little black specks she assumed were cows. A landscape completely foreign to her, which fit since the ranching lifestyle was equally foreign to her.

After washing her hands, she'd decided to call India, feeling guilty for her unintentional family neglect of her only sister, when two raps sounded on the door.

"Skylar? Sweetheart, you all right?"

Kade.

She stepped out and resisted throwing herself into his arms. Streaks of grease dotted his face. He looked cute and surprisingly, a bit perplexed.

"Hey. Sorry. I got roped into helpin' fix an old tractor with Blake and Chet and Remy. Then when Cam showed up I realized I'd left you alone for a coupla hours."

"Understandable. It's also understandable that I want to go home."

"Sky—"

"Don't worry. I know it's your family time. I won't whine and make you come with me. You can stay. No big deal. I'll call my sister to come get me, if you and Eliza wanna hang out."

Kade bent down until they were nose to nose. "That's what you think? I'd be pissed off about you tryin' to get me to leave here?"

She hadn't meant to sound petulant. She hadn't meant to make him mad either. "I realize you want to be with your family."

"Wrong. *You* are my family."

Before she could respond, footsteps echoed up the stairs. Kade grabbed her hand and towed her into the next room and quietly closed the door.

"What are you doing?"

"Findin' someplace private where we ain't gonna be overheard by everyone." Kade crowded her against the wall. "You wanna tell me why you've got that lost look in your pretty eyes and why you're hidin' out in the damn bathroom?"

Because I was adrift until you showed up.

"Sky?" he prompted.

"I'm tired, I'm so tired all the damn time and it's been stressful meeting your whole family at once."

"I imagine. Despite what you think, we can go home right now, if you want to."

She was ridiculously thrilled he considered her place home. She reached up to wipe a grease smudge from his nose. "Got a little dirty playing with your big boy toys, didn't you?"

"Yeah. Sorry."

"Don't be. It looks good on you." Sky let her fingertips wander over the angles of his face, cheekbones, jaw and up to his forehead. "Very, very good."

Kade stared at her in that way which made everything feminine inside her go all soft and moist.

"Anyway, Grama Kimi just absconded with Princess Eliza and she'd probably throw a fit if we attempted to leave." Skylar brushed a piece of hay out of his hair. He smelled good. Like earth and animals and machinery. Like home.

"Can't have Grama disappointed," he murmured.

"No." She continued to stroke his temple and the smooth section of skin in front of his ear, loving the chance to touch him however she pleased.

The air in the room seemed heavier, thicker with intent. His. Hers. For once, she didn't fight it. She embraced it. Encouraged it.

"Know something, Mr. McKay?"

"What, Miz Ellison?"

"The truth is, I looked lost and lonely because I *was* lost and lonely. I missed you. Even though everyone has been really nice and welcoming, it's not the same if you're not with me. Then I really seem like a whiner for feeling that I don't belong here with these people."

"You lumpin' me in with 'these people', Sky?"

"No. That's not what I meant."

"Then where do I fit in, darlin'?"

Hoping to lighten both their moods, she teased, "You fit in me perfectly."

"Cheeky woman." Kade turned his head and kissed her forearm. Then lightning fast, he pinned both wrists above her head with just one of his rough-skinned hands.

She squeaked with surprise. "What are you doing?"

"Enforcin' a new rule."

"Is this like the naked rule?"

"Yep. If you touch me, I get to touch you."

"You are touching me."

"Not where I wanna be touchin' you."

She wet her lips just to watch his eyes flare with desire. "And where would you like to be touching me?"

"Everywhere. But I can get real specific in a helluva hurry."

"Show me." She arched into him as he nuzzled her neck. "Please."

"Goddamn, Sky, I want you so fuckin' bad I can't think beyond hikin' up your skirt and nailin' you against this wall."

Her silent chant of *do it, do it, do it* throbbed in her blood so loudly she hoped he'd hear it.

Kade breathed in her ear, "I've been thinkin' about last night all damn day. Have you?"

"Uh-huh. It was the hottest sex ever."

"When I get you home, I'm gonna try my damndest to turn it up a notch or ten."

His mouth was like liquid fire on her skin. "Kade. I-I don't

173

want to wait until we get home. I want you now."

"Thank you, Jesus. I was wonderin' how fast and sweet I was gonna hafta talk to do this." He tugged at her skirt until it pooled around her ankles and he crushed his mouth to hers. His hand was between her legs, stroking her through her panties. He broke away momentarily to whisper, "I love the skirts you always wear. Not only do you look sexy as hell, nothin' like easy access to this hot body I can't get enough of." He kissed her again.

Skylar whimpered at the contrasting sensations. His tight grip on her wrists. The feather-light touches on her pussy as he sucked the air from her lungs and common sense from her brain.

Gradually his fingers slipped beneath the elastic and into the slippery wetness. He thrust his fingers inside her and she twisted from his hold.

Her freed hands zeroed in on his belt buckle.

"Guess I'm gonna hafta remind you who's in charge later."

"Fine. Whatever. Help me get these damn jeans off—"

Laughing softly, he said, "I love that you're impatient," and stripped the denim to the tops of his boots, clamping his hands on her ass. "Wrap your legs around my waist as I lift you up."

"I'm too heavy—" earned her four sharp smacks on her ass that stung like a bitch. "Hey!"

"More where that came from if you say shit like that again."

He hoisted her against the wall. His cock impaled her in one swift movement.

Skylar gasped.

"Ssh." He kissed her and began to thrust slow and steady.

She wreathed her arms around Kade's neck and held on.

They moved together, lost in each other, straining closer to that point of no return. His cock seemed harder, thicker, hotter as he didn't pull completely out. Made for a very intense intimate connection and one she knew she'd searched her whole life for.

Or did the *hurry hurry hurry* feeling stem from the chance they might get caught?

Maybe, but sex with Kade had an edge. His hands gripped

her butt, pushing, pulling, grinding and the constant contact with her clit sent her spiraling into a short, intense orgasm.

Kade swallowed her cries, never missing a stroke.

When she quit gasping, he put his mouth on her ear. "I love to make you come. It gets me off." His hips pistoned faster and he groaned against her throat. She felt each hot pulse as his cock emptied inside her. She realized she could feel it because he hadn't worn a condom.

Ah. So he had noticed her admission she was on the pill. It was just like him not to comment.

Even as Kade was trying to catch his breath, he panted, "Skylar. Marry me."

She whispered, "No."

"Worth a shot."

He smothered her laugh and set her back on her feet. Her underwear was ruined so she used it to wipe up the milky liquid trickling down the inside of her thigh.

Kade's eyes glittered possessively as he fastened his belt. "Is it chauvinistic to say I like seein' my seed runnin' down your leg?"

"Yes."

"Mmm. Then I'm really a pig because I sure like makin' love to you without a condom."

She rolled her skirt up, wondering why she wasn't icked out by going commando. In fact, it primed her for more sexy and naughty fun. "Look, I didn't tell I was on the pill—"

"We had an unplanned pregnancy, Sky. You don't gotta explain nothin' to me. But I'd like to think you woulda told me at some point."

Certainly not the reaction she'd expected. But she was slowly figuring out that just because Kade McKay was even-keeled, he wasn't the most predictable man she'd ever known, and maybe that wasn't such a bad thing.

"What do you say we get our girl and head on home?"

"Sounds like a plan."

They snuck back downstairs like a couple of guilty teens.

Outside, dinner was in full swing.

"Aunt C ain't gonna let us leave without eatin' first," Kade said.

"I am kinda hungry. We can stay, if you want."

A look of gratitude flashed in his eyes and he kissed her cheek. "We'll go right after, I promise."

After they loaded their plates, Kade was called over to talk to his dad, who was proudly holding Eliza. Skylar ended up sitting with Kade's cousins, Remy and Chet West. She knew them since their construction company had remodeled her store in Sundance, but for some reason, she hadn't made the West/McKay family connection.

The beefy guys were as equally fine looking as their McKay counterparts, but fair haired, fair skinned, bulky, like a band of Viking warriors, rather than the "black Irish" looks associated with the McKays.

Chet said, "Hello, Skylar. Our lucky day. I was hopin' a single woman would join us."

"One that isn't related to us," Remy added. "Speaking of related to us...Aunt Kimi has been cartin' around your beautiful baby." Remy leaned forward, his hazel eyes dancing with humor. "You could've told us Kade is her daddy. We can keep a secret."

"In this family? Right."

He smiled, flashing his dimples. "You're catching on quick."

"My cousins are socially inept, so I'll introduce myself. Blake West."

The man at the end of the table had a halo of golden curls adorning his deeply tanned face. His eyes were the color of melted milk chocolate. "Nice to meet you, Blake. Explain the family affiliation, even though I'll probably forget. Apparently pregnancy and childbirth has sucked out all my memory brain cells."

"My father, Darren West, is Kimi and Carolyn's brother."

"Are you in the construction business?"

"I help them out occasionally, but my main occupation is raising sheep."

"Sheep? Is it a family operation?"

"Just me and dad. We ain't land barons like the McKays, got a small spread that barely supports us. So my older brother, Nick, moved to Denver."

"Really? My sister just moved *here* from Denver. What does your brother do?"

"He's a cop. Upgraded to detective last year."

Ironic, considering India had spent time in the slammer in Mile High City, not that she'd share that tidbit, despite the McKays wouldn't think twice about tossing that in the conversation.

After a few minutes of polite chitchat, Remy said, "So what's going on with you and Kade? I hear he's living with you?"

Chet groaned. "Jesus, Rem. You're as bad as Aunt Genevieve. I can't take him anywhere, I swear."

A large shadow fell across the table. Sky looked up, expecting to see Kade, but Cam McKay hovered over her. The man was huge; he had to be at least six-foot-five. His shoulders were damn near as wide as the picnic table, yet not an ounce of fat clung to his enormous biceps and flat stomach. With his buzz haircut, camouflage pants and tight T-shirt, he epitomized the lean, mean, fighting machine depicted in the army ads on TV.

"Pull up a chair, Cam," Chet said.

Cam plopped down. He offered her a smile. "Have we met?"

"No. I'm Skylar Ellison."

"Nice to meet you, Skylar." He offered his hand. "I'm Cameron McKay."

Sky tried not to stare, but Cam didn't look much like his brothers, beyond having those same blue eyes. With dark blond hair, he resembled Chet, Remy and Blake more than the McKays, except for Carter. Still, he was striking looking, if a bit menacing.

"Who are you here with?"

"She's here with me, Cam, and if you don't let go of her hand I'm gonna hafta break yours," Kade said.

Cam brought her hand to his lips and took his own sweet time kissing her knuckles.

Kade growled.

"Just kiddin', K, sit down and chill out." Cam grinned. "Congrats are in order on your daughter."

"Thank you."

Kade sandwiched himself on her other side. "Glad to have you home, cuz."

"Good to be here, although it's a little weird seein' all the women and babies around my brothers."

She listened while the guys chatted, at obvious ease with each other on a level Skylar didn't understand. The only person she'd ever shared that kind of connection with was India, and only in the years since India became sober. When Kade put his hand on her leg and squeezed, she was touched he'd sensed her mood.

"If we set it up for Wednesday night, everybody oughta be able to come right? Kade? You in?" Cam asked.

"The Golden Boot? Yeah. I could swing by. We ain't gonna start hayin' until Thursday."

"All the more reason to celebrate. That part of ranchin' sucks ass."

"Which is why we're very glad we aren't ranchers," Chet said, and clinked his beer bottle to Remy's.

Cam added his longneck to the toast at the last second and said, "Amen."

Sky noticed Kade looking at Cam oddly. Was it surprising to him that Cam admitted he didn't want to ranch?

"You think Colt will come?"

"I dunno. He ain't stepped foot in the place in the year since he quit drinkin'."

"Maybe we oughta go someplace else, so he don't feel uncomfortable," Cam said.

Sky faced him. "That'd make him feel worse. Just invite him like you normally would. Either way, it's his choice."

"Thanks for the advice. I appreciate it. Six o'clock, Wednesday night, at the Golden Boot." Cam leaned over to give Kade an intimidating stare. "Skylar's smart, beautiful and throws good fillies. Remind me again, why she ain't got your ring on her finger?"

Chet and Remy both went, "Ooh."

"'Cause she keeps sayin' no."

Skylar blushed.

"Then she's even smarter than I thought," Cam said with a wink.

Amidst the sounds of more laughter, Sky heard Eliza crying. Kimi approached and Kade scooped Eliza in his arms before Sky stood.

"That's our cue to get home." Kade held out his hand to Sky. "Ready, sweetheart?"

"Yeah."

"I think she's just tired, son. If you want to put her down with the other babies…"

"Nah, she's been a handful this week. Skylar and I are both beat. Tell Aunt C thanks." He kissed Kimi on the top of the head. "See ya, Grama."

Once Eliza was in her car seat in the back of the deluxe cab, and they were driving down the dusty road, Skylar scooted across the bench seat to sit right next to Kade. She set her head on his shoulder and sighed.

Kade didn't say a word. He just wrapped his arm around her and smiled like he knew exactly what she was thinking.

Her last thought before she floated into sleepy contentment was maybe she wasn't so smart to keep saying no to this man.

Chapter Eighteen

The second they walked in the door, Eliza was all bright-eyed and bushy-tailed. When it became obvious the baby wasn't interested in napping, Skylar begged off to finish paperwork at the manufacturing plant.

Kade had noticed a few things outside Skylar's place that needed further inspection. He tied a hat on Eliza's head and dressed her in an outfit which completely covered her lily-white skin. Took him some time to decipher how the baby pack worked. Once he'd strapped her to his belly, facing forward so she could see the world, her legs kicked like a frog's.

"You like bein' outside. I'll bet you're gonna be a tomboy." He adjusted his ball cap and wandered to the old wooden barn. The building listed to the right in a bad way, presenting a serious hazard. It could collapse at any time. He'd talk to Skylar about knocking it down before the first snowfall.

A long prefabricated metal barn was kitty-corner from the house. It wasn't in too bad of shape, but it'd been jam-packed with all sorts of junk—antique machinery, tools, rusted paint cans and empty feed sacks. Rope. Lots of rope.

He unhooked a chunk of rope that wasn't too thick or too thin. He jerked a foot-long section of it between his hands. Plenty of give. Could use it for quite a few things. Might come in handy.

A flash of inspiration struck him. He knew exactly how he could put the rope to good use. He draped it over his shoulder.

Kade always did things with purpose, so it was nice just to meander, no destination or agenda in mind, talking to Eliza as they wallowed in the lazy afternoon. It pleased him Skylar hadn't cultivated the stereotypical suburban lawn, but allowed the landscape to remain natural. Rugged. A backdrop of long, gold and brown grasses, stubby groundcover the color of cinnamon, sagebrush, and the occasional yellow daisy popped up, all blended seamlessly past the barbed wire fence and across the pasture.

An oak tree with gnarled branches grew in the middle of the backyard. Usually only scrub oak survived and they never reached that size. He stopped under the canopy of shade and looked up. A sturdy branch stuck straight out from the thick trunk.

"Whatcha think, Eliza? Nice and peaceful in this spot. Shady. That'd be a perfect place for a tire swing, wouldn't it? Made outta one of them big tractor tires?"

She grunted.

"No? Would you rather have a wooden swing so you didn't get your pretty pink clothes coated with black rubber?" Her feet moved. Kade laughed and wrapped his hands around her chubby calves. "Wooden it is, though it'll be a few years before I'll let you swing on it, darlin'."

If you're even around.

He refused to consider he might not be living here in the future. He was making progress with Skylar, slow, but it was still progress. Whether she'd admit it was a whole 'nother story. Then again, earlier today, she'd admitted she wanted him. And she'd been willing to toss caution to the wind to have him. One week ago he couldn't fathom Skylar banging his brains out in a strange house, with strangers around, and chance they'd get caught.

Man. It'd been hot as hell, hoisting her against the wall. Feeling the hot, tight caress of her pussy around his cock without a layer of latex. Sky'd matched him thrust for thrust, move for move, kiss for kiss. Those noises she'd made in his mouth when she came...damn.

The self-assured Skylar hiding in his aunt and uncle's upstairs bathroom had knocked him for a loop. When she'd reached out, touching him so sweetly, telling him, and showing him she did need him on an emotional level as well as a physical one, he'd been tempted to blurt out—*Baby, I love you,* right then.

Luckily he'd refrained. Talk about spooking the woman. India might be of the *no pain, no gain* school of thought, but these days, Kade was more inclined to follow the old saying *slow and steady wins the race.*

Kade circled the perimeter from the house to the barns, to the granary and machine shed. He'd been pleased to find the chicken coop in relatively decent shape. He rested his boot on the bottom rung of the fence, scrutinizing the field. He studied the green patches of high grass, noting cattle or horses hadn't grazed in it for a number of years. It looked healthy. How much land did Skylar own? He racked his brain trying to remember if she'd told him.

"Baby girl, what's your mama's acreage?"

Eliza grunted.

"I know, never ask a cowgirl the size of her spread. If I could fence that area off, it'd be a perfect place for your pony. Still want a white one?"

She grunted again. Then Kade knew why she'd been grunting.

"Whoo-ee, are you Miss Stinky Britches. Let's go in and get you changed."

How one little thing could poop so much boggled his mind. By the time he'd bathed her, dressed her, changed his clothes and fed her, they were both yawning. Kade stretched out on the couch. Eliza was sound asleep on his chest and he didn't have the energy to move. Truth be told, he didn't want to move. It was an ideal way to spend an afternoon, at home with his family.

He tucked the blanket around her, kissed her sweet-smelling head and drifted away.

That's how Sky found them. Father and daughter snuggled together like it was the most natural thing in the world.

It is. He belongs with her. He belongs here. He could belong to you.

But would he? Despite what he claimed he'd written in the missing letter, part of her believed Kade wouldn't be here, with her, if it wasn't for Eliza. Another part of her believed the reason he'd become so sexually demanding was not in an effort to get her to open up to new sexual experiences, or to give him control of her pleasure, but so she'd willingly provide him with enough sexual variety that if she did accept his marriage proposal, he wouldn't be tempted to look elsewhere for the kind of kink he needed in bed.

If that's true, then why did he ask you to marry him before he revealed that side of himself?

Still, she couldn't deny Kade had lovingly brought out a side of herself she'd ignored her whole life—her sexuality. And the man hadn't exploited it; he'd reveled in it.

Sky was judging him harshly on either scenario. Why? So she covered her bases for when he (invariably) took what he wanted and bailed?

Lord. India was right. She could over-think everything.

One thing Skylar couldn't deny was Kade's commitment to Eliza. His actions spoke louder than words. She leaned against the doorjamb and watched them sleep for a good long time before she turned away.

An hour later she heard them stirring. She warmed up a bottle and put the finishing touches on supper.

Kade came around the corner, barefoot, wearing ratty surfer shorts, a threadbare tank top, sporting a five-o'clock shadow and his hair stuck out every which way. He looked so damn cute she grinned at him.

"What?"

"Nothing. You hungry?"

Eliza cried.

"Guess that answers that." Sky reached for her. "Gotcha covered, baby girl. Let Daddy eat."

She popped the bottle in Eliza's mouth and looked up to see Kade looming over her. "What?"

"This." He slid his tongue over the seam of her lips, until she opened her mouth for him fully. His kiss pacified and inflamed, both sweet and spicy. Kade eased back without a word, which was A-okay with Sky, since she was thunderstruck anyway.

The evening passed uneventfully, which was fine by her. She never dreamed she'd be so...happy to sit on the porch swing, holding hands and admiring the stars. When Eliza dozed off Kade put her to bed.

But the man who returned downstairs didn't look like Kade, the sweet, loving father. He looked like Kade, the dark, demanding lover.

Desire rolled over her like a hot summer breeze.

"Skylar. C'mere."

She walked to where he stood at the bottom of the staircase with his legs braced apart, his arms behind his back.

"Pick a hand."

"Why? Do you have a present for me?"

"A present of sorts. Pick."

"Ah. Okay. The left hand."

Kade's instant grin was decidedly predatory. He thrust out his arm. A length of rope dangled from his fingers.

"What's that for?"

"What do you think it's for?"

"A new clothesline?"

"Wrong. Try again."

"Are you going to tie something up?"

"Yep. You."

Her stomach pitched. "Why?"

"'Cause it's gonna be fun."

"Umm. Where is this private rodeo event going to happen?"

"Your room because that's what a four-poster bed was designed for, sweetheart."

"But, Eliza—"

"Is sleepin' in the guest bedroom."

"Oh." She swallowed hard. "What was in your other hand?"

He grinned again and held out...another length of rope.

"Hey! That's cheating."

"I already warned you I wasn't gonna play fair. Get upstairs. The nekkid rule is now in effect."

Her bare feet shuffled on the rug.

"Or would you rather I trussed you up, tossed you over my

shoulder and we played out my pirate and the wench fantasy?"

Skylar's mind created the image of Kade in a billowy white shirt, his gleaming chest muscles rippling like the sea. Knee-high glossy black boots gave way to tight breeches, which accentuated the size of his big...sword. His visage was topped off with a silky black eye patch and a shark-like smile.

He said, "That's a fine choice, me hearty lass," and started toward her.

"I'm going. But I don't mind telling you I'm a little nervous."

"You should be, darlin', 'cause I am a force to be reckoned with when it comes to ropes." To prove it, he snapped one rope low to the floor, and a crack reverberated through the air, loud as a gunshot.

Skylar took off like a bullet.

Kade waited a full five minutes before he followed her, as he let the scenarios run in his head.

Nothing painful. Nothing degrading. Nothing but her at his mercy.

A dark thrill zipped through him, potent as whiskey.

The bedroom door was ajar. Lamplight spilled across the carpet into the hallway. No candles. He'd been half-afraid candles would cast the room with a dungeon-like vibe and he didn't want her to be scared. Kade wanted Skylar turned on beyond compare.

She sat in the middle of the bed, knees drawn up to her chest, eyeing the ropes attached to the wooden posts, not with curiosity, or fear, but with resignation.

Before Kade spoke, or touched her, Skylar blurted, "You aren't going to whip me are you?"

"Not unless you aren't cooperatin'."

"Kade!"

He chuckled and placed his hands on her tense shoulders. "No whippin's, sweetheart, I promise. I'd never hurt you. Lay back." When she didn't obey right away, he nudged her.

Kade stretched her arms in a "Y", taking the opportunity to feel that soft, warm flesh beneath his callused hands. He tied her left wrist first, then her right and moved down to tie each of her ankles. He sat back and admired Skylar spread-eagled before him.

"Don't strain against the ropes or you'll get a nasty rope burn."

"Easy to say, not so easy to do when you're touching me like that."

"I haven't even started touchin' you."

He crawled up her body. Bracing himself on all fours above her, Kade kissed her. And kissed her. And kept kissing her until she relaxed into the mattress.

He pushed up on his knees and whipped off his shirt. As he returned to softly brush his lips over her cheeks and eyes and forehead and temple, he allowed her nipples fleeting contact with the hair on his chest.

Skylar moaned softly. "I like that."

"I know." He kept the same amount of friction on her breasts as his mouth journeyed down her throat. Scraping his teeth over the graceful arch. "Have I ever told you how much I love your neck? But especially this spot right here." Kade traced his tongue up her collarbone. "You usually push me away. Drives you so crazy that you can't stand it. Hard to push me away when you don't have use of your hands, ain't it?"

"Yes."

"Could you come like this? If I suck—" he let his breath drift above the area, "—right here?" Kade lightly flickered his tongue on the magic spot, sank his teeth into that tempting flesh and sucked hard until she bucked into him.

"Oh God."

Kade smiled against her throat, continuing to use his breath and lips and tongue and teeth. The only places he touched her were the tips of her nipples rubbing on his chest and his mouth on her neck. He'd tease her and retreat until a fine sheen of sweat coated her skin and he could smell that sweet, sweet cream gathered between her trembling thighs.

He hopped off the bed.

Skylar lifted her head. "Where are you going?"

"When you're nekkid and at my mercy? No place." Kade stripped off his remaining clothes. He reached for the spare ropes and brought them back on the bed.

"What are those for?"

"You'll see." He took the thickest one, a tan rope about two inches in diameter, made of coarsely twisted twine and snapped it between his hands. "Close your eyes."

"But—"

"Nothin' to be scared of, I promise."

The moment her eyes were shut, Kade dragged the rope over her naked body. Starting with the underside of her arms. Winding it around her tits. Across her belly. Between her hips. Knowing by the way her spine arched she enjoyed the contrasting tactile sensations of the bristly rope sliding against her soft skin. He didn't rush. The weight and texture of the rope left light pink stripes from her neck to her knees.

Kade swirled the softly frayed end over her clit.

"That tickles."

"I must not be doin' it right then." He flicked faster. "Better?"

"Uh-huh." He kept up the movement until her thighs became rigid and she cried out, "Oh God, oh, don't stop."

He pinched her left nipple as she started to come, and she bucked her hips up, begging for more than the feather-light touch of the rope—his fingers, his mouth, his cock. He watched her self-consciousness disappear as she lost herself in her body's response.

Finally she opened her eyes. "Wow. You *are* good with ropes."

"You ain't seen nothin' yet, baby." He tossed the thick rope to the floor and picked up the lighter, white cotton one.

"Kade. What—"

"Relax." He crawled off the end of the bed and stood between her spread-eagled legs. He slithered the thinner, softer rope down the tops of her thighs, from the crease of her hip to her kneecap. Up and down. Back and forth. When he journeyed further south and touched her toes, she jerked hard. He murmured, "Are your feet ticklish?"

"Ah. Yes."

Kade threaded the rope through each one of her toes. Then

he gently pulled the rope as his mouth connected with the vulnerable skin on her foot just inside her ankle. He tongued and suckled, while swirling the rope through her outstretched toes.

Her leg shook and her chest rose and fell rapidly.

Good thing Sky was tied up, otherwise she'd be kicking him in the face. He said, "Time for the other foot."

"Stop. I-I can't take it."

Kade ignored her. This time after winding the rope through her toes, he nibbled the top of her foot as he tugged, lightly licking the tips of her cute little piggies. He watched as gooseflesh rippled up her calves. When his gaze reached above her knee, he noticed the inside of her thighs were wet and slick with her juices.

He abandoned the rope with a growl. He flattened himself between her legs, slapped his palms on the inside of her thighs and set his mouth on her. Feasting on her moist, soft folds. Inserting one finger into her pussy, then two, then three. Feeling her cunt muscles pulse around his fingers as they plunged deep. Losing himself in the taste of her against his lips and tongue, her essence flowing down the back of his throat. Her scent settling on his skin, filling his lungs. His head, his heart, and his soul rejoiced with her pleading cries and sexy moans as Sky repeated, "please Kade" over and over. Kade hummed as he sucked her clit and she came in a gush of sweet, sticky warmth.

When she quit thrashing and throbbing, she lifted her flushed face to look at him, still lying between her legs. Kade licked his lips and said, "Mmm. I love doin' that to you. I love that you're tied up and I can do anything I want. I love..."

You. Baby, I love you so damn much it's killin' me to keep it inside. I wanna tell you. I wanna whisper it in your ear while I'm lovin' you. I wanna shout it to the world.

"Kade? You okay?"

"Yeah. Why?"

"You never finished the sentence. You love, what?"

Kade stared at the two spots of color the last orgasm had left on her cheekbones. Was that hope shining in her eyes? Or fear? Rather than chance ruining the moment, he grinned cagily. "I love that you're gonna return the favor right now, darlin'."

He shimmied up her body, placing his knees on either side of her ribs. "I've got a hankerin' to do a little sixty-nine action with you, but it'd be a mite difficult without usin' your hands." He ran his knuckles down the smooth skin of her face. "Ever had a tongue in your pussy while you were suckin' on a cock?"

She shook her head.

"Ever had your tits fucked?"

Again, she shook her head.

"These are perfect. Watch." Kade cupped her breasts in his hands and clasped them together tightly. "Arch up, baby, yeah, just like that." He slid his dick in the valley of her cleavage and grunted. "That's good." While strumming her nipples, he rocked his hips, slowly sliding in, dragging the sensitive underside of his cock over the hard bone at the base of her throat, then pulling back and surrounding his rock-hard shaft with soft, warm tightness. It was sexy as hell seeing the dark purple head of his cock vanishing into the creamy white flesh and peeping out the other side.

His eyes met hers. "Do you like this?"

"It's okay. I don't think I'd like you coming on my face."

"Oh, I'm not gonna come on you. I'm gonna come *in* you." He shifted back. "I want your mouth on me now."

Nodding, Skylar licked her lips.

"Tastin' you has got me so turned on. With as close as I am to blowin', this is gonna be a little rougher than last time." He reached for the headboard with one hand and held his cock in the other as he angled his pelvis over her face. "Open up."

She flicked her sassy tongue across the slit bubbling over with pre-come.

The tip of his cock passed over her teeth and her lips closed around the head. Instantly, the wet heat made his whole body shake. "That's it. Don't arch your neck. Take me in. All of it."

A devilish gleam entered her eyes and she hummed around his knob. It sent an electric charge straight to his balls.

"Jesus, Sky, you tryin' to make me shoot first thing?"

Her head bobbed, warmth enveloped his dick, followed by a

cool rush of air as she released him. Time and time again. Her mouth moved up and down the length in a continuous slide of heat and wetness.

Kade's thighs were clenched tight as he pumped his hips into her face. He loved to watch his cock tunneling in and out of her mouth. Loved to see the flush on her cheeks. Loved the feminine look of power and surrender in her eyes.

When she began to suck hard, hollowing her cheeks, well, Kade went a little crazy. He pushed a bit deeper, thrust faster at the visual of her lips stretched around his girth.

"Skylar." Careening over the edge of insanity, he plunged in and gripped her head, keeping it still as his cock emptied down the back of her throat. He groaned at the sensation of those strong throat muscles working as she swallowed until he had nothing left.

He slipped his cock from her mouth, and rested his head on her belly, catching his breath.

Her voice was just above a whisper. "I wish I could touch you. Kade, untie me. Please."

"No." Kade scattered kisses over her stomach, surprised his dick was raring to go again. "I'm gonna fuck you like this. Putting my hands, my mouth, my tongue and my cock anywhere I want to."

Skylar was unnaturally quiet.

He glanced up at her. "What? No secrets between us, remember?"

"Fine. Where all do you plan on sticking that big cock of yours?"

He grinned. "You've liked where I've put it so far." Kade curled his hands around her hips, and slid them to her spine and down to cup her butt cheeks. "You know how much I love this ass. Touchin' it, squeezin' it. Kissin' it. Does it make you excited to think about me slidin' my cock in your ass?"

No answer.

"There's something wickedly dirty and raunchy about doin' that. I'd be the first man to have that part of you, wouldn't I?"

Skylar nodded.

Kade moved so they were face to face. "Then I want it. I'm

gonna take it, Sky, and you're gonna love every fuckin' minute of givin' it to me. Not tonight. But soon. Very soon." His lips grazed her cheek. "For now, I need you again." Bracing his hands by her head, he slipped inside her in a single smooth thrust.

"Oh. Yes."

He fucked her hard and fast. Followed by slow and easy. Kissing her throat, her lips, tasting himself on her tongue. He built her higher and higher, holding back his darker needs to meet hers. When she came, the sweet aftershocks pulled him under, swamping him with such a mix of emotion he could scarcely keep in check.

While Kade's body still pulsed with pleasure, he whispered, "Skylar. Marry me."

She nipped his earlobe hard and said, "No."

"Maybe I oughta keep you tied up until you say yes."

"That wouldn't be fair."

"Why not?"

"Because I can't think straight when I can't feel my arms or my legs."

"That's because all your focus is on how great I make your pussy feel, which ain't so bad, near as I can figure."

"Cocky man."

"You know it." He lifted up and was surprised to see worry in her eyes. "I didn't hurt you, did I?"

"No."

"Then what?"

"You make me feel things I never thought I would, Kade. Things that are way scarier than being tied up and tied down and subjected to your every sexual whim."

Kade knew that confession wasn't easy for her to make. Rather than say the wrong thing, he said nothing as he gently untied her arms. He winced at seeing the red rope marks and feathered kisses over her wrists. He did the same thing for her ankles.

As he kissed her and she melted into him, he realized he'd been going about asking Sky to marry him in the wrong way. Of course she'd keep saying no, when she was naked and sweaty and on the downhill slide from an orgasm. That's not exactly the special moment they could share with their grandkids anyway. So Kade would wait and ask her again after he'd created a romantic scene, something she'd never forget.

Chapter Nineteen

When Sky parked in the driveway after work the next day, she was surprised to see Kade sprawled on the wicker chaise on the front porch, with his working hat pulled over his eyes. He didn't budge when she started up the steps with Eliza in her arms. "Kade? You okay?"

He groaned. "Tired. You wore me out last night, sweetheart."

Her entire body flashed with pure heat in remembrance of their bedroom antics. Kade tying her up and demanding her total submission. Him gorging on her until she whimpered and begged. Bringing her beyond the point of rational thought where nothing existed but his single-minded concentration on her sexual pleasure.

And what mind-blowing pleasure it'd been.

Even after he'd untied her and they'd seen to Eliza's needs, he'd been so sweet and so...loving. Cocooning his big, warm frame around hers as they fell asleep. A few hours later he'd woken to have his wicked way with her again. As they lay spooned together, he'd brought her top leg back over his hip as he entered her from behind. Kade's hand clasped hers, stretching their arms so they could grasp the headboard for stability as he steadily fucked her. His free hand roved, plucking her nipples, stroking her clit, while he licked and kissed the side of her neck. It still brought a delicious tingle when she recalled the masculine growls he'd uttered against her skin as he'd climaxed.

"Gaa!"

Kade removed his hat and his eyes flipped open. "Is that

Eliza speak for get up?"

Her arms flailed uncontrollably.

He grinned. "Come give Daddy some sugar."

Skylar passed Eliza over and Kade lifted her to blow a raspberry on her little round belly.

The baby squealed with delight. He murmured something to her that set her legs in motion.

"You are a really great father, Kade."

Without taking his eyes from Eliza's face, he said to Skylar, "Are you surprised?"

"No. Last year when we were dating you mentioned how jealous you were of all your cousins who were having babies."

"I did?"

"Numerous times. I thought you were feeding me full of bull since I'd never met a man who admitted he cared about that kind of stuff."

"Huh. I remember hintin' around that I was ready to settle down and have a family of my own. But you never took the hint. Then or now."

Her stomach flip-flopped.

Kade sat up. "Sorry. I'm a little punchy and too tired to rustle up anything to eat. How about if I take my best girls out for supper?"

"Really?"

"Yep, my treat. Steak and a cold beer sounds mighty tasty."

"Deal."

"You mind drivin'? I've been in my truck enough today and I'm really beat."

He hadn't reminded her of the long haul he drove every day to make her feel bad, but she did nonetheless. "I worry about you making that drive."

"You shouldn't."

"I do. Promise me you'll be careful. Promise me if you're too tired to drive by yourself you'll call me to come and get you."

"I promise." Kade stood and curled his hand around the back of Sky's head and kissed her. "I'm not complainin'. It's just the road home to you seems to get longer every damn day."

The road home to you. Right then, her day, her world felt complete. "Come on, cowboy. If you play your cards right, I might even bring home a slice of chocolate cake so I can fulfill your frosting fantasy."

Eliza slept on the way into Moorcroft, allowing them to share their respective days. Unfortunately, Eliza's nap meant she was wide awake in the restaurant. Wide awake and extremely fussy. They passed her back and forth, but nothing soothed their cranky daughter. Sky ate quickly while Kade bounced and cajoled Eliza. Then Skylar held the baby while Kade wolfed down his steak. The second Eliza let loose a shriek of distress, they exited the restaurant to the dirty looks of patrons who'd left their children at home so they could enjoy a quiet dinner out.

"Guess a candlelight dinner for three ain't her cup of tea," Kade said dryly.

The drive home wasn't any better. Eliza screamed in her car seat. She screamed in the house. She quieted down long enough to drink a bottle, but she threw most of it up on Kade. She was red faced and mad during her bath. Her legs were kicking, her back arching as Kade put clean clothes on her.

During the two hours of nonstop crying, Kade didn't try to pass the unhappy infant to Skylar. And it wasn't due to his male stubbornness, but Kade's desire to figure out for himself how to deal with Eliza when she wasn't all sweet smiles and cute baby coos. Which only made Sky more crazy about him because the man never gave up, never took the easy way out, even when he was exhausted.

After Eliza finally crashed, Kade flopped on the couch next to Skylar and groaned. "I'm whupped."

"I imagine. What time did you leave to go to the ranch this morning?"

"Four-thirty. I was already up after we...you know."

Sky smiled. Kade? Shy? After everything they'd done together? "After we did the wild thing?"

"For the *fourth* time, woman. I think I deserve to go to bed early tonight."

"Poor baby." Skylar grabbed his hand and kissed his knuckles. "Come outside and sit on the swing with me. The

195

moon is beautiful."

He cracked an eye open. "Just moon gazin'? No hanky-panky? You'll be a perfect gentlewoman?"

"If that's what you want."

They strolled onto the porch, hand in hand, and stared at the big, fat moon, a golden orb that rolled across the midnight blue sky. A gentle breeze stirred the persistent scent of sage as they set the swing in motion.

Kade exhaled on a sigh. "One good thing about you not havin' cattle around here yet. No barnyard scent."

"True." She paused. "*Yet?* You planning on bringing barnyard animals home, McKay?"

"Sure. I promised Eliza a pony. I think I promised to buy her a Corvette when she turned sixteen to get her to stop bawlin' tonight."

"Sucker."

"Well, it didn't work, so I don't think it counts. Anyway, I thought I'd talk to Cord about gettin' us a coupla horses so we can go ridin' when the mood strikes us. And that chicken coop is in good shape if you wanna try your hand at raisin' chickens. Ma has some great setters. She'd be happy to getcha started."

"Is this where you make a crack like 'horse feathers' to the city slicker when I say yes to ponies and hens?"

Kade snickered.

The swing creaked as they rocked. Night sounds surrounded them in a soothing outdoor lullaby.

He asked, "Can you smell that sweet scent?"

"Mmm-hmm."

"What kind of flower is that?"

She inhaled. "Which one? The faint floral of the petunias? The pungent pepper of the marigolds? The sugary sweetness of the sweet peas? Or the heavy perfume of the clematis?"

"You can tell the difference between all of them? That's amazin'."

"Not really. It's what I do. I'll bet if we drove by a field of cattle you could tell me which variety every one was and whose brand they wore."

"Probably. But I can tell you, with how the air feels and with the wind pickin' up, it's gonna be rainin' before too much longer."

"Then I'd probably better do this before we get soaked." Skylar gathered her skirt up and swung a leg over his lap, straddling him, pressing her chest against his and her lips on his surprised mouth.

Didn't take Kade long to get with the program. Didn't take him long to try to wrest control, either. He patted her ass in a signal to lift up. He yanked down his sweat bottoms and all that smooth male hardness rested against his belly.

She wiggled closer, proving she wasn't wearing panties.

"I like this naughty side of you. Maybe I oughta institute a no panties rule, like the nekkid rule."

"I'm game. Especially since I know how much you like the skirts I wear. Every time you see me you'll wonder if I'm going commando."

She swallowed his answering groan as his hands cupped her face. Rubbing his length against her cleft made her wet enough to push him inside.

"Jesus. That's always so good."

Sky sank her teeth into his bottom lip and tugged. "See? You aren't too tired. I'll do all the work. You just have to keep the swing in motion."

"I thought you said no hanky-panky?"

"*You* said no hanky-panky. I agreed to be a gentlewoman. And I'll be very, very gentle, I promise."

She kissed the strong line of his jaw up to his ear. "Let me rock your world, Kade, like you rock mine."

And amidst the creaking of the swing and the approaching storm she did just that.

Chapter Twenty

It poured all day. Coming to work on a rainy Tuesday depressed everyone in her employ.

But it was impossible to be depressed when Skylar relived Kade's glorious rainy morning wake-up call. Long, thorough kisses. His rough-skinned hands bestowing sweeping caresses over her bare skin.

Their naked bodies rolled and twisted in an unhurried lover's dance. Kade worshipped her breasts with his fingers, teeth and lips. Squeezing, suckling, nipping, dragging his morning beard across the hardened tips of her nipples. Circling open-mouthed kisses over every swell and curve until she damn near came just from the erotic heat of his mouth.

But he wasn't close to done.

Nothing was as lovely as the dreamy feeling of his tongue lazily penetrating her pussy in the hazy gray predawn. His silky hair teasing the inside of her thighs as he licked and lapped at the thick cream pouring from her sex. His fingers digging into her ass cheeks as he brought her to a gasping orgasm two times, before gently turning her over on the cotton sheets.

A cool breeze floated in the window, heavy with the dark scent of moist soil drenched in rain. The humid air settled on Skylar's heated skin, as soft and welcome as Kade's kisses.

Kade stretched her arms above her head and hiked her hips up, trailing his wet tongue down her spine a vertebra at a time. That naughty, wicked tongue kept right on going, between her cheeks, across her tailbone, down to the puckered rosette. The tip of his tongue teased the nerve-rich tissues, drawing tighter circles, wetter circles, probing her ass completely. He'd chuckled at her moan of approval.

Then Kade widened her stance and rose to his knees behind her, adjusting her pelvis higher, to his height and to his liking.

No hard, fast thrust. His entry was slow and sweet. Once his cock was fully seated, he began to stroke, a long withdrawal, a quick snap of his hips and he pushed that thick, hard cock in deep again.

She'd rested the left side of her head toward the window. A soft draft stirred the scents of rain, damp sheets, and Kade's sweaty masculine tang into an intoxicating aroma that left her mindless. Breathless.

His hands moved from gripping her hips to gripping her ass. He separated her cheeks, baring that tight little hole and whispered, "Watch me."

Skylar looked over her shoulder as he sucked his middle finger into his mouth, hollowing his cheeks. He slowly pulled it out, showing her it was good and wet. Then he placed it against her puckered flesh and slipped it in her ass.

"Oh."

Kade never missed a stroke as fucked her with his finger and his cock. Pleasure beat at her from all angles. When a second finger joined the first and he began ramming into her both places, she sank her teeth into her upper arm to keep from crying out as another climax erupted as fast and furious as a windstorm.

The sounds of skin slapping skin stopped abruptly as Kade stiffened. Liquid male heat coated her spasming interior walls in strong bursts, and his low grunt of male satisfaction made everything inside her preen. After he was spent, he layered his chest over her back and nuzzled the back of her head. "Good mornin', sweetheart."

"Skylar. Did you hear me?"

She blinked at Annie glaring at her in the doorway. Crap. "No. Thinking about something else. Sorry. What's up?"

"Phone. Line two."

"Thanks." She picked up the receiver and hit the flashing button. "This is Skylar Ellison."

"Where the fuck is my wife?"

"Excuse me?"

"Don't play stupid. Where's my wife? And my kid?"

"Who is this?"

"You know goddamn good and well who it is. Now lemme talk to that bitch Nadia right fuckin' now."

"I'm sorry, sir, but Nadia isn't here."

"The fuck she ain't. She ain't been home in three damn days. The only places she ever goes is work and home and she sure as shit ain't here."

She forced herself to stay calm. "I suggest if you think your wife is missing, you contact the sheriff's department and file a missing person's report." Skylar hung up.

Jesus. That man was a piece of work.

Nadia's words, *they're all just like him*, rang in her head.

Wrong. Kade wasn't like that. Not at all. He'd never shown a single sign of violent behavior.

She looked around her office and groaned. She'd fallen behind since Eliza's birth in keeping up with the piles of paper clutter. A dozen cardboard boxes were stacked against the wall. Suppliers' catalogues, trade magazines, junk mail, all stuff she needed to go through before she tossed it in the shredder.

Wasn't she the boss? Couldn't she make someone else do the drudgework for a change? Congratulating herself on her sneaky cleverness, Sky dialed Annie's extension and said sweetly, "Could I see you for a minute?"

Annie swung open the door, propped herself against the doorjamb. "I know that look, boss. No way. You've been puttin' off cleanin' this office for two months. I ain't doin' it for you."

"Dammit. How did you know? Please? I'll pay you extra."

"Huh-uh, not worth it. Besides, I already went through all this junk once and sloughed it off to you because I didn't know what the hell to do with it."

"That sucks."

"Buck up, little camper. This is why you get paid the big bucks. Don't forget, tomorrow is your day in the kiddie ward and you ain't passin' that off on me, neither."

"Why did I hire you again?"

"Because I'm a snappy dresser and I can smell bullshit a mile away."

"Speaking of bullshit...the last phone call. Did you know that was Nadia's husband?"

"Yeah. Caller ID. Third time he's called today, but he finally asked for you." Her eyes glittered. "Mean motherfucker needs to die. I offered to help Nadia pull a 'Good-bye Earl' on him, but she wouldn't go for it."

"You offered to kill the man with poisoned black-eyed peas?"

Annie grinned. "Or a poison kiss with a black powder Smith and Wesson. Whatever works."

Sky shook her head. "Forget I asked."

With a resigned sigh, Skylar plopped on the floor in front of the first box. An hour later ninety-nine percent of it was in the trash. She eyed the other eleven boxes. Maybe she ought to save herself a bunch of time and just chuck the whole works.

Nah. If she tackled one box a day, she'd be done in two weeks. Easy. Doable.

A visit to check on Eliza in daycare and she returned to work, steering clear of any more distracting wet daydreams about her favorite naked cowboy.

Kade returned home later than usual. Quieter than usual too. Looking exhausted again. He changed into an outfit similar to hers, ratty sweat shorts and a tank top since they were both out of clean clothes. He lavished attention on Eliza while Skylar caught up on mountains of laundry. They were running low on baby supplies and groceries.

She frowned. When was the last time she'd been to the store to stock up? At least a month ago. Before Kade moved in.

Had Kade ever picked up diapers and formula? She wandered into the living room and saw Eliza on a blanket on the floor and Kade lying on his side next to her.

He said, "I think she's gonna roll over soon."

"She's too young."

"Not accordin' to Brazelton. Lookit how fast she's kickin' them legs. Any time now she's gonna be rockin' and rollin', ain't you, baby girl?"

Eliza grinned and made a goo noise.

That girl was shameless when it came to charming her daddy.

"You know, I think she's teethin', that's why she's been so cranky."

"Could be."

"Isn't she supposed to be gettin' another round of shots at four months?"

"Yeah. I haven't made the appointment yet."

"Huh. Well, we don't want her fallin' behind schedule. Be best if it was taken care of right away."

Skylar crossed her arms over her chest. "Why don't *you* take care of it? Eliza sees Dr. Monroe. She's in Moorcroft. Set it up in one of the convenient Monday through Friday, nine-to-five timeslots, wait with other sick kids for two hours for an appointment that lasts ten minutes. This time *you* can hold her when she screams as they poke needles in her legs, since I know how much you love needles. And *you* can walk the floor with her for two days afterward because the shots always make her sick and cranky."

"Hey, now. Don't get defensive. I was just sayin'—"

"I know exactly what you were saying, Kade. You want to be involved with every little thing? Here's your chance. And while you're at it, why don't you pick up diapers and formula because we're almost out. And we're running low on food and laundry soap and cleaning supplies and everything else it takes to run this household." She spun on her heel and stomped to the laundry room.

Thwack. She threw the sopping wet clothes in the dryer. Stupid spin cycle wasn't working. Might as well wring the damn clothes out by hand or it'd take forever for the load to dry. She couldn't hang them outside since it was still raining.

By the time she'd squeezed out the excess water in the laundry tub, hung up the drip-dry items, started another load and swept up the last of the powdered detergent she'd spilled all over the floor in her fit of anger, Skylar had calmed down some. And realized she'd been a total jerk to Kade. The man always did everything she'd asked, a lot of times he did things before she even thought of them. He was nothing but sweet and cheerful, helpful and kind to her and to Eliza, and she'd snapped at him like a fishwife.

Wife.

Dammit, that wasn't a word she should use to describe herself or her relationship with Kade. She was not Kade McKay's wife.

And doesn't it bother you just a little? He hasn't asked you to marry him after he'd made love to you? Not since the night he tied you up.

No. That was not it. Unhappy if he asked her; unhappy if he didn't ask her. She was not that psycho and controlling.

Was she?

Yes, it appeared she was.

Argh.

Sky sucked it up and went to apologize to him. She found the living room empty. She dashed upstairs. No Kade. No Eliza.

Oh hell no. He hadn't gotten pissed off and taken off with their baby, had he?

Can you blame him if he did? Haven't you been afraid all along he'd take her or sue for joint custody?

She flung open the front door. Sure enough, his truck was gone. Sky unearthed her phone and dialed his cell number, a number she'd programmed in, but never called.

Didn't that just speak volumes about how much she wanted to prove she didn't need him?

Argh.

"Hello?"

"Kade? Where are you?"

"I'm in my truck."

"Is Eliza with you?"

"Yes, she's with me. Why?"

"What are you doing?"

"Goin' to the store." Pause. "Isn't that what you were anglin' for when you threw that hissy fit, not more than a half hour ago?"

Shit. Shame heated her cheeks. "It wasn't a hissy fit."

He laughed softly. "Yeah, sweetheart, it was."

She managed a smile. "Fine, it was. But I didn't expect you to drop everything and go right then."

"Well, I wasn't doin' nothin' else and it needed to be done, or else you wouldn't have made such a big deal about it, right?"

The man was so damn even-keeled. Why wasn't he barking at her for being such a bitch to him? Demanding an apology?

"Skylar?"

"Yes, it needed to be done. I'm sorry I snapped at you. Thank you for taking care of it."

"See? That wasn't so hard. And you're welcome."

"I'm just not used to help of any kind, especially not immediate help."

"That's another thing that's gonna change. Look, I wanna help out, but I need direction. I'm a longtime bachelor, darlin'. I'd live on chili and ramen noodles and wash clothes only when I was completely out of 'em if I was in charge."

"Good thing you have me, huh?"

"Very good thing, but you're foolin' yourself if you think the only reasons I'm with you is because you can cook and do laundry."

Are you with me only because of Eliza?

"Besides, sweet thang told me she had a hankerin' to ride in the truck."

She laughed. "She did?"

"Yep. She loves Gretchen Wilson. She already knows all the words to 'Redneck Woman'."

Sky pressed her forehead to the rain-slick wooden pillar on the porch. She resisted asking him if he'd grabbed the diaper bag. Or if he'd bundled Eliza up since the night air was damp. Or if he knew what kind of formula and diapers to buy. She really resisted asking him why he hadn't asked her to come along.

Because the sobering truth was, Kade didn't need her to come along. He could handle anything when it came to Eliza, with or without her.

Why didn't that thought make her happy?

Because she wanted him to need her, the way she was beginning to need him.

"Sky, we're at the store. We'll see you in a bit."

She clicked the phone shut and stayed on the porch, absorbing the warm rain, feeling bewildered, and a little bereft.

Chapter Twenty-one

Lights bobbed up the driveway. Kade's truck rolled to a stop. The door opened and a baby wailed. Skylar dashed down the porch steps before Kade had Eliza out of the car seat.

"What's wrong?"

"She's mad at me for some reason. She screamed all the way home. Again."

"I'm sure it's not you personally, Kade." Sky unbuckled Eliza, picked her up, and right away Eliza snuggled into her and quit crying.

Kade froze. "What did you do to get her to stop?"

"Nothing magical. Must be luck." She draped the blanket over Eliza to keep the rain off. Inside, while she waited for the bottle to warm, she changed Eliza's diaper and put her in her fuzzy pajamas.

After sucking down the bottle, Eliza fell asleep as if she'd been drugged, rosebud mouth slack, dark head thrown back. Sky settled her in her crib and returned to the kitchen.

Kade was drinking a beer, gazing out the back door. She saw six canisters of formula, three bags of diapers, a gallon of milk, a bag of apples, a six-pack of beer and a chocolate cake.

Hmm. She hadn't given him a list, but still, slim pickin's. "Kade? You okay?"

"No. I never knew how damn hard it was to shop with a baby. Like a dumbass I took her out of her car seat, thinkin' the car seat would take up too much room in the cart. So I'm holdin' her, tryin' to steer the cart with one hand. I made it to the baby aisle and loaded up her stuff. By the time I reached the bakery, she was screamin'. She screamed in the dairy aisle. She screamed in the produce section. All these people were starin' at me like I was the worst parent ever—or glarin' at her like she was one of them bratty kids you hear all over the store. I grabbed beer and booked it to the check-out."

He drained the bottle and set it on the counter. "And Eliza was the damn Energizer Bunny—she just kept on a goin'. The checker couldn't wait to get rid of us. I loaded the pitiful amount of groceries in the cart and realized I couldn't push it, hold her, and unlock the truck door, even if it hadn't been rainin'. I had to ask the carryout boy to help me. With five lousy bags."

Skylar circled her arms around his waist, pressing her face into the middle of his back, hoping she was giving him half the effortless comfort he always offered her. "Shopping is hard. I usually leave Eliza with India when I go to the store to stock up."

"Wish I'da known that. No, I'm glad I learned firsthand how hard it is just to do simple things when you're cartin' around a baby." Kade turned into her embrace and tilted her face up. "I'm sorry I wasn't around, Sky. For everything. For your pregnancy and her birth, but mostly because you've had to do all this stuff yourself and it ain't fair."

"Stop beating yourself up. Let's move forward, not back."

"Okay. Does that mean—"

A blinding reflection of headlights flashed in the window behind Kade. Skylar looked over her shoulder. A car had pulled up by the outside fencepost and cut the lights. "What the hell?"

"What?"

"Who is dropping by at ten at night? Were you expecting anyone?"

"No."

"I don't like this. Not at all." She scurried out of the house and made it halfway up the gravel driveway, when the rear car door opened. The *chink chink chink* of glass bottles hitting rocks echoed back to her.

"Hey! What are you doing?" She began to run. "This is private property!"

The car was thrown into reverse, narrowly missing the

fence. The engine gunned, muddy water and gravel sprayed her from head to bare toes as the vehicle fishtailed down the driveway and out of sight.

"Goddammit!"

A large hand landed on her shoulder and spun her around. "What the hell do you think you're doing?"

"Didn't you see that car? They were dumping garbage and who knows what else."

"And you ran out here to confront them?"

"They were trespassing. What if they'd tried to break into the plant? Or tried to dump something toxic that'll cost me thousands of dollars in clean-up costs?"

"Jesus Christ, Skylar, what if they would've pulled a gun out and shot you?"

She went utterly still.

"Bustin' a couple of underage kids for drinkin' ain't worth your time and sure as hell ain't worth your life."

"I-I—"

"Don't you ever do anything like that again, do you hear me?"

Feeling like an idiot, Skylar twisted out of his grip and raced back to the house. She'd reached the tiny strip of grass in front of the porch, when again, she was jerked around. This time Kade hauled her to her toes. "Let me go."

"Not until you answer me. Don't you ever take chances like that, do you understand?" He shook her a little. "Do you have any idea what the thought of anything happenin' to you does to me?"

She whispered, "No."

"It rips me clean apart."

"Kade."

"Don't. Just don't." He dragged her into his arms and squeezed her so tightly she couldn't breathe. He kissed the top of her head as he muttered in her wet hair. His mouth grazed her forehead. Her temple. Her cheek. But when he reached her lips, his mouth didn't graze; it devoured.

Sky kissed him back as ferociously. With need. Frustration.

Every negative emotion fed their passion. Fueled their urgency.

Kade released her. He yanked her tank top over her head. Dragged her shorts down her legs. Tore off his own clothes.

"Just like this. Dirty, angry and wet." He didn't wait for her response. They half-fell to the soggy ground with a splash.

In the downpour of the cool rain, Sky swore she could see steam coming off their heated bodies. Kade pinned her hands above her head. She was lost to any kind of reality beyond his solid weight pressing into her. She shrieked when his mouth latched onto her nipple and sucked it with enough force it hit the back of his throat.

Skylar said, "Please, please, please," and hooked her ankles in the small of his back, pumping her hips to urge him higher.

The slick head of his cock slipped over her clit and then all that thick rigid maleness surged inside her.

A gasping sob burst from her lungs.

Kade put his mouth on her ear. "I wanna hear you."

Sky knew neither of them would last long, it was too intense. The need too sharp. She craved that orgasmic rush, she burned for it. She arched and bucked and thrashed against his thrusting body demanding, "More. Kade, please."

His cock jackhammered into her. Hard. Fast. Deep. Water sloshed around them. He growled, "Let me hear you. Scream for me."

That did it. The tight coil unraveled. She screamed until every throbbing pulse slowed to nothing more than a dull throb. She blinked away the rainwater and opened her eyes, to see Kade staring at her.

"God. Skylar. I-I—" His whole body convulsed as he came with a roar. Afterward, he buried his face in her neck even when he still shook.

The rain fell steadily. It was startlingly peaceful, in the aftermath of such an emotional storm, hearing the water droplets pinging on the metal downspouts. Smelling the parched earth beneath them soaking in every drop of moisture. Feeling Kade's rough fingers braceleting her wrists. Feeling him hot and hard inside her. Listening to their labored breathing returning to a normal cadence.

Yes, there was a certain contentment accepting that not only had she given this man control of her body, he'd taken control of her heart.

Kade had fucked Skylar like an absolute animal, in a mud puddle, on the front lawn.

And she didn't seem to mind.

A primal sense of satisfaction howled inside him and he couldn't wait to take her again. Mark her as his.

He released her wrists and lifted his upper body to look down at her.

She brushed the wet hair stuck to his forehead and palmed his cheek, allowing the pad of her thumb to trace his lips. She didn't say a word. She didn't make any move to...well, move.

Kade opened his mouth to speak and she shook her head. Then Sky kissed him with sweetness and passion, which got him all hard and needy and desperate again.

She preferred this be a wordless encounter? Fine. What he planned to do to her would probably make her pretty damn speechless anyway.

He eased his cock out of her body and rolled to his feet. Kade helped her up, then snatched their discarded sodden clothes, leaving them on the porch. He led her up the stairs, past her bedroom and straight into the bathroom.

With the hall light on and the door cracked open, there was no need to turn on the overhead lights. She stepped in the shower and cranked the handle, giving him time to snag what he needed from his shaving kit.

Kade pulled the shower curtain back and joined her under the warm spray.

As she rinsed her hair, he lathered up a washcloth with lemon sage scented soap and began to wash her. The graceful line of her neck. Then her full breasts. Her belly. The flare of her hips. Down each leg.

Wordlessly, he urged her to turn around. Kade swept the suds across her shoulders. Over her back and spine. When he reached her pear-shaped butt that drove him insane with lust, he pressed closer to her. The water cascaded over them, sending soapy swirls to their feet and down the drain.

He pushed her hair to the side and spoke against her wet skin. "Skylar. Your ass is mine tonight. I'm gonna fuck it, right here, standin' up in the shower." His teeth tugged on her lobe and she shivered. "I'll make it so good for you you'll be screaming again. We'll go as slow as you want, but goddamn I need you like this. I need a part of you that's just mine."

Sky released a soft sigh and rubbed her face against his razor-stubbled cheek. "Will it hurt?"

"Maybe a little at first." Kade kissed the tender skin below her ear. "Are you worried?"

"Maybe."

"Don't be. I've got plenty of lube." His excitement caused his stuttered breath to drift across her damp skin. She shuddered and made that little squeaking moan that drove him insane with lust. "You liked havin' my fingers and my tongue teasin' you there."

"True." She paused. "Would you let me do the same thing to you?"

Whoa. Not the question he'd expected. "You mean, strap on a rubber cock, stick it up my ass and fuck me with it?"

"Yeah."

"Baby, if that's something you wanna try, I'm game."

"Really?"

"Really. Ain't nothin' wrong with doin' anything that brings us both pleasure." He whispered, "What happens in our bedroom or in our shower or on our front lawn ain't nobody's business but ours."

She laughed the bellish sound he loved and his heart damn near burst.

"Let me have you like this, all warm, soft and slippery wet."

When Kade dropped the bar of soap Sky looked at him with a mischievous grin. "Is this where you tell me to bend over and pick it up?"

"Smart ass." He sucked her lower lip and bit down gently before releasing it. He'd crowded her to the back of the tub. "Turn around and brace your hands on the wall."

Soon as she did, Kade placed her right foot up on the

corner ledge. He took his time smoothing his hand over the outside of her ankle, up her muscled calf and the curve of her thigh. He reached for the lube and squeezed a good amount onto his fingers. Pressing his chest to her back, he licked the water beading on her shoulder as he fingered her hole.

Skylar's body tensed as he inserted the first finger, followed quickly by the second. Kade thrust in and out, stretching her, spreading the lubrication high and wide, kissing her neck. His cock ached as her muscles automatically clamped down on the intrusion.

"Breathe. Push out. That's it." He twisted deeper, fluttering his fingers open and closed, loosening.

"Do it, I'm ready. I wanna feel all of you. Please."

Carefully, he removed his hand.

As the water beat down on the sexy arch of Sky's back, he grabbed the lube again, generously coating his shaft from root to head. Once again he was behind her. Breathing hard, anticipation thundered in his blood. Aligning the tip of his cock to that hidden entrance, he pushed just the thick head in past that rigid ring.

"Oh. Wait."

"It's okay. No rush." Right. Kade's legs shook with the need to slam into her until every inch of his dick was buried balls deep in that tight channel. He slid his hand around her hip, down to her pouting clit, slicking his fingertip through her juices. "Better?"

"Much. I love the way you touch me."

"Which is a good thing because I love touchin' you, Sky." He sank his teeth into the slope of her shoulder, flicking his finger over her sweet spot, as bit by bit he breached her resistance, sliding his cock up that hot, vise-tight channel. The scrape of those untried anal walls on every throbbing inch of his hard cock caused him to grit his teeth and keep it slow and steady.

She moaned.

"Baby, I'm in all the way. Relax. I'll let you get used to it before I move. How does it feel?"

"Full. Burns a little. But in a good way."

"Know how you feel to me?" Kade put his mouth on her ear. "It's so fuckin' hot, havin' my cock in your ass. Knowin' no other man has been here. Feelin' these muscles grippin' me."

A shiver moved through her and gooseflesh broke out across her body.

He rocked his hips. Each thrust followed by a slow retreat until just the cockhead remained inside. The words *slow slow slow* repeated in his mind.

"I need to move faster. Like now. You're so damn tight..."

"Then move faster." Skylar turned her head and licked the droplets caught on his stubble. "The water is getting cold anyway. Keep me warm, Kade. Make me burn. Don't be a gentleman, be a wild man. Show me." She placed her fingers over his on her clit and slid their joined hands into her wet, clenching sex.

He plunged harder. Over and over. Never pulling completely out, but not holding back.

Sky gasped and thrust against his invading cock as she fucked her pussy with their entwined fingers.

The constant push/pull of his shaft, and the tight ring of her anal muscles squeezing his glans on the downstroke had his balls drawing up. But it was Skylar's orgasm that sent him over the edge. He came so hard when her cunt and ass spasmed around his fingers and his dick, that he felt his cock had split in two and he was fucking her both places at once.

"Fuck. Oh fuck. That's so fuckin' good." Kade's forehead dropped onto her shoulder as another short orgasm blindsided him and shorted out his brain.

Icy needles on his spine roused him. The water was freezing and he was still buried in her ass. He angled around to kiss her as he pulled out his softened cock.

She hissed in his mouth but returned his languorous kiss.

Kade ran his hands over her wet body, gorging his senses on the tactical contrast from her soft, sweet-smelling skin to her slippery skin. He loved making love to Sky in a bed, but there was something very erotic about the heat and slickness of making love in water.

"Let me dry you off and then we'll go to bed."

"I hope you mean to sleep, because I don't know if I'm up for another round."

He smiled against her shoulder. "I mean sleep. But I ain't gonna lie. I want you in my arms. I wanna hold you until mornin'."

Sky angled her head and kissed his temple. "I'd like that."

"Me too, sweetheart. I'd like that a whole lot."

Chapter Twenty-two

Another good thing about having a baby: no need for an alarm clock. Skylar yawned, set her feet on the floor and glanced over her shoulder at Kade...who was staring at her, a sleepy, goofy smile on his rugged face.

"Mornin', beautiful."

Her insides melted. Lord. It should be illegal to look that good at the crack of dawn. "Mornin', handsome."

His grin widened. "Handsome? Why, Miz Ellison, I do believe that's the first time you've ever called me that."

"Yeah? Well, you are handsome, McKay, but don't get a swelled head."

"Too late, dependin' on which head you're talkin' about."

"Ha ha." She hopped up and lifted Eliza from her crib. Once again Skylar experienced that melting sensation, seeing her sweet baby's face. "Ooh, aren't you all charming smiles like your daddy this morning?" She kissed the top of Eliza's head and hugged her close.

"Bring her here."

"She's probably hungry."

"We both know she'd be squawlin' if she was." Kade rolled to his side and patted the mattress. "Hey, baby girl. Come see Daddy."

Eliza turned her head and grinned at him.

"She's shameless." Sky crawled on the bed and set Eliza on her back between them.

"What can I say? She loves me."

So do I.

Her body, her mind, even her blood went absolutely still. Kade didn't notice. He was smooching Eliza's cheeks, blowing raspberries on her neck, and letting her pull his hair.

Oh God. It was true. She loved Kade McKay.

Her skeptical side demanded, *since when?*

Maybe from the start when he'd fainted upon seeing Eliza. Or when he'd insisted on moving in. Or when he'd proven his love for their daughter had no boundaries. Or when he demanded Sky's complete sexual surrender to him and never abused her trust. Or when he showed with actions, not just words that he understood her, accepted her, and still liked her. Or because he was an eternal optimist, he kept asking her to marry him, even when she kept saying no.

Dammit. Except Kade hadn't asked her again last night. After making love to her in the rain. After he initiated her not only into the dark pleasure of anal sex, but showing the side of himself that was closer to an animal than to a man. Revealing a harsher, darker side she suspected he tried very hard to hide. Yet, he'd shared it with her.

"Sky? Ah. A little help here?"

Eliza had two fistfuls of Kade's hair, her arms were flailing, her feet randomly kicking him in the chin and neck. Sky peeled Eliza's fingers open and the baby made a protesting squeal. "I know you like to pull Daddy's hair, but he shouldn't let you, because we don't want you to get a bad reputation at daycare, do we?" She gave Kade an arch look. When he smiled smugly, she refocused on Eliza. "Speaking of...shall we get a start on our day, snooks? Since I have to be in early?"

"And here I was hopin' you could crawl back in bed for a bit."

She lifted her eyes to his. "Are you serious?"

"Always serious when it comes to gettin' you nekkid and between the sheets."

"No way." When he opened his mouth to institute the naked rule, Sky held up her hand. "I'll take a rain check."

"We already did it in the rain once, but I'm up for another round."

Such a satisfied male smirk. She smirked back. "You know what I meant."

"Are you sore this mornin', sweetheart?"

"A little. But it was worth it. Man, was it *ever* worth it."

His blue eyes became heavy lidded with pure lust. "I'll say. One of the hottest nights of my life. Here I was hopin' you'd play hooky and we could laze in bed. All. Damn. Day."

She blushed. "Aren't you going to the ranch?"

Kade squinted at the rain beating on the window. "I told Dad and Kane I wouldn't be over if it was rainin'. Not that I'm complainin' because we need the moisture in a bad way. No point standin' around doin' nothin' there when I could be here. You want me to hang at home with the hair-puller?"

"No. Actually, today is my turn in daycare. Even though I'm woefully behind on office work, it wouldn't be fair if I didn't pull my weight."

"How many munchkins?"

"Eight including Eliza."

"Hell, I ain't doin' nothin'. How about if I do your stint in daycare so you can get caught up."

"You're joking."

"No, I'm not." His gaze narrowed on her. "Why? You think I can't do it?"

Crap. "It can get kind of crazy."

"Crazier than takin' care of a couple dozen newborn calves in the snow and havin' them and their mommas all bawlin' at the same time?"

"No. Different."

"You don't think I can do it, do you?"

Lie lie lie. "It was sweet of you to offer, Kade—"

"Sweet, my ass." He bounced off the bed. "I'm doin' it. I'm gonna be the best damn daycare worker you've ever seen. And I'm so gonna make you eat your words at quittin' time, boss lady."

"Right."

"Wanna bet?

She snorted. "That's a sucker bet."

"Then why don't you put your money where your mouth is?" Kade leaned forward. "If I win, you do something for me. If you win, I do something for you."

"Fine. What do you want if you win?"

His wolfish grin appeared. "I want you to blow me in my truck while we're drivin' down the road."

Skylar blinked at him. "Oh. My. God. You didn't just come up with that off the cuff, did you? How long have you been planning something kinky like that, Kade McKay?"

"With you? Since the day we met. The fantasy has just gotten more specific since I know how damn good you are with that sexy mouth of yours." Kade wrapped a section of Sky's hair around his finger. "What about you? What do you want if you win?"

For you to ask me to marry you again.

Dammit. She could not, would not, sound that damn needy. Sky considered him for a second before she smiled. "I want to tie you to the bed."

"And?"

"And what is unclear about that?"

"Be specific, 'cause if it's tie me down and leave me there without playin' any naughty sex games, well, darlin', that ain't happenin'."

"There'll be sex games, cowboy, don't you worry about that."

Kade kissed her square on the mouth. "Deal. Now excuse me, I gotta get ready for work. I hear my boss lady is a real hard ass."

Sky said, "Baby girl, I think I created a monster."

"He's great with kids."

If one more person said that to her today, Skylar was going to scream.

Annie said, "Instead of doin' arts and crafts, he's teaching them to throw a rope. And at naptime, he had them drape their blankets over the desks and pretend they were camping out, Old West style. He even got Joey to fall asleep."

She growled.

"And, he promised to bring them a pony to ride next time."

Sky slapped her hands on the desk. "Annie. Why are you barging in here and telling me all this when I have work to do?"

"Because I knew it'd drive you crazy." Annie offered her a benevolent smile. "Don't you think you oughta tell Kade how you feel about him?"

"Yes. No. Hell, I don't know. I mean, I will when it's not so complicated."

"Don't seem so complicated to me, but then again, I'm just a country girl. You love him, he loves you, get a preacher and get married. Simple."

Skylar slumped back in her chair. "What makes you think he loves me?"

"He's here, on his day off, takin' care of kids that ain't his, in order to help you out? Sugar, if that ain't love, plain as day, I don't know what is." Annie left and closed the door.

A couple hours later Kade was outside dumping garbage when an old Dodge truck pulled up to the outer gate, not in the general parking area.

The bearded guy behind the wheel poked his head out the window and studied the building from top to bottom, side to side. Like he was casing the joint.

The behavior raised Kade's hackles. Still, he decided to give the guy the benefit of the doubt. The man disappeared inside the truck cab, then sat up. He tipped a bottle of booze and took several long swallows. Then he jumped out of the truck, puffed up his chest and all Kade's doubts were fully realized.

This guy was trouble.

Kade intercepted the man about thirty feet from the front entrance. "Something I can help you with, buddy?"

"I ain't your fuckin' buddy. Move."

"Whoa. Then how's about you tell me who you are?"

The man sneered. "How's about you back the fuck off, and lemme handle my business."

"See, that's where I have a problem. What goes on in that buildin' is my business so you're gonna hafta tell me yours before I let you step another foot on this property."

"My wife is in there. I wanna talk to her. Now get the hell outta my way."

"What's your wife's name?"

"None of your business."

"Again, it is my business. Tell me her name and I'll get a message to her."

"I'll give her the message myself, asshole. Move."

"No. What's your name?"

"What the fuck is it to you?"

Kade was beyond pissed. "Wrong answer. Get in your truck and go home."

The man's beady black eyes shrunk to pinpoints. "You can't keep me from my family. She took our kid and she's hidin' out in there and I got rights."

"I don't give a good goddamn about your rights. Get off this property. Now."

"Or what?"

"It involves my boot in your ass, buddy."

"Bet you'd like that you fuckin' pervert."

The steel door banged open and Skylar stormed out. "What is going on?"

"You!" The guy brushed past Kade, menace in every ounce of his posture.

Rather than take a chance this idiot might hurt Skylar, Kade jerked him to a stop by the back of his shirt.

The man twisted, leading with his fist. He clocked Kade in the jaw with enough force that Kade stumbled back. The guy came after him again, swinging and missing, then driving a punch straight to Kade's sternum.

"Fuck!" Kade launched himself at the idiot. They fell to the soggy ground and Kade landed a solid right to the man's mouth. Blood burst from the guy's lip. Kade followed through with another right, but the guy rolled and Kade's fist connected with mud. Before Kade regained his balance, the man hit him in the side of the head.

Even though he'd gotten his bell rung, Kade automatically swung low and heard the *whump* of air as he punched the guy in the stomach. A splash followed as the man fell into a puddle.

"Enough!"

When Skylar moved to stand between them, Kade jumped up and blocked her from the man's long reaching arms, even when the guy was curled up on the ground. "Stay back. You have no idea what this guy is capable of."

"I had no idea that *you* were capable of this kind of behavior."

Stung, he said, "He took the first swing."

"I don't care. Step aside. I'll handle this."

"The hell you will." Kade dropped his voice. "Get in the goddamn building, Skylar, right now."

"Last time I checked, I owned this place and you do not get to dictate to me here. So back off."

"No. I will not let you put yourself in a dangerous situation because you think you can handle it."

Skylar's eyes were as cold as he'd ever seen. "I'll handle it my way and it won't be with physical violence like you've handled it."

"There ain't any other way."

She sidestepped Kade and addressed the prone man. "Rex. Get off my property and don't come back. If I see you within fifty feet of the front door, I'm calling the sheriff."

Mud-covered Rex scrabbled to his feet and shuffled back to his pickup, amidst mutterings of lawsuits. He gunned the engine and was gone.

Kade seethed. Hadn't she learned her lesson last night about purposely putting herself in danger? How did Skylar know the idiot didn't have a gun in his truck? He could've pulled it out and started firing at her and gone after everyone in the building. He growled, glaring at her for her short-sighted decision to let the guy go.

Without turning away from Kade, she pointed to the building. "See those kids plastered to the window? Kids you spent all day caring for? They've been watching you beat the shit out of another man. Every single one of them has had to deal with domestic violence in some form. This is the one place they shouldn't have that fear. You brought that fear to them today in Technicolor."

"I didn't. *He* showed up here lookin' for a fight. I gave him one."

"You should've walked away."

"I didn't do a damn thing that was outta line. I'd do it exactly the same way if I had to do it over again."

"Is that macho cowboy bullshit supposed to impress me?"

"No, it was supposed to protect you. I was just defendin' myself, and you, and what's mine."

"I don't need you to defend me."

"You really think you would've stood a chance at keepin' that guy under wraps if he'd've come after you? Were you gonna try to reason with him?"

"Yes."

"Give me a goddamned break," Kade snapped. "That guy was pissed off, outta control and lookin' for trouble."

"No, you're out of control. You're a hundred times more trouble."

"What the fuck is that supposed to mean?"

"Just like I suspected, the little bit of control I allowed you wasn't enough. Now you want all the control in my life and take it at the first opportunity." Skylar spoke through clenched teeth. "You're not content to call the shots in the bedroom any more. You want to do the same here. Guess what? Not happening."

Kade could not believe she'd thrown that in his face. Control wasn't the issue and she damn well knew it. "Well excuse the fuck outta me."

Her eyes narrowed.

"I'll put aside your ignorant, wrong and just plain damn petty insult and give it to you straight. This is about safety, not control. And guess what? Your security measures are piss-poor, darlin'. First, that guy shouldna been able to get that close to the building. Second, he coulda waltzed right in the front door. Know how I know that? Because I've done it several times. No one stoppin' me, no security inside or out. You, or whoever is in *control* doesn't even lock the goddamn door during workin' hours."

Skylar's icy glare continued.

"This is a business. If you've hired women with a history of domestic violence issues, you oughta be more vigilant about security issues than normal, not less. Alarms on the doors and windows. A gate with a code box to keep out trespassers. You already have a damn gate, hell, you have *two* gates, why would you leave them open night and day? You've got kids in there, Sky. You've got *my* kid in there. And the way it sits, ain't nothin' stoppin' an angry ex or a pissed-off boyfriend from stormin' the joint with a gun and killin' every last person in there."

"That wouldn't happen. Not here."

"Wrong. It happens all the time and you know it. So you'd better fix your security problems pronto, because after this incident today, I ain't about to let you put my daughter in danger any more."

Skylar bristled. "What are you getting at?"

"Just what I said. Fix the problems or I'll yank Eliza out of here so fast it'll make your head spin."

"You wouldn't."

"Don't fuckin' push me on this because I'd do it in a fuckin' heartbeat. And yeah, if you wanna be technical, I'm exercisin' my parental *control* and right to remove her from a potentially dangerous situation. I'll make sure my kid don't become another tragic statistic because you have too much pride to admit you are wrong."

Footsteps splashed up next to them. "You two oughta take this inside."

"We're done," Skylar pronounced.

"Done? What the hell do you mean *done*?"

"Oh, honey, you have a gash on your jaw," Annie said to Kade. "Why don't you come in and I'll take a look at it?"

"I'm fine. Probably had worse." Kade rubbed the sore spot

and his fingers came away bloody. Sucker did hurt. "I gotta take off pretty quick anyway." He didn't bother to hide the anger in his eyes. "Think about what I said. And don't wait up for me tonight."

"Where are you going?"

He said, "Out," and walked away from her without looking back.

Out.

Damn him.

Why did he make her feel like she was in the wrong when he was the one who'd been involved in a fistfight with her employee's husband in the parking lot of her business, in front of her employees? And then he had the balls to tell her how she'd been putting everyone—including their child—in danger?

He'd threatened to take Eliza away, just like she'd feared.

Why had she believed Kade would be different from any other man who'd been in her life? Charm her and then take what they wanted and leave her broken.

Kade isn't like that.

Yes, he is.

Chase him down and hash it out.

No, let him cool off first.

Talk about a split personality.

"Sky, you should go back in. It's five o'clock."

"Did everyone see what happened?"

"Pretty much. Dee shooed the kids away, but Nadia watched the whole thing."

"How is she?"

"Mad. Scared. Embarrassed."

"I'll talk to her and try to calm her down before she leaves."

As she trudged inside, Skylar wondered who was going to calm her down.

Chapter Twenty-three

"What the hell happened to you?"

"I don't wanna talk about it." Kade signaled the waitress and held up Cord's bottle of Budweiser.

"Where's Buck?" Cam asked with a snicker. "I gotta admit, it's funny as shit he's changed his name after all these years."

"He's sick as a dog. I wasn't at the ranch today and he didn't answer his cell, so I called Ma and she said he's got a bad cold, chills, fever, the whole works. Been in bed since yesterday."

"That sucks. But I'm glad he stayed away. I don't need to drag that shit back to Iraq with me."

Chet said, "When you leavin' again?"

"Day after tomorrow."

Blake whistled. "Damn short trip."

"Yeah, but what can you do? Better'n nothin', since Ma threatened to hop a flight to Baghdad if I didn't get my ass home soon. Been damn near three years since I've been here."

"A lotta shit's happened since then."

"No kiddin'. Good and bad. I almost made it for Carter's weddin'." He knocked back a swallow of beer. "Didn't know about Dag until the day before his funeral. Same with Uncle Harland."

"How much longer you think you'll be over there?" Colby asked.

"At least six months. Then I hafta decide if I wanna re-up."

"Why the fuck would you wanna re-up if you had the

choice not to?"

"Jesus, Remy, way to be a prick," Chet said. "Cam's like platoon commander. A real war hero."

"Hero. Right." Cam concentrated on peeling the label off his beer bottle. "Eatin' sand, gettin' shot at, arrestin' soldiers, filin' a million fuckin' reports, patrollin' hopin' I don't get shot at some more, serious hero shit there."

No one said anything while the waitress brought another round.

Kade took a long sip of beer. It loosened some of the tightness in his shoulders from his huge blowup with Skylar. His pride stung way worse than his jaw and his gut, not that he'd share that with anyone. "I take it Colt ain't comin'?"

Colby shook his head. "A.A. meetin' tonight. He don't miss 'em. And thank God for that."

"Think maybe you oughta be thankin' Kade. If it weren't for him, who knows what might've happened to our wayward brother," Cord said.

"It wasn't my doin'. I just drove him to rehab. Colt made the decision to go there and get sober all by himself."

"Well, I appreciate it, and if I haven't said thanks for lookin' out for him, I'm sayin' it now. Not knowin' what was goin' on around here, especially after what went down with Dag, really sucked."

"Sucked pretty bad watchin' it happen, so in some ways, Cam, you were lucky not to be around."

Quinn and Bennett walked in and Cord waved them over.

After they were seated, Quinn leaned over and said to Kade, "Where's your ropin' partner in crime?"

"His meetin' night, I guess. He ain't gonna make it."

Bennett pushed his hat back a notch and smirked. "Quinn almost didn't make it tonight either."

"Why not?"

"Yeah, Q, why not?"

"Shut up, Ben. Nobody fuckin' cares."

"Come on, bro, it's a funny story."

"Not to me. It ain't funny at all."

Kade noticed the grim set of Quinn's mouth and had the perverse hope his cousin had a fight with his wife. Be nice if he wasn't the only one at the table with woman troubles. He cast a covert look at Cord and Colby, both happily married to sweet women who wouldn't snap at them for anything, least of all for acting like a man protecting what was his. Skylar's words echoed in his head: *Is that macho cowboy bullshit supposed to impress me?*

"It can't be that bad," Cord said.

Colby laughed. "I recognize that hangdog look, we've all been there, you longer than all of us combined. Spill it. What was it Libby wanted you to do?"

"She's on this kick where she's tryin' to find an *activity* we can do together as a couple."

"Sex is a couple's activity," Chet said. "Hell, you shouldn't need nothin' else."

"Amen," Cord said, chinking his bottle to Colby's.

"Spoken like a single man, Chet," Quinn replied. "Libby says what we do on the ranch don't count. So ridin' horses, four-wheelers, checkin' cattle, and cookin' ain't a possibility for couple time."

"What is?"

Quinn chugged his beer. "This is so damn embarrassin', can we drop it?"

A chorus of *no*'s broke the smoky air.

"How long you been married again?" Kade asked.

"Seven years. Been together since high school, so it's like twelve years and that just proves that she knows how to push my damn buttons. The woman ain't gonna let up on me 'til she gets what she wants, which is my total humiliation."

Remy angled closer. "She ain't makin' you wear funny clothes in the *bood-war* is she? Dressin' you up like an Indian chief? Or makin' you wear a saloon girl costume with fishnets, spiked heels and pantaloons while she straps on a six-shooter and plays the part of the gunslinger?"

Dead silence.

"Jesus Christ, Remy, what the fuck is wrong with you tonight?" Chet hissed.

"Thanks a lot for the mental image of Quinn dressed up as Mae West," Cam said dryly. "My cousin as a drag queen—worse than combat nightmares for me for sure."

Cord shook his head. "My brain sort of froze up at the word 'strap on', to be real honest."

Kade choked on his beer.

"Pantaloons?" Colby frowned. "Where'd you even hear that word, Remy? A John Wayne movie?"

"Bein's Remy is freely usin' the words *pantaloons* and *boudoir* in casual conversation, I'm wonderin' just how deep his western whorehouse fantasy goes," Blake said.

"Fuck you all very much."

"See, compared to the weird shit they're thinkin' up, the reality ain't that awful, Q." Bennett hid his smile behind his beer bottle. "So, you tellin' 'em, or am I?"

"Fine." Quinn blurted, "Libby signed us up for some damn hippie pottery class."

"Like in... Writin' love words an' shit?" Chet asked with horror.

"No," Quinn said, "Pot-ter-y."

"Pottery?" Cord repeated. "Like makin' flowerpots outta clay?"

"Yeah."

They all tried not to laugh, but once Cam's infectious whoops of laughter rang out, then it was pointless to stay somber.

Blake clapped him on the back. "At least you got out of it tonight."

"Don't think Libby ain't gonna be makin' me pay for it. So, Cam, I hope you appreciate me bein' here, 'cause I ain't gettin' any pussy for the next week."

"Yeah? Least your wife didn't trick you into fuckin' her without a condom so you'd knock her up again."

All eyes turned to Colby.

"That's right, Channing cut me off for over a week, then *bam*, nailed me but good."

"Why you complainin' about gettin' nailed?" Chet asked.

228

"Because she didn't have an easy pregnancy with Gib. Don't know why the hell she wants to take a chance again so soon."

Cam said, "I figure she's tryin' to keep up with Gemma and Macie on the baby races. Them two, I swear. Tryin' to populate Wyoming."

"Keep 'em away from AJ." Cord gave a mock shudder. "Much as we wanna have another kid or two someday, that ain't *to*-day."

"You tellin' us everything is perfect between the newlyweds?"

Cord grinned. "Absolutely fuckin' perfect."

Kade wondered if they noticed he hadn't tossed in his two cents. Probably not, he'd always been the quiet one of the boisterous McKay/West bunch. Preferring to listen rather than to talk, letting his twin muscle his way into the spotlight while he remained in the background.

As Chet, Remy and Blake yammered about the single life, Kade made wet rings on the table with the bottom of his beer bottle. Being stuck in limbo with Skylar was worse than dating. Might make him pussy-whipped, but he'd gladly take a damn pottery class with the woman he loved, even if he hated the idea. If it was important to Sky, then it was important to him.

Why couldn't Quinn see that? No wonder he and Libby were having problems. Much as he hated family gossip, it'd shocked him when Skylar relayed the conversation she'd had with his cousin's unhappy wife during the barbecue. In fact, Sky seemed pretty damn shocked at how much private information his family disclosed to her in a few short hours.

What she didn't realize? That was *not* his family's way to blab about personal issues...unless they considered her part of the family, which appeared to be the case with Sky.

So why couldn't Sky see that? Why was she so damn resistant to a permanent relationship with him? Why couldn't he just buck up, tell her he loved her, and they were tying the knot whether she liked it or not?

You're taking control in every aspect of my life.

Yeah. That caveman behavior would go over like a club to the head.

"Kade? Buddy? You still here?" Cord asked.

He looked up guiltily. "Sorry, just thinkin' about something else. What'd I miss?"

"Ben said Chase scored a ninety-one in the final go round in Lewiston on Sunday afternoon. Ended up in third place."

"Cool. Which circuit is that?"

"Dodge. The PBR had an off week, but you know him. He's obsessed with bull ridin' so he found another event to feed his habit."

"Glad to see my little cuz is keepin' the McKay name alive in the world of rodeo," Colby said.

"Rumor has it Keely's makin' quite a name for herself on every circuit too."

Dead quiet.

Cord slowly lowered his beer. "You'd better be explainin' that statement, Bennett, right fuckin' now."

Cam and Colby shot him menacing looks too.

"Whoa whoa whoa, guys, I ain't trash talkin' your little sister. I'm sayin' cousin Keely is gettin' a reputation as a miracle worker when it comes to non-surgical physical therapy alternatives with rodeo injuries. Chase said Justin Donahue told him that the Wrangler Sports Medicine team wants her to quit school and go to work for them full time for a helluva lot of money."

"Then why didn't Keely tell us about that this weekend when she was home?" Colby demanded.

"She told me." When they all turned and gaped at Cam, he said, "What? You guys don't listen to Keely most of the time any way."

"And you do?"

"Yep. I always have. She's been too damn smart for her own good since the day she was born."

Must be a girl McKay thing, Kade thought, because he knew even at four months, Eliza understood everything he said to her. He and Sky would have their hands full for the next two decades if Eliza was anything like Keely.

Chet, Remy, Ben and Blake drifted to the back room to shoot pool and were suckered into a tournament. Luckily the various women who'd been circling their table like sharks in a feeding frenzy followed the single guys into the back room. Quinn ended up talking to an old friend up at the bar, then he took off, leaving Kade with Colby, Cord, and Cam.

They discussed upcoming cattle sales, the start of haying, Carter's impending art show, the hunting season, military life and horses. Kade was surprised to see two hours had passed.

Cam wandered into the back room to watch the pool games.

"How's it goin' with Eliza?"

Kade smiled at Colby. "She's something else."

"How's it goin' with Skylar?"

"Shitty."

"That don't sound too good." Cord set his forearms on the table. "You wanna tell us what's up?"

"Look, no offense, guys, but I doubt either of you had to go through any of the junk Sky and I are dealin' with right now."

"What kinda junk do you mean?" Colby asked. "Dealin' with havin' a baby type stuff?"

"No, figurin' out relationship stuff."

"Why the hell would you say we don't know nothin' about that?"

Kade scowled at Cord. "Didn't you tell us that everything between you and AJ is perfect?"

"I meant now. It sure wasn't always that way, especially not on my end."

"Get out. AJ's so sweet sugar wouldn't melt in her mouth."

Cord snorted. "That tongue of hers can be laced with arsenic, and she ain't afraid to put me in my place. You weren't around, but I about did the dumbest thing ever and let AJ get away from me."

Colby nodded. "Channing disappeared for damn near three months after I got busted up in Cheyenne. I didn't know if I'd ever see her again or if she'd even want a crippled-up former rodeo star."

"Seriously?"

"Yeah. I don't know why you think we had it easy. Hell,

none of us, includin' Carter, had a smooth go of it with our wives. Fact is, I'd say most men are dumbasses when it comes to this sort of relationship junk."

"That's encouragin'. Maybe I do need another beer," Kade muttered.

So, armed with liquid courage, Kade gave his cousins a run-down on everything that'd happened—from dating Skylar the previous summer, to the recent confrontation at Sky Blue.

Both men were quiet until Kade couldn't stand it any longer. "What?"

"Let me get this straight. You've been crazy about Skylar for over a year, when you found out you knocked her up, you moved in with her to learn how to be a father to Eliza, the sex is off the charts good, and you've asked her to marry you numerous times, and you're lookin' out for her safety?"

"Yeah."

"Buddy, I hate to tell you this, but there ain't a whole lot more you can do," Cord said.

"Geez. Thanks a fuckin' lot for that stellar advice."

"For once I agree with Cord," Colby added. "It seems you ain't the one with the problem. Skylar is. And if she can't see what's right in front of her face, K, then maybe you oughta give her some distance so she gets a different perspective."

Kade blinked. "What do you mean? Walk away? Move out?"

"Maybe."

"No way. I'd miss her and Eliza like crazy, and goddammit they both need me, even if that stubborn woman won't admit it."

"I wasn't ready to admit I needed AJ until she left me," Cord offered.

"With Channing and me, time away just reinforced the truth that we belonged together."

"You guys ain't kiddin', are you?"

"How many years was AJ right in front of my damn face and I didn't notice her? And even after I'd fallen for her I didn't want to admit it to her or anybody else, but mostly to myself how I felt about her. We can be our own worst enemies."

"I'll betcha Skylar would figure it out pretty damn quick

how she feels about you if you weren't around. It don't hafta be permanent, just for a coupla days. Besides, ain't we startin' hayin' the south section tomorrow? You ain't gonna wanna drive sixty miles at ten o'clock at night after you've been on a tractor for sixteen hours, just to turn around eight hours later and do it all again."

"Colby's right." Cord pulled his ringing cell phone from his shirt pocket. "Hey, baby doll." He grinned. "Really? Don't move. Ah-ah-ah, no buts. I'm on my way."

"What's up?"

Cord stood and threw a twenty on the table. "Gotta go."

"Right now?"

"When your wife calls and says the kid's sound asleep and she's naked in bed, sorry guys, you lose every time. See ya tomorrow and good luck, K."

"Thanks."

Colby squinted at the bar clock. "I'd probably best get on home. See what trick my darlin' wife has up her sleeve for tonight's sexcapades. Funny thing is, she thinks I don't know what she's up to, so I'm not playin' hard to get." He clapped Kade on the shoulder. "Good luck."

Kade pondered their advice as he finished his beer. Why did men and women have to play games?

Then again, being straightforward and honest hadn't done him a bit of good either.

Chapter Twenty-four

After saying his good-byes to his cousins, Kade walked down the street to his truck. The promise of an early fall teased and the evening air was chilly. Clouds covering the moon made the night seem even darker than normal. He'd hunkered into the collar of his coat and didn't see the man step out of the shadows until it was too late and Kade smacked right into him.

"Hey. Sorry."

"You'd better be sorry, you son of a bitch."

"Excuse me?"

"No excuse for you because I know you were fuckin' my wife, McKay."

Was this man drunk?

"What kind of loser fucks another man's wife?"

Kade attempted to back up. "Wait a second, pal, you've got the wrong man."

"The hell I do." The big bear of a man pressed closer. "I followed her, so I know she was meetin' with you."

"Me? Since when?"

"Two months ago I saw you and her laughin' and jokin' in that restaurant downtown. Then you two snuck into that massage parlor and didn't come out for a coupla hours. We all know what kinda shit happens in them places."

"See, now I know you're mistaken, buddy, because I've been livin' out of town for the last year."

"Makes it convenient when she sneaks away to meet you, which I know she's still doin' 'cause she ain't around at night. And when she is she's damn secretive, which pisses me off."

"I'm tellin' you, it wasn't me."

That information didn't calm the man down; it incensed him. "I know what I saw. And I saw you."

Shit. This was where family resemblances sucked. The man this guy had seen might've been any one of Kade's cousins. The man could've been Kane. That was the most likely explanation, even when Kane had a strict *no married women* policy. It was unlikely the guy would buy the laughable "I have an identical twin" argument, but that didn't matter. Kade wouldn't roll on his brother or his cousins anyway.

Before Kade uttered another denial, the man hauled off and punched him in the eye like a champion boxer. Pain exploded in his head and he staggered back.

"How'd you like that? An eye for an eye, fucker. That'll teach you to keep your eyes off my wife."

While Kade was trying to regain his equilibrium, the guy delivered a wicked uppercut that rocked his jaw so hard his teeth clacked together and he bit his tongue. "Keep your mouth offa her."

Kade curled his arms around his head, attempting to protect it, when the guy slugged him in the gut with enough force to knock the air from his lungs. Through the pain Kade realized he was getting his ass kicked and he couldn't stop it. He dropped to the pavement in defeat.

"Stand up and fight me, you fuckin' pussy."

A car door slammed, followed by bootsteps thumping down the sidewalk. "Hey! What the hell is goin' on?"

"Walk away. This ain't your concern," the man said.

"The fuck it isn't."

Colt.

Why was Colt here? Kade tried to say his name but nothing came out.

"Last chance to get gone or I'll give you some of what he just got."

"Big talk."

"I'm more than talk, sheep-fucker."

"Bring it on, cocksucker."

More bootsteps scuffled on the cement, preceded by loud shouts. Kade heard it all through a haze of pain.

"Colt? What're you doin' here? Oh, shit. Kade? Man, you all right?" This from Blake.

Colt said, "I was on my way inside the Golden Boot and I saw Kade get sucker-punched."

"Is this the fucker who did this to him?" Cam demanded.

"Yeah."

The man said, "Let me go."

"Fuck that. You started it."

"We're gonna finish it. Still feelin' tough?" Ben taunted.

"Not when the odds are six against one."

Kade pushed himself to a sitting position and said, "Let him go."

"What?" Remy said. "We all wanna take a shot at him so he knows he messed with the wrong fuckin' family."

"You're all McKays?"

"No, some of us go by the name West. Heard of us?"

The man said, "Yeah, you're all a buncha fuckin' psycho cowboys."

"Then you know we ain't gonna let this slide."

"Enough. Let him go. He thought I was someone else." Kade tried to look up at the guy. Shit. He couldn't see. "His choice. He walks away and stays away from all of us or we go to the sheriff's office and I file charges."

"This some sort of all for one and one for all bullshit?" the man sneered.

"You bet your ass."

Cam shook the big man like a rag doll. "What's it gonna be, hoss?"

"I'm goin'." After Cam released him, the guy slithered into the darkness.

"Jesus, Kade. He did a number on you. I think that cut above your eye needs stitches."

"Screw that, I fuckin' hate needles. It'll be fine."

"Is your mouth bleedin'?"

"Probably. He didn't knock any teeth out."

"That's reassurin'. Need some help up?" Cam asked.

"Yeah."

Cam and Colt hauled him up and leaned him against the brick building. "Thanks." The movement made Kade dizzy and he closed his eyes.

Chet said, "Want us to make sure you get home okay?"

"Nah, you guys get goin', you have a longer drive. I'll get him home," Colt said. "I owe him."

Murmurs of agreement followed and Kade knew they'd all left. Although, after two fights in one day, he couldn't muster the energy to wave good-bye.

Lighter footsteps approached, accompanied by *click click* of metal chains.

"Whatcha think, Indy?" Colt asked softly.

"I think he's bleeding like a crack whore and looks like dog shit. What is it with you cowboys and fighting all the damn time?"

Kade cracked open his good eye. Great. Skylar's sister. "What the devil are you doin' here?" He saw India shoot Colt a look and managed to turn his head to see Colt's response.

Colt mouthed something to her and she shook her head.

Silence.

"It wasn't a trick question," Kade said.

India sighed. "I'm here because I'm Colt's A.A. sponsor. Tonight was the first time he planned on going into a bar since he sobered up last year. I hung out in his truck so we could talk about it afterward."

"I didn't know you were his sponsor."

"No one knows. Colt wants it kept confidential information, which is his choice, so you can't tell anyone, not even Skylar."

"Well, that'll be easy since she's pissed as hell at me."

"Why?"

"Long story."

"Does that mean you ain't goin' to her place tonight?"

Kade gestured to his bloody and mud-covered clothes. "No

choice. All my stuff is there. You guys go on. I'll be fine to drive myself."

"You can't see out of your right eye, how are you supposed to drive thirty miles? In the dark?"

"I'll manage."

"We'll take you."

"I need my truck tomorrow."

"Fine. Colt can drive your truck. I'll drive my car. He needs to follow someone who knows the way in case you fall asleep and I'll bring him back to town."

Colt said, "Toss me your keys."

Kade dug them out of his pocket and pushed off the building to follow Colt to his truck.

India's hand on his chest stopped him. "Huh-uh. You're riding with me."

"Great."

India didn't speak until they were halfway home. "You know Sky is going to freak out when she sees you all bloody?"

"I figured she might since it's the second time she's seen me like this today."

"This is one of the reasons she refused to date cowboys when she first moved here because they're always getting in fights."

His laugh was more grunt-like than humorous.

She shot him a look. "So it shocked the hell out of me when you and I crossed paths—"

"Crossed paths? You cornered me in Sky's house like I was a stray dog in the chicken house."

"If the shitkicker fits..."

Kade snorted. "Sky still doesn't know about your threatening little chat with me that day, does she?"

"No. You think she's gonna get pissed off that I was doing my sisterly duty? Wrong. But it was damn shocking to learn that Eliza's father is not only a cowboy, but one of the notorious McKay cowboys."

"Yeah, that's me, one of the damned." He sighed. "I'd crash

someplace else tonight if I could, but everything I own is at her place."

"What's going on with you two?"

"Who the hell knows? She's mad. Thinks I overstepped my bounds today."

"Did you?"

Kade explained as neutrally as possible.

A full minute passed before India responded. "Lemme ask you this: Do you know the real reason why she's so upset?"

"Because I bucked up and pointed out the security issues with her business and she thinks it's none of my business to be worryin' about hers?"

"Close. But no cigar."

"Then what?"

"Let's break it down and see if you can't put it back together correctly." She offered Kade an impish smile. "As an A.A. and N.A. counselor, I'm big on folks finding their own solutions. The answer means more if they figure it out themselves.

"Now, I'm sure my sister has told you about Ted, and how he used her and robbed her blind. Once he'd gotten what he'd wanted from her—most of Sky's money—then he divorced her."

"But see, that's where what happened today don't fit. I don't want anything from her." Immediately after he voiced the denial, he made the connection. His queasy feeling multiplied. "Goddammit, I threatened to take Eliza from her."

"*Ding ding ding!* Give the man a prize for guessing the correct answer."

"Christ. How could I be such a fuckin' idiot? I'd never take Eliza from her. Never. I just wanted Sky to see how seriously she oughta take the safety issues at the plant. I've been tryin' my damnedest to make the three of us be a real family, not tear us apart. To show her I ain't goin' anywhere."

"You can talk until you're blue in the face and she won't believe you."

"Why the hell not?"

"Because she's the type who needs what she calls 'tangible proof'."

"I asked her to marry me so I could put a damn ring on her finger. What kinda concrete proof could be better than that?"

"There is one thing that you could do...never mind." She shrugged. "You thought I was joking around with the no pain, no gain comment? I wasn't. Come talk to me when you've figured it out."

Great. More games. More puzzles. More reasons for him to take his cousin's advice and lay low for a while.

India didn't speak further until she pulled into the driveway and parked. "I knew you were a different kind of man when you barged into her life and offered her everything she never thought she'd have. After I figured out the McKay family connection, I asked Colt about you. He told me you're the most honest, kind, and forthright man he's ever known. He says you cared enough to save him when no one else did."

Embarrassed, Kade looked away.

"Skylar doesn't need saving in the same way, but she needs you. Don't let her fears chase you away, Kade. Fight for her."

"I'm a little tired of fightin' at the moment."

"I can imagine."

Kade stared at Skylar's front door before he faced India. "You ever heard the phrase 'nice guys finish last'? It's true. Been true my whole life. So, maybe it'd be nice for me for a change, if someone thought *I* was worth fightin' for."

He climbed out of the car leaving India in stunned silence.

Chapter Twenty-five

Heeding Kade's advice about her impetuous behavior, Skylar didn't race down the porch steps when a set of headlights appeared at the end of the driveway. She paused in the doorway until she recognized India's car. What was her sister doing here at eleven o'clock at night? Then Kade's truck pulled up, but Kade didn't jump from the cab. Colt McKay did.

What the heck?

The sight of Colt helping Kade out of the passenger's side of India's car finally spurred Sky into action.

"What's going on? Omigod, Kade, you're bleeding!" Her heart rate kicked up, her stomach lurched as she looked at his battered face. "What happened?"

"Can we get him inside first?"

"Oh. Right." She held open the door.

Kade shrugged off Colt's help. "I can walk."

He passed by without looking at her and headed to the kitchen.

She followed him, even when it was apparent he didn't want her to.

Colt said, "If you've got a first aid kit, please get it."

"Okay." She turned but India snagged her arm. India's eyes searched Sky's face. "Please don't be stupid. This man is hurting and not just because he was in a fight. He needs you tonight. Forget whatever else happened today, be there for him—"

"Indy?" Colt called.

"Coming."

By the time Sky brought the kit, a bag of ice rested on the upper right half of Kade's face. She scrutinized his swollen mouth, the bumps and bruises on his jaw, the deep gash above his eyebrow. Her gaze tracked the splotches of dried blood on his cheek and the long line of brownish-red trailing down his neck.

Don't cry, be strong. She inhaled slowly and was amazed her voice didn't shake. "Does it hurt?"

No answer.

"Let me see." Sky's stomach made a seesawing sensation as she inspected the deep cut. "I take it you opted for no doctor and no stitches."

"Didn't seem that bad."

"Well, it sure isn't good." She brushed a bloody clump of hair from his forehead, over and over, at a loss for what else she could do to fix this for him. "I probably need to clean it before I can put on a bandage."

"Fine."

Colt dropped Kade's keys on the table. "Since you're in capable hands, we're gonna head back to town."

"Thanks. Both of you. I appreciate your help."

"No problem." India turned to Sky. "Is Eliza sleeping?"

"She's upstairs in our room, if you want to take a peek."

"I will. Don't worry, I won't wake her."

"I'll wait outside, India," Colt said as they both left the room.

Sky ripped open an antiseptic wipe and lowered the ice pack. She winced. His eye was completely swollen shut and his eyebrow had a deep gash, which was still oozing. She dabbed around the area. "What happened to you?"

"A guy jumped me outside of the Golden Boot. He thought I was someone else. And before you ask, no, I wasn't drunk and pickin' fights."

"I wasn't going to ask that." But Sky wasn't surprised Kade was defensive. She'd taken him to task on his violent behavior earlier in the day and she knew he wouldn't appreciate her apology now. "What's the other guy look like?"

"Not a scratch. He caught me off guard. I'd be in much

worse shape if Colt hadn't come along when he did. My cousins showed up at the end." He hissed. "Shit that stings."

"Sorry." Sky wiped the area three times before she was satisfied it was clean. She attached the bandage. The sound of the front door closing and an engine starting let her know she and Kade were alone. "It should stop bleeding now. You want something for the pain?"

"Nah. I'm good, thanks."

She used a warm washcloth to gently clean his face and neck. Rather than relax into her touch, he tensed up. "I'm trying not to hurt you, Kade."

"It's pretty much a given that you will, even when you don't think you are."

Her hand froze. Was he referencing something besides his injury? "Kade, please listen to me. Can we talk about this? I'm so—"

"Forget it. That's probably good enough anyway."

Stung into silence, Sky dumped water out of the Ziploc, adding more ice, and rewrapped the cold pack in a clean kitchen towel. "Here. This should help with the swelling."

Kade stood. "Thanks for patchin' me up. I'm tired and I've gotta be up early so I'm headin' to bed."

While Sky paced alone downstairs, pretending to clean the kitchen, wondering why she was such an idiot about this relationship stuff, she heard Eliza fussing on the baby monitor. After she picked her up, she realized Kade wasn't in their bed. She wandered into the hallway. The door to the bathroom was open, but the door to the spare bedroom was closed.

So, he'd opted not to sleep with her tonight.

Can you blame him?

A loud thump sounded from inside the room. What if he'd hurt himself because he had too much pride to ask her for help?

You would know about being too proud.

The stupid voices in her head always offered advice way too late.

She took a chance and knocked. "Kade? You okay?"

"Fine. Hang on a second."

Eliza squawked.

Kade opened the door. His gaze landed on Eliza and he smiled softly. "Hey, baby girl. What's the ruckus?"

At the sound of his voice, Eliza turned her head.

"She's probably hungry. She didn't finish her last bottle."

"Sorry I didn't hear her. She okay? Not sick or anything?"

"Not as far as I can tell, besides her crying jags the last couple days. I think you were right. I think she's teething."

"I'd offer to take the midnight shift, but I thought she'd shriek if she caught sight of my ugly, beat-up mug in the middle of the night. And to be honest, I'm in more than a little pain right now."

Sky didn't respond; she was too busy staring at the duffel bags next to the bed. He stiffened when he realized she'd seen them. Somehow, she swallowed the lump in her throat and asked, "What's going on?"

"I'm gonna be busy at the ranch for a few days." He shuffled his feet and looked anywhere but at her. "After what happened earlier today, and now with this, I decided we could both use a break."

You decided? What about me? Don't I get a say? Don't we? Her hold on Eliza increased.

"You can reach me any time on my cell. I probably won't check my messages until late, but if it's an emergency, you can call my mom and she'll track me down." Kade stroked Eliza's cheek. "Gonna miss you bad, sweet thang. Be good for your mama, okay? I'll see you soon."

"You aren't going to try and take her with you?"

"No." His pain-filled eyes searched hers. "I'd never take her from you, Skylar."

Oh no. What was going on with them? When had they returned to polite strangers? "I thought..."

"I know what you thought and you were wrong. Some things that were said in the heat of the moment shouldn't have been said at all."

Immediately she wondered, things like, *marry me?*

Eliza protested her hungry state and Skylar took a step back. "I, ah, need to feed her." She started down the hallway.

The door closed softly, but it echoed in her head as loudly as if he'd slammed it.

After Skylar got up with Eliza again for her two o'clock feeding, she couldn't go back to sleep. She paced in the hallway outside Kade's room, wondering if it was the best thing for him to be sleeping alone. What if he had a head injury? Weren't you supposed to check on concussed patients every few hours? Rather than risk waking him by knocking, she quietly opened the door and tiptoed into his room just to double check on him.

Kade was splayed in the middle of the bed. His right hand held the bag of ice on his right eye.

Sweat beaded on his skin. She leaned over to place her hand on his forehead. Damn. His skin was hot to the touch. The poor man was burning up, no wonder he was completely naked. Sky went to the bathroom and returned with two wet washcloths.

She perched on the edge of the bed, which woke Kade up. "Skylar? What's goin' on?"

"Sorry. I didn't mean to wake you. I came in to check on you and your whole body is feverish. How do you feel?"

"Like I got the crap kicked out of me."

"You did. I thought you might like it if I cooled you down a little."

"You don't have to."

"I know. I want to. Please. Let me do this for you, okay?"

No answer.

Well, he hadn't barked *no*. That was a good sign. "Do you feel nauseous?"

He shook his head and groaned. "Except when I do that."

"Then don't do that," she half-chided. "Hold still. I'm going to move this ice bag aside for a bit." She sucked in a harsh breath and it froze in her lungs. Oh man. He was on track to a serious shiner.

"What?"

"Nothing. Just relax. This cloth might be cold at first."

Skylar began with his forehead. Avoiding his swollen eye,

she sponged the sharp planes of his face, cheekbones, temples, his generous mouth, lingering on his strong jawline. She wiped the long line of his neck.

He sighed deeply.

She continued across his collarbones and shoulders. Down his pectorals. He hissed, not with pain, when the nubby washcloth drifted over his nipples and the disks hardened into little points. Skylar realized since she'd handed Kade control of their interludes, he'd never allowed her to spend much time exploring his beautiful, strong body. She hadn't lingered on learning how he liked to be touched above the waist. She hadn't traced the delineated muscles of his abs and stomach with her tongue. Which was a damn crying shame, and a situation she'd rectify pronto.

Skylar admired his meaty biceps and thick forearms as she ran the washcloth along his brawny arms. The back of his hands were scarred and scabbed; the palm side of his hands were callused and rough. The hands of a working rancher. She knew these strong hands could rein in a thousand-pound horse, or fix barbed wire fence or even knock a man out cold. But she also knew how unbelievably gentle these powerful hands could be on her body. On her face. On their child.

She switched washcloths and finished his torso, his rib cage, the flat belly and his narrow pelvis, spending time on that sexy, sensitive strip of skin stretching from hipbone to hipbone. Skylar circumvented his groin even when his full erection indicated he enjoyed her ministrations.

Kade's legs were dusted with dark hair and were all sinewy muscle. She swept the cloth down his thighs, repeated the process for his ropy calves, but she avoided his feet. When she finished, she half-expected he'd be watching her intently, but his eyes were closed. His breathing wasn't slow and easy, but choppy, restless. She knew he wasn't asleep.

Sky angled over his mouth and very very softly kissed his swollen lips. Then she followed the exact same path with her hands and mouth over his body that she had with the washcloth. Just as slowly. Just as thoroughly.

By the time she finished, his cock was weeping for her attention. Using the slick fluid leaking from the tip, she wrapped her fist around his hot, rigid shaft and began to stroke.

"Skylar. You—"

"Let me do this for you. Please. I can't stand that you're hurting. Let me make you feel good. Let me give you back some of what you always give to me." She flicked her tongue down the corded muscles in his throat. When she reached his upper chest, she began her sensual assault.

Kade arched into her and his left hand twined in her hair.

She drove him crazy, went a little crazy herself, licking and playing with his nipples. Digging her nails and her teeth into his warm, pliant flesh. She suckled and bit every inch of skin on his pecs as she jacked him off. Building from a slow steady pace to a fast one that elicited his near growl of impatience. His hips bumped up, his balls were walnut tight at the root of his sex. And when that thick cock jerked in her moving hand, she bit down on his left pectoral, sucking with enough force to leave a hickey. A big hickey. Sticky warmth poured over her fingers and Kade groaned long and low, slightly pulling her hair, as the pulses intensified and then, tapered off. Then stopped.

Still squeezing every drop of come out of his cock, she sought his mouth, trying to convey without words what was in her heart. Still kissing him, she used the washcloth to clean them both up.

Sky untangled from his embrace and replaced the ice on his eye. His breathing slowed, but he didn't reach for her. She tiptoed out. He needed his rest, and whatever they needed to say to each other could wait until morning.

But the next morning, when Sky woke up, Kade was already gone.

For Kade not being able to see out of his right eye everything in his life was finally crystal clear.

When Skylar had come to him so sweetly the previous night, it'd been all Kade could do not to demand her submission, mount her like a crazed beast and fuck her senseless. But he knew her taking the initiative in offering him loving comfort cemented the bond between them.

Especially after he'd seen love bites she'd left all over his chest. Suck marks. Teeth marks. Indentations from her fingernails. By showing him her ferocious, possessive side, she'd been marking him as hers.

Time to return the favor on a more permanent level. He called his cousin Colt, knowing he was up with the damn chickens these days, and Colt happily gave him the phone number he needed.

Kade dialed. No hello, no niceties, he just said, "I've got a brilliant idea how I can prove it to her." He held the phone away from his ear. "Yeah, I know what time it is. I don't give a shit if you're not a mornin' person, you said to come talk to you when I figured it out. Hey, you're the one who said, *no pain, no gain,* so can't blame anyone but yourself for stickin' your nose in this. I'm takin' you up on your offer. Yep." Pause. "How the hell should I know? You're the expert. You've got roughly ten hours. I'll be there after work."

He called Colt back. "Hey, cuz. Remember how you're always sayin' if I need anything, just holler? Well, here's your chance. I'm gonna be hollerin' real loud tonight and you've been elected to hold my hand."

Chapter Twenty-six

Day One of Kade's absence from her life was bad.

Day Two of Kade's absence from her life was worse.

But Day Three? Day Three was absolutely intolerable.

Eliza was beyond cranky. Skylar suspected the baby missed her daddy and decided to make Mommy pay for it by disrupting the entire daycare. Disrupting it to the point Skylar had to sequester Eliza in her office all day, which meant she hadn't gotten a damn thing done. For three days.

Not only that, Nadia had called in sick for the last two days, which threw Sky Blue's schedule off. The other employees were grouchy because they had to pick up the slack and work on a Saturday. Even India had snapped at her, babbling nonsense about nice guys finishing first, recognizing a good thing, and ending with India threatening to put a boot in her ass if she was too stupid to know she had to fight this time. And all she'd called for was to check on the stock.

Skylar couldn't concentrate and screwed up the quarterly sales figures four times before she closed the file. Needing a mindless task, she spread out a blanket on the floor, plopped Eliza down with her favorite toys, and waded through the boxes of junk while keeping an eye on her fussy daughter.

Annie barged in. "Glad to see you're finally takin' care of that stuff. It's a fire hazard."

"Something you need?"

"Two things, actually. Where's the purchase order for the bottles?"

"Which bottles?"

"The hand lotion bottles. The plant in Cheyenne says they never received the order."

"Bull. I sent it three weeks ago."

"Well, they never got it. And the original order form is not in the file." Annie braced her shoulders against the doorframe. "Is it possible with all that's been going on, you only think you sent it?"

Yes. "No."

"What do you want me to do?"

"What are my options?"

"Send another purchase order and pay the rush charge."

Skylar shuddered. That'd put a big dent in the already small profit margin. "Or?"

"Or wait until you get through those boxes to see if you accidentally tossed it in there during your rant about the ridiculously high prices of plastics and were looking at switching bottle manufacturing companies."

"Funny. Pay the damn rush charges. What was the other thing?"

"Nadia wants to talk to you after lunch break."

Skylar looked at Annie. "Thank God she actually showed up today. Do you know what she wants to talk about?"

"I have an idea."

"Something you're going to share with me, Annie?"

"No. But as long as you're already in a pissy mood, I might as well tell you I heard what Kade said the other day and he was right about external safety issues around here." When Sky started to protest, Annie stopped her. "Don't bite my head off. We've talked about this. I oughta say, I brought it up and you ignored me. As the owner you make sure all the internal safety equipment surpasses OSHA standards. All the MSDS are up to date. But, that's not all there is to creating a safe work environment. Most of your female employees have been in bad situations with men, including myself, which you knew when you hired us. So, I don't understand why we have a security gate we don't use and no alarm system whatsoever."

"Um? Hello? Because we're out in the middle of nowhere?"

"Sweets, you're a great boss, but you have the attitude bad

things don't happen in Wyoming. Bad things do happen here, less frequently than in LA, but we're still somewhat untamed in the Wild West. In some respects, cowboys are like them gangbangers, never backin' down from a fight, always lookin' for a way to avenge themselves when they think someone done them wrong. Especially if they were wronged by the woman in their life. Like Nadia's husband. Are you denying that is a potentially volatile situation?"

"No."

"Don't deny that if you had this exact same business in LA, you wouldn't dream of leavin' the door unlocked or the gate open. Those security type things woulda been the first things in place."

The truth punched her in the gut like a freight train. Holy crap. Annie was exactly right. Kade had been right. How could she have been so oblivious? Because she was seriously overworked?

And whose fault is that?

Annie kept going. "I figured you'd take care of the oversight after you gave birth and Eliza was on the premises, things'd change and you'd see the external safety problems. But you haven't."

Half in a daze, Sky asked, "Then why didn't you just handle it? Order the security components, hire the installers? You *are* the office manager."

"We both know that's a courtesy title. You're the owner, you're in control, and you make no bones about that. I can't even order the damn lotion bottles without your approval."

Hadn't she sworn she'd delegate rather than do everything herself? Especially after Eliza's birth? And here she was stuck in the same pattern she'd been stuck in her whole life? Would she never learn she wasn't superwoman?

"Go ahead and snap off a smart question like, 'If you feel so unsafe and unappreciated here, why are you still working for me?' "

Skylar absolutely recoiled.

Annie shook her finger. "What's wrong? Why aren't you defensive? Full of pride. Glaring at me, unwilling to admit when you're wrong?"

Hadn't Kade accused her of the same thing? She swallowed, but her voice still was barely audible. "Because I was wrong, Annie. Fix it, however you see fit, okay?"

"Good." Annie sidestepped a pile of papers and slammed the door.

Startled by the sound, Eliza started screaming.

Sky wished she could scream right along with her.

She was still sitting on the floor an hour later when Nadia knocked. "Is this a bad time?"

"No. Come on in and pull up a piece of carpet."

It surprised Sky when Nadia plopped down. But she focused on Eliza. "She's a beautiful baby. She has your cheekbones."

Skylar tried to remember in the last month if anyone had mentioned Eliza resembled her in any way. She heard Kade's rumbling voice, *She has your cute little upturned nose. I'm hopin' she gets your freckles too. And your laugh. I love your laugh.*

"She has your disposition."

"Marvelous. I'm the picture of well adjusted, aren't I?"

Nadia sent her a panicked look. "No. I meant, she's very vocal."

"Thanks. I think."

"Trust me, that's a good thing, to not be afraid." Nadia wrapped her arms around her up-drawn knees. "Look. I want to apologize for putting you in a bad position all these months by asking you to lie to my husband."

"It's understandable."

"No. It's not and I'm sorry I missed work the last two days. But after Rex showed up here...and Eliza's father..." Sky's gaze snapped up. "He did the right thing, when it wasn't the easiest thing. When most people don't get involved. I hid behind the blinds and watched a man I didn't know from Adam stand up to Rex, because he was trying to protect you and everyone in this place, including me—who he didn't know from Adam—I realized it was past time I stand up for myself."

"Really?"

She nodded. "Hiding out, hoping Rex will go away won't change any of the problems and isn't the example I wanna set for my boy. The reason I was gone the past two days is because I talked to a lawyer. Then I went to the sheriff and told him what happened out here and about some other stuff Rex threatened to do. I filed a restraining order against him. A piece of paper isn't armor, but it shows Rex I'm done being afraid of him. And we're done. For good."

"I can't tell you how happy I am to hear that." She grabbed Nadia's hand. "Are you really okay?"

"Yes. I feel more in control of my life than I have been in years."

"I'm glad, Nadia, I really am."

"All thanks to you."

"To me? I appreciate the sentiment, but you were the one who took that first step. It's easier not to change." How well she knew that. She let her head fall back against the wall. "I've done some things wrong, things I plan to change as soon as possible. I thought you were coming in here to quit, and I was all ready to whip out my spiel about how I intended to beef up external security and do some things differently around here to get you to stay."

"Quit? I'm not going anywhere. This is the best job I've ever had. We all think that." Nadia rolled to her feet. "You give us more than just a good paycheck and a great place to work, Skylar. You show us how to be strong. You give us confidence in ourselves. No matter what mistakes we made in the past, what's been done to us, you've shown us we don't have to live there, we can overcome it, change, and work toward a better future. We deserve to live our dreams the same as anyone else."

She slipped out the door leaving Sky staring after her, feeling a little more at peace with her business, and her relationship with her employees, but not having a clue how she could make things right with Kade.

With everything that'd happened, the mindless sorting of paperwork was a welcome reprieve. Except the phrase, *we deserve to live our dreams*, hung in the air and stuck in Skylar's brain on a continuous loop. A life with Kade and Eliza was her dream.

When she reached the bottom of the fifth box, the corner of an envelope—stuck in yet another safety supply magazine— poked out. Before her fingers connected with the smooth white paper, she knew. This was the letter Kade had sent.

Sky flipped it over. No return address. Post marked Gillette, WY...two months ago. Using a pen, she slit open the top and dumped the letter on the floor. She unfolded the single piece of lined notebook paper. The blocky printing filled up half the page:

Skylar—

I'm probably the last person you expected to hear from. I hope you won't crumple this up and will give me a chance to explain.

After the bad way it ended with you last year, I needed time to re-evaluate some things. I moved to a remote section of the ranch, which is why I haven't approached you before now.

In the year I've been alone on the range, I've had time to think about what happened between us. What I did wrong. I can honestly say I'm ashamed of myself. My intention wasn't to deceive you, but to get to know you.

When I get back into town in the next month, I'd like to call you, maybe meet for coffee (or chocolate cake?) and see if time has healed the rift I caused. I believe there's still something worth exploring between us, something worth working out, something worth fighting for. I'd like to start fresh.

I hope you don't find this out of line, and I'm saying this from my heart. Being with you changed me. Time and distance haven't changed my feelings for you. But I hope the same time and distance have changed yours for me and you'll give me— us—a second chance.

All My Best,
Kade McKay

Kade wanted her. It was right there in black and white. He'd wanted to be with her *before* he found out about Eliza. No ulterior motive. The sweet, honest man had thrown his heart out, not knowing if she'd slice it to ribbons in her paper shredder.

Fat chance of that. Now that she had his heart she was keeping it safe forever. So, despite their rocky start, they'd finished what they'd begun not a month ago, but a year ago, they'd fallen in love, the forever, permanent kind of love she never thought she'd find or deserve.

Sky didn't realize she was crying until the tears splashed on the page.

She had the overwhelming urge to shout it from the rooftops: He likes me! He really really likes me! *Likes?* He loves you.

You love him; he loves you. It's the most simple thing in the world.

Was it?

Yes.

Eliza squealed and Sky glanced at her.

Her daughter batted those big blue eyes, flashed a gummy grin...and rolled over.

"Eliza Belle McKay! How long have you been able to do that?"

The baby made a gurgling sound suspiciously close to a laugh.

Still sobbing through her laughter, she said, "Wait until your daddy sees your new trick. He's gonna be over the moon."

And Sky couldn't wait another second to tell him everything. She picked up her babbling baby and ran out the door. "Annie!"

Her coworker raced out to see Sky sprinting away from her office. "What's wrong?"

"Nothing. I'm leaving to fix another thing in my life."

"Are you coming back today?"

"I hope not. So you're in charge. Get used to it." Halfway down the hall, Sky stopped and turned to look at her friend. "Is it really that simple?"

Immediately Annie smiled. "Yes, honey, it really is."

Skylar found Kimi and Calvin's place easily enough, and felt another punch of guilt that she'd never been here before. That was something else she'd prioritize, making time for family, their family of three, and the McKay/West bunch that was such an important part of Kade's life. Maybe sometimes she and Kade and Eliza could stay overnight here, so Kade didn't have to drive so blasted far. Heck, she'd move here and make the commute to Sky Blue if it came right down to it.

She started up the short sidewalk the same time a dark-haired man exited the house. They nearly collided and both took a step back. Neither said anything as they eyed each other.

"Hey, Skylar. How are you?"

This didn't have to be awkward. "Good. You?"

"Tired." He bent down and peered at Eliza.

But Eliza's little feet didn't kick with happiness. She didn't coo and smile. She stayed still and watchful.

"She knows I'm not him, don't she?"

"Yes." Sky kissed the top of Eliza's head. "She's Daddy's girl. Daddy has her wrapped around his little finger."

"My brother is a lucky man. She's beautiful." Kane smiled. "You look just like your mama, doncha, sugar?"

No surprise Kane was still a total charmer. "Everyone says she looks like Kade."

"Then they're not lookin' very hard."

"Speaking of Kade...where is he?"

"He's finishin' up the south hay field. Why?"

"I need to talk to him."

Kane straightened. "Now? Can't it wait until later tonight when he's done?"

"No."

Skylar half-expected Kane to get in her face. Demand to hear why she was interrupting his brother's workday.

But he didn't. He positively grinned and chucked his niece under the chin. "I figured that might be the case. When you track him down, tell him I'll finish up tomorrow. Ma sent me out to ask if you needed help carryin' anything in the house."

"That'd be great. There's a portable crib in the back seat."

After Skylar deposited Eliza with grandma and grandpa, she leaned against her car door and studied the map Kimi had drawn.

Kane sauntered over. "Got an idea where you're goin'?"

"Not a clue."

He chuckled. "Throw away that map. Ma goes a little overboard. It's easy to find. Go five miles east on the gravel road. Turn right at the first four-way. Two miles later on your right, you'll come to a barbed wire gate. Go through it and follow the tire tracks along the fence line until you see dust and tractors."

"Much easier." She smiled at him. "Thanks."

Kane gestured to Sky's Subaru wagon. "You takin' this?"

"Yeah. Why?"

"'Cause with the rain there's a couple places you might get stuck." He pointed to a dented and muddy red Dodge. "Take my truck. Keys are in the ignition. Leave it here when you're done."

"But...what will you drive?"

"Colt can come and get me, no biggie." Skylar's distrust must've been obvious because Kane said, "I'm sure you're wonderin' why I'm doin' this. You're here to make things right with my brother, or else you'd be willin' to wait until he's done workin', right?"

She nodded.

"Good." Kane sighed. "Look. I never apologized for how I treated you on our date last summer, me bein' such a dick and all. When you started seein' Kade I'll bet you thought I had a miraculous personality change, huh?"

"In hindsight, it should've been a big tip off you were two entirely different men."

"Well, I ain't surprised Kade jumped at the chance to redeem us both. The poor guy's had no choice but to put up with the fallout from bein' my twin. With women who scream at him in public because I didn't call them back. Hearin' come-ons and put-downs just because we look alike. Guys pickin' fights with him because they think he's me and I've done plenty to piss lots of folks off around here. It ain't never been fair and I never cared until last year."

Skylar waited for him to find the words to finish.

"Dag dyin' sucked. But you know what was worse for me? Watchin' my brother, who'd always been the backbone of our family," Kane's voice dropped an octave, "seein' Kade losin' hope. He cut himself off from everybody. I'd never seen him hurtin' so bad and I've never been so ashamed of myself for havin' a part in it. Yeah, I know he should've come clean with you. He made a mistake. Probably threw him for a loop because he hardly ever screws up. He always does the right thing."

"He's a good man. A great man. He's the very best man in the whole world."

"Glad someone finally recognizes that. Make him happy, Skylar."

"I intend to."

Chapter Twenty-seven

Kade didn't pay attention when his brother's pickup parked next to his along the fence. He looped another pass in the field, trying to stay awake. On his third round, he saw Skylar standing beside Kane's truck. He snapped upright, half-afraid he'd fallen asleep and was dreaming of her.

Then the apparition waved.

Holy shit. That *was* Skylar.

In the south hayfield.

Why?

Sweet Jesus. Something bad must've happened.

His heart slammed into his throat as his brain raced through all the awful scenarios. Kade managed to park the tractor next to the nearest fence. After shutting it off, he hopped to the ground and sprinted across the stubbly field.

Skylar met him halfway.

He clamped his gloved hands over her shoulders. "What's wrong? Are you okay?"

"Yes, I just—"

"Is Eliza all right?"

"She's fine. She's with your mom."

"So the rest of my family is okay too?"

"Yes."

"Then what..." He took a deep breath. Everything was fine. Thank God. "Sweetheart, why are you here?"

She bit her lip and glanced away. A nervous gesture? From the always confident Skylar?

"What's goin' on?"

"Eliza rolled over today."

He blinked with confusion and then he grinned. "She did?"

"Yeah, and little miss was mighty pleased with herself. You weren't there to see it. All I could think about was how you deserved to be there for every milestone in her life—big or small. And how badly I wanted you there for every damn one, not just for her, but for me, too."

Sweet Lord, she looked like she was going to cry. "Hey, it's all right."

"It is now that I'm here with you." Sky wrapped her arms around his waist, pressing against him as if she was trying to crawl inside his skin. "So I showed up because I missed you, Kade. I missed you so much. And I couldn't wait another day to tell you that I love you. I love you like crazy. With all my heart, all my soul, with everything I am. Please. I'll do anything to make this right. Please come home."

Kade closed his eyes and squeezed her tightly to make sure it wasn't another dream. "Say it again."

"I love you. And I'm sorry, you were right about a lot of things. Not just the security stuff, which I have taken care of, much to my employee's relief. What I accused you of was wrong. I panicked. Deep down I knew you wouldn't take Eliza from me. Then you were gone and I didn't know if it was for good. And I didn't know how to make it right. So all I can do is ask you to forgive me for being a pride-filled idiot, for not trusting you, or trusting in this."

"If you've forgiven me for the Kane thing, I can forgive you." He hooked a piece of flyaway hair behind her ear. "Skylar. I love you. I love you so damn much." He just held her. Loving the way she fit him so perfectly in so many ways.

Finally, she said, "You aren't going to leave me, ever, are you?"

"Nope."

"How long would you have waited for me to realize that?"

"Oh, fifty years, give or take."

She looked up and her eyes were so serious.

"What, sweetheart?"

"You really are a true gentleman cowboy. A good guy, honest, steadfast, loyal and true."

"You're makin' me sound like a damn preacher or something. I am who I am, Sky. Who I've always been."

"I know. That's who I want. That's who I love. And I'm too damn practical, because I suck at this kind of romantic stuff. But I did try to make this be special and spontaneous and..." Skylar stripped off his gloves and grabbed his hand. "Dammit. Come here. I have something to show you." She dragged him to where she'd spread out a yellow blanket on the flat spot of ground between the ditch and the fence line. A red cooler anchored one corner of the blanket. Centered on the plastic cooler lid was a bunch of wild flowers. "Here's our romantic celebration. You like it?"

The woman who claimed not to be a romantic...had picked flowers for him? "Yeah. It's great."

"That wasn't a very convincing *great*, Kade. Sit down."

He shuffled his feet and sighed.

"What?"

"I don't wanna sit on your nice blanket."

"Why not?"

"I'll ruin it. If you hadn't noticed, I'm covered in dust and grime."

"Hmm." Sky gave him a head to toe once over. "Then you'd better take off your dirty clothes."

Surely she was joking. "Sky—"

"If you hadn't noticed," she mimicked, "I'm trying to seduce you. But I'm fine with skipping the mushy romantic stuff and getting straight to the hardcore sex."

"What?" He glanced around. "In the middle of the damn field where anyone can see us?"

"Yep."

"No way."

"Oh. I see. It's okay when you make *me* strip down so you can have your wicked way with me, any time, any place. Need I remind you we had sex in my front yard, McKay?"

Shit. He was so totally screwed.

The triumph shining in her eyes made him half-wary and completely hard. Skylar fisted her hands in his shirt and pulled his mouth down to hers for a fiery kiss that should've set the hayfield on fire.

Kade groaned. God he loved kissing this woman. *His* woman. He loved her taste. He loved the way she curled her tongue against his. He loved the softness of her lips. He loved the sharp nip of her teeth. Mostly, he loved the fact she loved him.

She broke her mouth free but not her hold on his shirt. "I want you."

"And I want you. I always want you. Let's go back to the house, I'll get cleaned up, Ma can watch Eliza for a bit longer and we can—"

"No. Right here, right now."

"But I don't think—"

"Know what I think? That you don't *want* to think. You want a woman who will drag you off that damn tractor to fuck you in the weeds any time she pleases." Sky brushed her lips across his ear in an erotic glide that made him shiver. "You want a woman who doesn't care if you're covered in dirt because she plans to fuck you in the mud like an animal anyway. You want a woman who gets all hot and bothered by your possessive primal male declaration of 'I protect what's mine' and then balls your brains out in the barn."

His cock went rigid.

"I like the way you smell, fresh off the ranch. I like the way your tired muscles feel, flexing beneath my greedy hands." She licked his throat. "I like the way you taste. Everywhere."

"Sky—"

"Kade," she imitated his tone. "The naked rule is in effect. Strip."

"Wait a sec—"

"Nope." Buttons flew as she ripped his shirt open.

"Skylar!"

She'd focused on unbuckling his belt as she rained kisses down his belly. "Damn T-shirt. Why do you have to wear so many layers of clothes?"

Why *did* he? Hell. He could not think. "Ah. Um. Protection from the bugs and sun."

"This little scrap of cotton isn't gonna protect you from me."

Kade groaned again.

"Fine. Half-naked works. You want to leave your boots on?"

Kade's head was spinning with, *what the hell had gotten into her?* Followed by, *why are you resisting?*

"I take that as a yes." *Zip.* His fly was undone. *Yank.* His Wranglers and boxers were down past his knees. She looked up at him. "Are you gonna lay back on that blanket?" When he didn't move, her eyebrows rose in challenge. "Or am I going to have to push you down?"

Somehow, he managed not to stumble and ended up flat on his back, his cock sticking straight up like a divining rod, as he stared at the stunning cloudless blue of the big Wyoming sky.

Then an even prettier Sky was above him. "With your jeans around your boots, you're hobbled, cowboy. You can't get away from me."

"You put your hand or your mouth or your pussy on my cock and I guarantee I ain't gonna try to get away."

She grinned, looking as carefree and wild as he'd ever seen her. "Have I mentioned that I love you?"

"Once or twice, but I wouldn't mind hearin' it again. And again." He reached for the tie on her hair. The shining waves fell around his face like a curtain of silk. He crushed a handful of the sweetly scented strands and inhaled deeply.

She slowly unbuttoned her blouse, letting it flutter to the ground. Her rosy nipples were completely visible through the lacy pink bra. Skylar threw her leg over his hip, scooted back and lifted her skirt.

He caught a glimpse of a dark triangle of curls between her milky white thighs. "Good Lord. You ain't wearin' panties?"

"Nope. Since you usually rip them off anyway, I took them off in the truck."

"Hopin' to get lucky, were you?"

"I already knew I was the luckiest woman in the world when I saw you on the tractor. When you came running across the field to meet me."

"Sweetheart—"

"Let me finish. I didn't think it was possible to fall in love in a month. But I do love you. Not because you're Eliza's father but because you're you."

"A month? I gotcha beat, babe, by a country mile. Do you know I've been in love with you since our second date?"

"No, but I figured it was a possibility when I found that letter you sent today."

"You found it? Where?"

"It'd been shoved in a pile of junk mail. I've gotta say, for the strong, silent type, you certainly have a way with sweet words."

His cheeks heated. "You didn't think it was dumb? Or corny?"

"It was beautiful. And hopeful. And perfect."

Kade twirled a section of her hair around his palm as he composed his thoughts. "If you hadn't found that letter, would you be here?"

"Yes. It wasn't that I thought you were lying about writing it. It's just the way I am, Kade. I'm the type of person who needs proof in order to believe."

"Believe what?"

"Believe you were with me because you cared about me, and wanted me for me, not just because of Eliza."

"I only told you that about a dozen times. You want more tangible proof that I love you?"

"No. That's not what I meant."

"Hang on." In one quick movement he whipped off his T-shirt.

Her eyes narrowed on the square of white gauze on the left side of his chest. "What happened? How did you get hurt?"

"Self-inflicted. It's not completely healed, so you can't touch it yet." He peeled the adhesive tape and lowered the protective gauze so she could see his brand new tattoo.

Skylar's eyes widened, then pooled with tears. "Kade. You did that? For me?"

"Yep."

"Why? You hate needles."

"When you came to me the other night, and left your marks all over me, I knew they'd fade and I wanted to prove that you're a permanent part of me." He glanced at the puffy red skin, and the heart with *Skylar* scrolled in the center.

She squinted. "Is the outline of that heart supposed to look like...barbed wire?"

"Yeah. Your sister has a bizarre sense of humor."

Tears splashed on his chest. Her mouth trembled.

"Baby, don't cry."

"But I don't deserve you."

"See, that's the thing, you do. Believe you deserve me, because I finally believe I deserve you. All you have to do is look in my eyes to know the truth. I'll always be your tangible proof." Kade wiped her tears and curled his hand around her face, bringing their mouths together for a long kiss. He rested his forehead to hers. "Skylar. I love you."

"Show me. Please. Show me now."

"That I can do." He braced his arms behind him as she lowered herself until they were joined completely. He kissed her as she rode him, slow and easy, sweetly. She freely and lovingly gave him all of herself, and she showed him tenderness he didn't know he'd needed.

In one magnificent burst, the explosive physical pleasure they always brought to each other became the true intimacy they'd both been searching for because it came from love.

He flopped back, still inside her, taking her with him so she was sprawled across his chest.

Scarcely a heartbeat passed before she put her lips to his ear and demanded, "Marry me, Kade McKay."

"About damn time you came to your senses, woman."

"So, is that a yes?"

"Absolutely, it's a yes."

For the longest time, Kade was content to lie in the middle of the land he loved, with the woman he loved. He was content to just...be. To exist in the moment of perfect happiness and look forward to going home.

About the Author

To learn more about Lorelei James, please visit
www.loreleijames.com or send an email to
lorelei@loreleijames.com or join her Yahoo! group to join in the
fun with other readers as well as Lorelei James at
http://groups.yahoo.com/group/LoreleiJamesgang.

Ridin' the edge of lust is fun—until someone falls in love.

Cowgirl Up and Ride
© 2008 Lorelei James
A *Rough Riders* book.

Goody-two boots AJ Foster has waited her entire life for her dream cowboy Cord McKay to see her as more than the neighbor girl in pigtails. Now that she's old enough to stake her claim on him, she's pulling out all the sexual stops and riding hell-bent for leather—straight for his libido.

Divorced rancher Cord has sworn off all women...until innocent AJ suggests he teach her how to ride bareback—and he realizes she doesn't mean horses or bulls. Between his responsibilities running his massive ranch, missing his young son and dealing with the sexual shenanigans of his brother and cousins, Cord is more than willing to take AJ up on her offer. On a trial basis.

The fun and games tie them both up in knots. AJ isn't willing to settle for less than the whole shootin' match with her western knight. But for Cord, even though the sexy cowgirl sets his blood ablaze, he's determined to resist her efforts to lasso his battered heart.

Sweet, determined AJ has the power to heal—or heel—the gruff cowboy...unless Cord's pride keeps him from admitting their relationship is more than a simple roll in the hay.

Warning: this book contains: raunchy sex scenes that'll work you into a lather faster than a winded horse, graphic language, resourceful use of baling twine, ménage a trois, and yippee! hot nekkid man-on-man-lovin'.

Available now in ebook and print from Samhain Publishing.

Enjoy the following excerpt from Cowgirl Up and Ride...

He sighed, primed to leave, when Amy Jo darted onto the dance floor with some fresh-faced buck who had three extra pairs of hands.

Rather than go home to watch lousy TV alone, he settled in and watched her. She'd two-step a couple of numbers with one guy, flit to the bar for a fresh drink, and drag a new dance partner to the floor.

Cord hid in the darkened corner for over an hour, tracking every enticing sway of her slim hips, every smooth glide of those long legs, every exaggerated shoulder roll, every sexy chest shimmy, every toss of that sleek platinum hair. Not once did Amy Jo acknowledge him, even though she was as hyper-aware of him as he was of her.

Her sexy little ass shake turned him on more than if she'd been buck-ass naked grinding her crotch on a brass stripper's pole.

When she was alone at the bar Cord moseyed up behind her. "Evenin' Amy Jo."

She tossed him a quick grin and granted him a not so quick once over. "Surprised to see you in here, Cord. And it's AJ now, not Amy Jo."

"My mistake. Why the name change?"

"New attitude, new name." She resumed drinking her beer.

Cord scooted close enough to catch a whiff of her sunshiny scent. He noticed sweat beading on the curve of her neck below her ear and had the strangest desire to place his mouth there and gently suck the salty droplets clean away.

A beat passed and she didn't acknowledge him.

"I didn't know you liked to dance."

"There's a lot you don't know about me."

I'd like to learn. Every. Damn. Thing.

"Who are you here with?"

Amy Jo—AJ—faced him fully. "Who are *you* here with?"

"No one."

"That why you came looking for me? Can't find anyone better to hang out with?"

"No. Didn't know you thought so highly of me."

She shrugged.

The classic brush off—a pointed reminder on why he avoided the bar scene. He flashed her a fake smile. "Anyway. I came by to say hello. I'm headin' home and I wondered if you needed a lift."

AJ arched a slim brow. "You offering to give me a ride, cowboy?"

Cord curbed his response, *you can ride me any time, any place, as long as you want, cowgirl,* and cleared the lust from his throat. "Yeah."

The band announced the next tune, Willie Nelson's "Always On My Mind" and AJ shook her head at yet another eager, happy-handed cowboy approaching her for a dance. "Thanks for the offer, but no."

"You sure? You've been drinkin' pretty heavily the last couple of hours. Probably shouldn't be drivin'."

"How would you know how much I've been drinking?"

"Because I've been watchin' you. Closely. Every step and every sip, darlin'. I couldn't take my eyes off you and you damn well know it." Her confidence slipped; he moved in. "You *like* that I've been watchin' you, sweet Amy Jo."

"AJ," she corrected softly.

"You like that I've been watchin' you, sweet *AJ.*"

"So while you were watching, did you see anything you liked, McKay?"

"Oh yeah." His gaze landed on her lush mouth.

"Right. Give me a break."

Cord managed to drag his eyes back to hers. "You callin' me a liar?"

"No. I'm calling your bluff."

"Meaning?"

"Meaning, I know you'll look your fill, burn my clothes away with your sexy eyes, but you're too damn polite to do anything more than gawk at me."

Cord nearly choked, "*Polite*?"

"Polite. Responsible. Chicken. Whatever." She stared at his lips and ran her pink tongue over her teeth. "Tell me, Cord, don't you ever just wanna say to hell with what's expected of you and do what makes you feel good?"

"Every damn day."

She reached up, letting her fingers fiddle with a button near his shirt collar. "Then tell me why you don't?"

"I'll tell you anything you wanna know, baby doll, as long as you answer a question for me first."

"Okay."

"Look at me."

When AJ's lust-filled eyes met his, it took every ounce of restraint not to smash his mouth to hers, hike up that sassy excuse of a skirt, spread those silky thighs wide, and nail her against the closest paneled wall.

Focus.

"Can I buy you a drink? Like the shot you did earlier?"

"You wanna see me do a blowjob?"

Cord froze.

She laughed. "See why I won forty bucks?"

"Just for sayin' that raunchy word out loud?"

"No. For doing it."

He lifted both brows. "Doin' what?"

"Giving them a group blowjob. See, the object is the same with the drink as it is with the act, shoving the glass in your mouth as far as it'll go, keeping a tight grip with your lips. Then you tilt your head and suck hard and deep, bracing yourself for the warmth spilling down your throat as you try to swallow it all."

He growled, "What game are you playin' with me, little girl?"

AJ stood on the tips of her boots. "I haven't been a little girl for a long time, Cord McKay."

"Believe me, I noticed."

"About damn time."

If he leaned in a fraction of an inch, he could lay a hungry kiss on those ripe lips, not innocent like the flirty smooch she'd teased him with last year. Would this bolder AJ take the initiative?

She didn't. Instead, she lifted a shaking hand to his cheek. Her fingertips delicately traced the outline of his neatly trimmed goatee, lingering on the short hair above his upper lip. A chaste, yet erotic caress to make his cock stand up and take notice if it wasn't already rock-hard.

"No games. If you want to play with me, all you have to do is ask. I'll be here tomorrow night, waiting for your answer."

AJ spun on her bootheel and vanished into the sea of bodies on the dance floor, leaving Cord McKay absolutely pole-axed.

GREAT
CHEAP
FUN

Discover eBooks!

THE FASTEST WAY TO GET THE HOTTEST NAMES

Get your favorite authors on your favorite reader, long before they're out in print! Ebooks from Samhain go wherever you go, and work with whatever you carry—Palm, PDF, Mobi, and more.

Samhain
Publishing ltd

WWW.SAMHAINPUBLISHING.COM